I0577932

THE REVENGE OF
BILLY BUCKLER

BOOKS BY RILEY CAIN

The Halloween House: 31 Putrid Poems and
Rotten Rhymes for October

Banshee Rising

The Curse of Silver and Sunlight –
Benjamin Blake Book I

RILEY CAIN ON SOCIAL MEDIA:

TikTok – @RileyRealm31

Instagram – @riley_writes4u

BlueSky – @rileycain

X – @RileyRealm

THE REVENGE OF BILLY BUCKLER

BENJAMIN BLAKE BOOK II

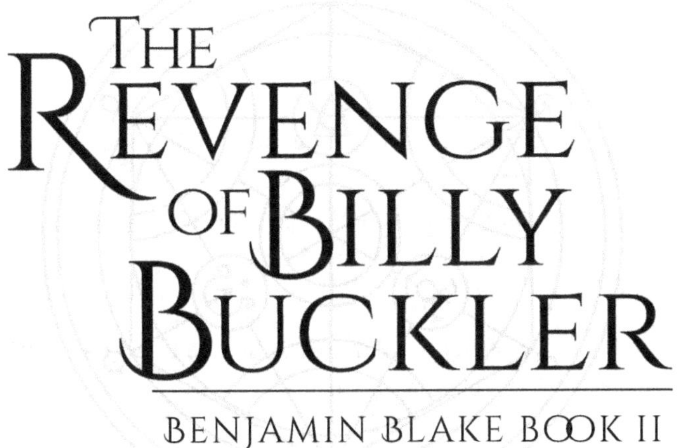

RILEY CAIN

First published in 2025 by The Riley Realm

Copyright © 2025 by Riley Cain

All rights reserved. No part of this publication may be copied, reproduced or transmitted in any form by any mans without prior written permission of the author, except for brief quotations in a book review.

This is a work of fiction. Any resemblance to actual persons, living or dead, events, or locales is entirely coincidental.

ISBN: 978-1-7393718-2-1

Cover design and illustration by Alba Esteban/Alestura Design and Alexis Sierra

Book design by Alba Esteban with layout by Paula Nolan PEN GRAPHIC DESIGN

For Cassie
'Though she be little, she is fierce'
Shakespeare

WHERE TO BEGIN

It began with a hanging.

That's the way Benjamin Blake told me his tale of pirates and magic the very first time, right here in the theatre.

It's a good line, isn't it, such an exciting way to start. It appealed to the actor in me immediately, of course. I pictured myself delivering that line from the stage to captivate an audience made breathless with anticipation. Between us, I think Benjamin has a flare for the dramatic, that's why he comes to my performances so often.

Anyhow, I recall it was at the end of another successful run for me at the Lyceum when Benjamin visited and offered that grim opening to the story of Billy Buckler's revenge. I had shared news with him of my next leading role, in The Pirates of Penzance – I have quite the singing voice – and that prompted something in him. Sitting there in your seat, he took on that faraway look of his and the stillness that comes whenever he remembers episodes from long ago in his vampire life.

Even now I can hear him whisper it.

'It began with a hanging.'

Well, you can imagine, I was chilled and intrigued by that all in the same instant. Normally tales end that way, you understand. But that's because, like you, I am mortal, and I simply forgot in the moment that Benjamin's stories are of the night world and hardly ever obey the rules of the stories of day.

So it was with Billy Buckler. His story was just getting started on the morning of his execution. Because from the beginning, before the beginning, in fact, the most sinister use of magic was involved in the pirate's tale, the likes of which even Benjamin had not encountered. And over the days after – no, I'm forgetting again – over the nights after, it became all too clear the revenge of Billy Buckler would not die with the man.

What was that revenge, you ask? Well, after Benjamin's colourful opening it would be unfair to spoil the surprise, wouldn't it? What I will tell you is that by the end, the true end as Benjamin told it, you will understand just as I did how close England came to ruin in the autumn of 1779. All thanks to pirates, a touch of magic and many, many murders.

I will try to tell it just as he did.

Are you ready?

1

It began with a hanging.

On the dank November morning ordered by the court, it seemed all of London was turned out for the single purpose of witnessing the traitor brought to his final judgement. From the walls of Newgate prison to the gallows at Tyburn miles away, dawn found a crushing multitude impatiently waiting, a swarming mass of humanity drawn to the day's grisly business. Like a great river to challenge the breadth of the Thames, the people surged, roaring as one in a furious swell of bodies, each competing for the best viewing point or perch, all driven by a shared anxiety of missing the event of the year and hungry for the chance to boast later of having been there to see it. Tall men were cursed and abused for blocking the view, their hats struck off by angry swipes while those smaller, be they men, women or children, were cruelly elbowed aside. The more adventurous of the spectators, arms and legs thrown wide, rode atop the wave of humanity, whooping for joy at the occasion until they were cast down and swallowed by the throng. The weak found themselves trodden underfoot by the ever shifting mass, their tortured protests drowned amid the greater clamour rising between the buildings.

Safe there above the fray, at high windows and on rooftops that had been hastily rented from homeowners along the procession route, the rich in their powdered wigs and shimmering gowns looked on, at once amused and disgusted by the antics of the crowd below. Sipping party wine from fine crystal glasses, they scoffed at the unruly peasants, yet shared with them the same shivering anticipation for the opening of prison gates and a first glimpse of the man whose final day had come at last.

A man? A mere man? The crowd gossips insisted the term could not be applied to this prisoner. No. How could one mere man lay claim to the terrifying litany of crimes laid before the court these days past? How could a mere man have escaped the might of the king's navy for so long to sink ship after ship in his monstrous campaign of piracy? Surely the many vessels lying beneath the waves around England's coasts had carried more treasure than any one man could lust for. And perhaps the greatest question of all, how could any English man commit such acts against his own country in a time of war with rebellious American colonies? The wretched figure set to emerge from the bowels of Newgate this morning could correctly be labelled 'pirate!', 'traitor!', 'villain!', even 'devil!'… but not 'a man'.

At the prison walls, a harsh scraping of wood on stone drew the attention of the crowd, turning all heads in gasping expectation to the towered entrance where a widening line of darkness between the gates drove the masses to new heights of frenzy.

'He's coming!'

Word raced through the body of humanity like a wildfire.

'He's coming!'

The news sparked great cheers and piercing screams as the jostling among spectators became unbridled.

'Here he comes!'

Voices altered quickly to boos of protest for the first sight, not of the condemned man, but rather a line of soldiers in red tunics which emerged from the place of detention to begin forcing a path through the crowd. With musket stocks the soldiers beat cruelly at heads and limbs and bodies until the swell reluctantly parted, offering a signal for the advance of two ponies, terrified and rearing, from the gateway. Clopping uneasily forward at their driver's urging, the animals strained in drawing into the light the prison cart and the lone passenger it conveyed.

The sight of that bound and hooded form proved more effective than a regiment of soldiers in forcing the crowd to retreat. With eyes locked on the terrible scarecrow-figure, the tide of citizens rolled back, its innumerable voices chilled abruptly to silence. For a moment the only sound to hear was the slow clatter of ponies' hooves on the roadway.

Uncertainty and fear ruled all hearts as the cart trundled free of the prison and began to cut its own passage. But all at once, through the awed hush, a voice far back in the crowd, and made bold by the safety of distance from the convict, called forth.

'Show us the traitor's face!'

The cry was met by the emboldened demands of others, all for an unmasking, until the greater part of the throng regained its voice and chorused, 'Show us his face! Show us his face! Show us his face!'

Unsettled by this fresh din, the ponies fought against their reins, threatening to bolt in panic while the soldiers once more found themselves under pressure to maintain the line of division between crowd and cart.

It was in the instant the troops were most beset that a headstrong youth breached the cordon to rush forwards. Spurred on by eager cheers from those who understood his intention, the boy launched himself at a wheel of the vehicle and, using the spokes as a ladder, he propelled himself to within reach of the transported man. His hand whipped up and seized the canvas material of the hood, and in a flash, the covering was pulled aside.

Diabolical eyes, blazing in a cruel face marked by a furious hate for the whole world, peered back into the boy's and froze him. In an instant the youngster took forever into his nightmares the murderous features of the prisoner.

The pirate Billy Buckler.

Under the buccaneer's savage glare, turned worse by a long jagged scar that narrowed eye and lip to an angry sneer, the boy toppled back onto a soldier already reaching to pull him down. The pair spilled to the roadway, their crashing tumble the only sound as again the crowd held to a stunned silence. With manic eyes, Billy Buckler watched soldier and boy fall until, wickedly amused, his face gave over to a twisted grin and he turned his attention to the multitude of faces arrayed before him in shared horror.

And he laughed.

Billy laughed and the mad sound of his laughter drove the crowd farther back, encouraging him all the more in his crazy merriment. To his left he turned, laughing harder as the people recoiled and babies cried, to the right, where a woman shrieked at the terrifying spectacle, and to the windows above, he laughed at the rich who were less rich because of the piracy of Billy Buckler.

A lone soldier advanced and snatched up the fallen hood. Determined to put an end to the show, he mounted the cart and reached forward to conceal the pirate's face. Billy, watchful as a viper even as he howled on in his bonds, waited for the opportune moment. With the soldier just inches away, the pirate crashed his forehead brutally into his nose and blasted him aside.

The action brought an eruption of renewed vigour from the crowd. Infuriated at the attack on one of the king's men, the people bellowed and lost all fear of Buckler. Hateful threats were issued, angry fists shook, and a volley of rotten vegetables flew on the air. And through it all, as ponies were whipped furiously for urgent progress, Billy Buckler's laughter continued.

'Hanging's too good for him,' a man protested, and the pirate laughed.

'Repent, sinner,' a voice demanded, and he laughed the harder.

'Take all my jewels for one kiss, Billy Buckler,' a besotted woman pleaded, and he threw back his head and laughed hard enough to shake the heavens.

'I watched you die, Billy Buckler!'

That voice, that voice was so familiar it sank Billy's laughter beneath a knowing smile, and he looked to find a man stepping from the crush into the road. The tattered remnants of a naval officer's uniform under wild hair were all he needed to recognise an old enemy blocking the way.

'Captain Faulkner.'

'I shot you,' the ragged man spat, and Billy saw how the once fine sailor, now shambling and drunk, had kept the pistol he held in good working order. Under the captain's thumb, the mechanism clicked audibly through the shocked hush surrounding.

'With that self same weapon,' Billy admitted as fresh chuckles rose in his throat for the captain's show.

'The same,' Faulkner assured.

Buckler was already laughing again as the weapon drew up, and his glee became louder as he watched soldiers leap to tackle Faulkner. Red tunics swarmed over the raging man and he fell beneath them, bellowing in frustration as his weapon was prised away and he was hauled from the roadway amid a renewed baying from the mob. The hangman would not be denied today, and the knowledge gave Billy cause to laugh again.

So it continued for the last of the route to Tyburn, the crowd's hysteria competing with his relentless laughter until the gallows prepared for the pirate's end loomed into sight. But even then, spectators would long remember, even in the shadow of the Tyburn Tree with its hangman's rope, Billy Buckler hitched in the throes of his laughter. Still he chuckled as the soldiers hauled him roughly from the cart to march him up the steps to the platform, and how he giggled when the noose was drawn to his face. There was even a leering smile for the nervous preacher who avoided his gaze and instead faced the crowd to offer a final prayer against sinful wickedness.

Only when Billy looked past the holy man to a great viewing gallery beyond, and to the honoured spectators it held, did the last traces of amusement melt from Billy Buckler's face. What replaced it was a churning hatred reserved in his heart for the man he now saw, the most important guest of all today. Just yards off, the King of England himself, King George III, sat in quiet contemplation of the prisoner, and met the pirate's eyes with stern appraisal.

Bedecked in gold and lace and ribbons of royal finery, the king remained motionless among his children and courtiers as he fixed his face on that of the despised criminal. Solemnly he considered the man who had brought such grief to his realm. For an undying age, it seemed to those standing witness to the staring, king and killer eyed one another as though in silent contest until, at last, and with a dismissive sniff, the king tapped his ornate walking stick on the boards and nodded for the preacher to continue.

Shifting his own gaze while the rope was pulled harshly about his neck, Billy Buckler considered the four children seated regally about their father. There was little Princess Elizabeth, held protectively close by her older sister Charlotte, and there Prince Edward so wide-eyed, while the eldest of them, George junior, Prince of Wales, worked so hard to imitate his father's imperious look.

Such pretty children.

The buccaneer glared with the hunger of a wolf on each, and the most dangerous of smiles formed on his lips for them.

'Does the prisoner have any last words?' the preacher asked coldly of him.

Billy Buckler looked briefly to the corner of the gallows where a pair of gravediggers dragged his rough wooden coffin into view. At this his smile grew wider yet and he turned again to face the royal family.

'I'll be revenged on the whole pack of you!'

The trap thundered open and the rope cracked tight.

There came a terrible silence.

2

Night drew on and brought with it the ghost. As ever, he came with the rising of the moon, faithful to his legend – his was a tale whispered by each generation of guards at the Tower of London these past one hundred and thirty-four years. He was the Boy of the Tower, and again as always he drifted through shadow, gliding along the stone battlements, there to peer east as though welcoming the night and Mistress Moon. The ghost boy stood, just as told, apparently lost in watching the pale lunar crescent pull free of the land to spill its silver beams on Thames water, hypnotised by the beauty of the spectacle, his face just as pale and, perhaps, even warmed by those first rays of moonlight.

Some versions of the story held the spirit to be a former inmate of the Tower, executed at the chopping block years ago and watching across the water ever since for rescue that would never come. Others insisted the boyish frame of the phantom marked him as one of the tragic Princes of the Tower, murdered centuries ago by his jealous uncle the king and now forever searching the dark for his brother and a blessed release from this final cold prison.

Such colourful stories made the phantom chuckle to himself. The tales were colourful, so wild, and so wrong. But they were useful. They kept mortals at a frightened distance from his secret reality. He was no aimless spirit, and the Tower was not his prison, it was his home, and had been for all those whispered years. An old guardroom beneath one of the watchtowers of the curtain wall, bricked up and long forgotten, had become his most comfortable refuge from the daylight world.

He had chosen the Tower of London quite deliberately, indeed most logically. During those first nights of wandering alone and free through streets and alleys, it was obvious to him the city would change and grow in time, but when he looked on the Tower of London, he perceived in its ancient walls and turrets a place forever unchanging. It was a fortress against time as well as enemies. The perfect home for a vampire.

Be about your business, Benjamin Blake.

To his scolding inner voice, Benjamin gathered himself from idle thinking to steal effortlessly over the castle wall and into the gloom below, smiling as he left superstitious guards at fires crackling against the chill of ghost stories. Tonight he had other things to occupy his attention besides memories and the beauty of the moon.

The business at hand lay east, across rooftops lining the river towards its bend at Blackwall Reach. It was there, a point where ships were forced to navigate slow turns to and from the capital, that the mortal remains of Billy Buckler were currently displayed. Caged in a gibbet of iron by royal decree and hauled to the highest warehouse along the Reach, the body hung as food for crows and a stark warning to all seafarers.

Piracy will not be tolerated.

To dark imaginings of Billy Buckler's lifeless form swinging on a night breeze, Benjamin raced across the tiles to his rendezvous with the pirate. His night existence meant he must surely be the only soul in all London to have missed the dread face of the buccaneer – and his misbehaviour at Tyburn. Through daylight's confinement to his resting place, Benjamin had lifted his ear in frustration to the distant clamour of Londoners while envying their witness to the last eventful journey of the legendary pirate.

Now he sped on to make up for lost time, quickening his pace to flit between chimneys and steeples on the way to his own private viewing.

Beneath his course, London drew on its glittering

cloak of evening. Candles flickered in a thousand homes against the dark and the city began to glimmer at his passing. A dance of enchanting sparkles played from homes he had watched grow over his ageless years, their ranks flanking pavements and roads which replaced the tracks and paths of former times, now grandly renamed for the era of the Georges as avenues and crescents and squares. Best of all for a travelling vampire, the improvements of time offered wider rooftops and perfectly-fitting slates, the ideal route for his journey this night and countless others.

Only once on his way did Benjamin pause. Drawn abruptly to halt above dark gardens running down to the river's edge, all thoughts of pirates were driven aside as he squatted by a perilous edge to peer on the black water's flow.

And, as so many times before, to listen.

The call was ever the same, far off and near in the same instant, secretive and sing-song from beneath the rolling current. It came again, catching a soft breeze as it rose to him from the depths.

I'm here.

Crescent-shaped scars on Benjamin's right hand prickled with memories of a witch's sharp nails and the book of magic she had killed and died for.

Sometimes the call of the Grimoire Adefina Corvus was louder, sometimes softer, never distinct but always in reply to the moon. When beams dappled black water it called.

I'm waaaaiting.

But the wide, deep river held the book fast where Benjamin had lost it when a vampire was young and clumsy.

Had that been the best solution, he asked himself. Had fate played a part in his trip and stumble in sending the grimoire splashing to its hiding place, secure from dark forces? Or had the witch's volume itself worked magic and slipped his grasp to lie in wait of rescue by another sorceress? He could not tell from that soft, teasing voice whether the book called blindly to the long dead Adefina or to some other witch, only that it could indeed be heard by others in the night world. In one hundred and thirty-four years of possessing its magic, Benjamin had faced many spell-weavers drawn by the grimoire's whispering.

Noting the latest site of calling, but refusing to add to a century's worth of fruitless searching now, he pressed on.

He aimed at last towards a distant line of buildings which marked the bend at Blackwall Reach. Here the looping Thames was the border between city and lawless countryside. Beyond the last weak glow of scattered lights, full and pressing night offered cover for ghosts and highwaymen.

And, perhaps, even pirates.

In his years of nocturnal life, Benjamin had lost count of those spirit inhabitants of the supernatural world he had met and tangled with in the city's dark places. As for highwaymen, he had crossed paths with precisely two. But of the third group, he had never had so much as a glimpse, not a single pirate in over a century.

He knew well of buccaneers, of course. When, years ago, their exploits had filled London's news sheets and pamphlets, he had excitedly consumed the tales and thrilled to each notorious name: Blackbeard, Anne Bonney and Calico Jack. Over a far horizon of imagining sailed villains of the sea whose adventures were filled with cannon smoke and the gleam of hidden treasure. But that was sixty years ago, he reminded himself, a golden age lost to history and the warm waters of the Caribbean. The tale of Billy Buckler was far, far colder by contrast, a modern horror story told every day in the blood of sailors washed up on England's shores.

For an entire year Billy and his crew of the Ghostmaker had transformed navy maps to a clutter of shipwrecks in their wake. Seafarers coursing English waters scanned in fear for the Ghostmaker's flag, a half-skull pennant cleaving through a sea mist said to rise as Lucifer's own protection for brazen

Billy. No accurate tally existed of souls claimed by the pirates' reign of terror. The number remained a terrible mystery the sea held to itself.

None, likewise, could place a true figure on the booty stolen away by the Ghostmaker in its time. Tales fantastic filled conversations in the port taverns of England, of jewelled rivers and coin mountains, stories that grew ever more colourful as they spread to the ale-houses of the capital. Yet not the barest hint of treasure had ever been found, no pearl or ruby, not a single doubloon to offer a clue to the hiding place of the pirate hoard. The only map, it was rumoured with knowing winks and nudges, was securely locked in Buckler's head, and the hangman's rope had put paid to that. The pirate captain had not uttered a single word to his jailers during the long months in Newgate, and in his final laughing madness he had carried the treasure's secret location with him to Hell.

What strange behaviour for a man about to die, Benjamin thought as he slowed towards the Reach. Could it be that Billy had considered his silence to be a last defiant gesture? Had denying England its lost wealth been the revenge roared from the gallows?

Not much farther now. Through the shadow of a church spire, Benjamin drew close enough to the lip of warehouse roofs to see thick beams extending into space beyond. These were the hoists for bringing up ships' cargo to the upper floors. And somewhere beneath one of the wooden cranes Billy Buckler waited, suspended in his man-shaped prison. With a supernatural tremble of anticipation, Benjamin edged forward, his mind tingling to visions of a lifeless form, lazily swinging and blindly staring into eternal darkness.

He had taken just a few steps when a great commotion rose from below. Metal and wood worked together to throw up a terrific clatter and disturb the wharf's silence. A terrified whinny of horses coupled with galloping hooves added to the din and signalled the hurtling pace of some vehicle.

Benjamin moved quickly to overlook the streets of the warehouse district. Within the black canyons he spied at once a speeding wagon drawn by two horses, the beasts frothing under the whip of a dark man bent to the reins. As the wagon sped between a warehouse and churchyard, directly under Benjamin's vantage point, he caught sight of a second man in the rear of the vehicle. This figure crouched protectively over a canvas-draped bundle as he aimed a pistol back along the roadway. The weapon erupted with an explosion that lit the night and blocked all other sound for a moment. Benjamin watched the path of a small lead ball where it cut the air towards a target emerging in pursuit.

A horse and rider hurtled after the wagon in a break-neck chase. Similarly armed, the caped man in the saddle ducked the whistling shot past his head and levelled his pistol to return fire in another blast of flame and smoke. His aim was more precise, and the bullet he sent found the rear gate of the wagon, punching an ugly hole in the right side to an alarmed cry from the passenger.

Hunter and prey flashed on, the sound of action rapidly fading between the buildings. Benjamin's mind raced in search of explanation as he strained vainly to see more of the receding chase. Abruptly suspecting this dramatic occurrence was in some way linked to the pirate's resting place, he darted rapidly towards his destination. He halted to overlook the river, and down at a beam stretching from his feet to a point in dizzying space above the dock. Held there by a length of chain, the cage turned slowly on the air, broken wide open and creaking on loose hinges. Benjamin peered in wonder at it, with its shattered lock and hanging gate.

The gibbet was empty.

3

Bodysnatchers!

In a flash, Benjamin mentally reworked events he had witnessed moments before.

Lured by the great price of coins Billy Buckler's corpse would surely fetch among trophy hunters, resurrection men had crept up soon after dark to spring the buccaneer from his cage. Discovered in the act by the lone rider, a guard or another snatcher denied his prize, the chase had begun and perhaps continued still, many miles off, with shots fired back and forth over the pirate's shrouded body lying in the wagon.

If Benjamin felt any satisfaction at having read the situation so clearly and correctly, it was immediately pushed away by the knowledge he still remained the only one in all London not to have seen the infamous pirate captain. Frustrated, he kicked at a tile and cursed ill luck.

But maybe he was not the only one after all, he thought, as fresh sounds reached his ears. Along roads cutting from all sides through the district, vampire senses caught the movement of horses and people, many people, drawing close. Were these yet more visitors arriving in the vain hope of viewing Billy?

Benjamin crouched to await the newcomers.

The dock came alive with forms emerging from the night. Men walked alone or in silent groups to assemble between warehouses and the river. Benjamin counted twenty men on foot before he spotted others approaching by different means. Eight on horseback travelled from the north to meet the rest beneath the gibbet.

Examining the group as it gathered to stare upwards with grumblings for empty graves, Benjamin easily found clues to their collective identity in the hardened and dangerous faces turned his way, by the ragged coats and broad hats they wore, and the swords and pistols crossed in every belt. Recalling those tales of long ago, it was all too clear to him. Here be pirates!

He felt a giddy excitement in the moment. This was becoming quite an occasion indeed. Having come in search of a single pirate, here he stared down on a group of thirty or more in one night! But what was the purpose of this solemn gathering?

His question lingered as men turned in silence to fresh sounds of yet another approach. Barely a minute behind the horsemen, a dark carriage trundled slowly into view along the churchyard boundary to press to the centre of the waiting buccaneers. At its halting, the vehicle's door opened, and Benjamin watched a small barefoot girl, African by her features, as she jumped to the ground to hurriedly unfold a small set of steps. Her duty performed, the little one stepped back to hold the door for the only other passenger.

The man who emerged from the carriage, like those others greeting his arrival, was villainous of face and appearance. Beneath a broad-rimmed hat his features were deeply lined by years of blistering sea-spray and sun, and held eyes permanently narrowed by a trade in cruelty. Pausing above his compatriots on the first step, he examined the scene gravely and tugged with finger and thumb at his sharpened beard when he spied the empty gibbet.

'Where's the captain?' he demanded furiously, dropping to the roadway to face each man in turn.

The pirates of the Ghostmaker shifted uncomfortably and avoided the speaker's glare, unable to answer the man whose fingers shifted to toy with twin pistols at his waist. Into the awkward silence came the sound of trotting hooves.

A lone rider, the very man who had chased the speeding wagon, guided his steaming mount among the buccaneers. He spurred the beast quickly towards the unanswered pirate and swung from the saddle.

'Mr Pyke, sir,' the breathless rider said with a sharp salute.

'Report,' Pyke ordered.

'The captain is stolen, sir, taken by grave robbers.'

The crew erupted to furious outrage at the news. A disordered howling of violent threats issued against those who dared lay hands on Billy Buckler. Promises of torture and death flew while swords and pistols thrust to the night sky amid grisly curses.

A shot burst over the protests, a thunder-crash of warning to silence ill-disciplined ravings, and all eyes came once again to the man named Pyke. Only Benjamin looked elsewhere, shifting briefly to regard the smoking bullet hole shot unknowingly into the hanging beam inches from his face!

'Secure your flapping jaws!' Pyke growled, enforcing his order with a maddened glare. Taking time to consider matters, his attention travelled between the gibbet and pirate faces looking to him for the next course of action.

'What's to be done, sir?' a voice pleaded now on behalf of the crew.

By way of answer, Pyke turned again to the lone rider.

'Mr Davy,' he said, 'can you identify those who have stolen from us?'

'Aye, sir,' came the reply. 'I saw one face, and left

my mark on their cart, a shot-hole through its rear gate.'

'Excellent,' Pyke barked, 'then our plan remains on course. Take three men, Mr Davy, find them grave robbers and take back what was stolen from us.' Here he drew a long dagger from his belt and added, 'By way of compensation, give 'em some slow steel.' His fellow sailors growled in hearty agreement. 'The rest of you will follow the hunt through London. Meet tomorrow night as arranged at the Gravediggers tavern. And let every man here remember well, we stick to the plan. Understood?'

As one, the crew roared, 'Aye!' and Benjamin marked well the name overheard – the Gravediggers tavern.

'Now for the rest,' Pyke said, and somehow his vague words were enough to force a renewed hush among the assembly.

Reaching into a pocket of his tattered coat, the pirate drew forth a tiny cloth bundle for all to see. Sight of the parcel provoked dark whispering and nervous pointing among the crew, and rapidly blinking eyes tracked Pyke's movements closely.

Stepping between his comrades towards the deserted churchyard, Pyke stared off into the gloom beyond its walls, and it was as though he searched there for something known only to him. He spread fingers to look once again upon the bundle and examined it keenly by touch and sight. When next he turned back and glanced at the waiting crew, it seemed to Benjamin he fixed for a brief spell on the little servant girl standing obediently by the carriage door. The moment passed, and with sudden and deliberate motions, Pyke drew back his arm and launched the parcel far into the churchyard's sucking black depths.

Like all, Benjamin tracked the arc of the parcel through the air, spying it where it hopped off a headstone and split asunder. Just before the tiny contents flew apart and tumbled beyond his vampire sight, there was just enough time to catch a glimpse of a stone, a dry twig bound up with roots and what appeared to be a small animal bone. Benjamin stared on in confusion, listening as Mr Pyke shouted on a phantom breath after the offering.

'Loa!' His voice ran hollow to the night as he raised his arms high. 'The one who is the Gatekeeper, come! I summon you! Come!'

For a time, there was nothing, merely the echo of the pirate's command rolling back between the buildings. But as the last of his words faded there appeared a first small hint of movement, a bare motion of shadow on the ground within the churchyard. At the limits of vision, something shifted across the ground and began to...grow.

What came formed as a devilish bloom. Ivy strands of night pierced dusty earth to creep in all directions from the resting place of the dead. One after another, oily strips emerged to test the night air and snake along. Spidering forms reached, tip-tapping against grave markers, and gripped eagerly their solid edges. More ragged strips appeared, bigger than the last, until a huge flowing mass was evident, its parts moving as though individually fuelled by knowing life, though all were clearly born of a single source. And that source, when at last it appeared, was a giant black cloak, torn to countless living strips flowing and billowing as if underwater and not on the dry land it covered. Most terrible of all, at the very heart of the surging mass came the features of a dark man, appearing from the pit rolling about. All over, the skin of the growing man was that of a native of Africa or the West Indies, and blended to the cloak in which he existed. All, that is, but for his horrifying face. Under a tall hat bedecked with a single raven feather, the man's features shone white, painted from forehead to upper lip and from ear to ear as a half-skull mask, with the closed eyes spared to look all the more like empty sockets of death.

'Wake!' Mr Pyke demanded of the monstrous

slumbering figure. 'Wake, Baron Samedi!'

The eyes of the demon flashed wide to the calling of its name, and brought fearful hisses from the pirates. Fixing its deathly gaze upon the gathering, the figure made to speak, and its voice boomed without breath from the depths where it dwelt to spill far and wide across the river.

'By stick and stone, and root and bone, I am come!'

4

A crushing silence greeted the Baron.

All stared in wide wonder, and tongues were stilled. Only pirate hands moved, slipping nervously to pistols and swords. Even Benjamin, in his lofty hiding place, though well aware of dark magic, was held transfixed to peer amazed on this giant man-creature of the shadows. And all the while the phantom, unmoving in its ever shifting robe, stared from under his top hat in waiting, daring someone in the throng of pirates to address him in his terrible greatness.

'Who,' he thundered at last, 'who summons Baron Samedi from the crossroads of death?'

'Baron,' Mr Pyke ventured boldly to answer, 'I do. I call you again. And you will serve me again.'

Baron Samedi's movements in reply were sudden and violent. Cloak strands lashed out about him. Grabbing markers and earth, they crushed stone to dust in an instant in hauling forward. Ragged strips stabbed the ground and launched the spirit on, and the Baron charged towards the churchyard wall and crossed it without pause as one carried on the back of a monstrous scuttling spider.

The pirates cried out in one terrified voice and staggered back from the dreadful advance, drawing weapons with no more than a hope they could defend against the awful spectacle. Only Mr Pyke held his ground in the path of the racing spirit, his face set hard, his own weapons holstered and untouched.

The Baron reached the dock and towered over the buccaneer, his cloak spilling as liquid shadow across the ground to encircle them both. Nose to nose, the pair stared on one another in shared hatred.

'Villain,' the Baron's sneer was long and slow, and his painted face filled with a boiling revulsion for the one who called.

'Slave,' Pyke responded just as slowly, and he peered with contempt at the creature floating above him.

Infuriated by the insult, the Baron roared and launched forth his robe-limbs.

Curling black tentacles lashed towards the gathered pirates, found the weapons they held and snatched them away before any man could react. The vast armoury was turned inwards in a blinking, and Mr Pyke was encircled head to toe by sword tips and pistols.

The pirate made no attempt to draw his own weapons in defence but merely offered a tired smile for the Baron's actions. When at last he did reach, it was to a pocket of his tunic as a floating pistol cocked and came to press against his head. Ignoring the threat, he drew forth an item and offered it between finger and thumb to his opponent.

'You know the arrangement,' he reminded the spirit as he lazily turned over in his hand a small corked bottle for the Baron's consideration.

The Baron tipped his head towards the empty gibbet swinging above.

'There is no captain for my work, I have no use for a bottled spell.'

'That is not your concern,' Pyke snapped angrily. 'I will deliver the captain as promised. You serve as agreed and all will go free.' He added with a knowing smirk, 'Or don't, the choice is yours.'

Looking on the empty bottle as a hateful thing, the rage in the Baron's face began to fade. Eyes which had previously burned furiously washed over with a defeated sadness and the Baron accepted his orders. He faced Mr Pyke again and reached to clutch the glass vessel offered. The night sang with a chiming of weapons discarded to the road.

'I will serve,' the Baron muttered bitterly.

'You know the first man we seek,' the buccaneer

instructed darkly, 'and the power we need. Find him, take it.'

Spurred by the pirate's instructions, the Baron sprang forward, robe-legs propelling him over the carriage roof and to the facade of a warehouse. Black strands pulled him effortlessly aloft, and his form merged with the sky as it sped towards the city. Behind, vampire and pirates looked on in awe at his passing.

'Jump to it, you scurvy collection,' Pyke barked at the distracted crew. 'We have work to do!'

Hastening to retrieve fallen weapons, the pirates of the Ghostmaker moved to obey. Horsemen charged away while those on foot split up to vanish quickly into the cover of shadowed streets, leaving Mr Pyke to re-enter his carriage ahead of the little girl as horses were whipped up to bring the vehicle trundling into the night.

Silence returned and found Benjamin alone in struggling to comprehend events so bizarre in the mortal and supernatural worlds that they forced a soft question from his lips.

'What is going on?'

5

ounding from his place, Benjamin cut the night between rooftops.

The fading sounds of pirates reached him from all directions, but his attention held to the dark form racing away across the tiles. Who or what was this nightmare creation Baron Samedi? What was the nature of the power holding so powerful a figure to these criminals of the sea? And what dark purpose was served by his "arrangement" with the Ghostmaker's crew?

The hunger for answers drove Benjamin on in pursuit of the demon shadow.

As fast as he could travel, he pushed hard to gain on the Baron where the spirit raced effortlessly amid the chimney pots, climbing, swinging, gliding with lightning pace west and towards the heart of the city. Where buildings gave way to leafy squares his spidery cloak propelled him far over open ground and the Baron became for a moment a great jagged blackness against the night sky. Returning softly to earth, his rapid progress continued in a rustle of black garments.

Benjamin tore on, his night vision keeping the ghostly shape fixed. The next neighbourhood was reached and the Baron climbed again, spilling over the rooftops like ink, oozing between stacks and darting from house to house on his way.

A low wall served as the perfect springboard for Benjamin's return to the roofs, vampire nails digging deep in hauling him to a high point where he paused to relocate his quarry. There, disappearing across the slates beyond, the Baron's cloak swept over the lip of a building, luring Benjamin on. Nimble as a cat, he sprang after, scaling a tall chimney pot for a clearer view of the demon below where he vanished around the corner of another home. Benjamin dived, floated and jumped from surface to surface in pursuit, rounding the corner in search of the Baron's route.

And he found nothing. The Baron had vanished.

Alarmed, Benjamin sank into shadow as protection against ambush, and from there he scanned the night. High and low he searched for a sign of the dark man's passing, the slightest flicker of movement to betray his position. For the longest time the only motion was the gentle rolling of chimney smoke as the silence of the night pressed in.

A sudden flapping of birds disturbed from their

roost broke the moment. It pulled Benjamin's gaze to a point to the left and below where, for barely a second, the figure of the Baron shifted against the darkness.

'Got you.'

Benjamin sped on, reaching the spot where the phantom had moved an instant before, only to discover he had vanished again. Benjamin frowned at such a trick in this of all places. For here, on a roof space flat and wide, was an oasis of light to make concealment practically impossible. The source of illumination was a large raised skylight through which lantern-glow from the dwelling beneath poured up, forcing shadows to retreat to the very lip of the roof on all sides. Only one strip of darkness held against the gleam, that from a partially opened door granting access to and from the upper part of the house, a door whose hinges offered the tiniest squeal in closing as Benjamin looked on.

Advancing cautiously on the barrier, he passed close to the skylight and, looking below, he saw a pool of candles playing on some jolly gathering of mortal men, the light sparkling on glasses as they were raised to laughter. Benjamin quickly dismissed the festivities and stepped on towards the doorway where he paused, night senses probing for signs of movement. Detecting none, he slipped inside.

A short flight of steps led the way, descending to the musty interior of an attic. The space ran empty but for breathing cobwebs and a mouse which scurried across the rafters from Benjamin's arrival. Through a forest of support beams, a narrow walkway led to a second door, no doubt offering access to the main part of the house. Benjamin crossed the distance quickly and stopped again, his ears seeking past the door for any indication of wandering mortals, a servant on his rounds perhaps, or worse, the Baron haunting the corridors of this home. Satisfied by stillness, Benjamin moved easily between door and frame.

A short corridor stretched away, illuminated weakly by a single candle on a side-table. Nothing moved here, but sounds of the happy gathering drifted up from a spot where the corridor opened onto a high gallery. Benjamin advanced through dancing shade and chose a dark corner to view the proceedings.

Settling down by the gallery's rail, he found his place to be located directly below the skylight, and above a long dining room. The chamber was dominated by a broad table bearing the remains of a hearty feast and surrounded by wigged gentlemen drinking joyously as they conversed. No sign of the Baron's presence was evident here. Believing himself misdirected, Benjamin was on the point of withdrawing to search elsewhere when a drunken outburst from among the celebrants stopped him.

'Tell us more of Billy Buckler, my Lord!' the shouting voice demanded.

'Yes! Yes!' Another drinker agreed through a loud belch. 'Remington, we simply must have more details!'

The requests were met by cheers of assent from the rest and backed by a rhythmic pounding of fists on wood as the guests urged the man at the head of the table to speak.

At last Lord Remington banged his tankard down on the table, once, twice, thrice.

'Order in the court!' he bellowed at his guests, all of whom laughed mightily at his joke amid splashing ale.

'He'll hang us all!' a joker cried and the laughter increased the more.

'Enough, gentlemen,' someone pleaded finally, 'let us hear from our good lord the judge.'

Lord Remington nodded in his seat for the due respect shown and afforded all present a moment to fall silent in expectation of his words.

'Gentlemen,' he at last addressed the faces turned to him, 'I believe this day I have looked into the eyes of the Devil himself. There can be no other description for that which I saw brought to my court these past days, none! Billy Buckler, I tell you, would far better to have burned as a possessed soul than hanged as a common criminal!'

Like the assembled guests, Benjamin tuned a keen ear to the judge's words. Everywhere he went this night, it seemed, Billy Buckler intruded as the sinister focus of events.

'I looked into the prisoner's face directly,' Lord Remington continued, leaning in to fix each guest with his own stern glare, 'and as God is my judge, a spark of hellfire lay within that pirate's eyes.'

'Terrifying,' came a reply, whispered and trembling.

'Were I not a justice of the Admiralty these many years,' Remington answered, and here he puffed out his chest and straightened his dress-wig officiously, 'I might indeed have been terrified.'

'Bravo!' the group cheered and drank a toast to the great law-giver.

Benjamin watched the revellers give over to renewed celebrations, and as they drained cups and howled for more ale, he worked to understand the trail that had led him here. But even as he did, vampire senses tickled urgently and pulled his gaze sharply from the feast. He turned upward to the skylight and caught the lingering presence at the glass.

Peering down on the gathering with flaring eyes,

Baron Samedi drifted and shifted on the air like a bad dream.

In an instant Benjamin was off and running, retracing his path back towards the roof. His rapid progress snuffed out the lone candle, and the attic was a moment's blur in his vision. Mere seconds later he was outside once more and seeking in vain for hidden demons. But the Baron was gone again.

Frustrated, Benjamin looked about for a trace, any clue to the dark form's whereabouts. No sound or movement offered a hint, no scent on the air came to offer help. The slates recorded no footprints, and chimney smoke rose undisturbed by any passing. The night and everything in it held to perfectly stillness.

The moment's clarity reached Benjamin, pushing through agitation to go deep to a vampire's understanding.

True concealment in the dark comes from stillness.

Benjamin held fast and probed the motionless night.

The telltale sign he hoped for came from far off, beyond the roof's edge. At the end of a terrace of dwellings opposite, where the last chimney stack climbed high, the Baron perched like a monstrous bird of prey, unmoving and almost entirely lost to sight against the clouds. It was motion that betrayed him, the gentlest floating of his gown to make it possible for Benjamin's silvery vision to pick him out. There the creature squatted, wrapped in his cloak, apparently lost in watching the night. But, as Benjamin looked on, he perceived through those black caressing rags how the Baron held a hand before his face, and in that hand, turning over and about in spindly fingers, he held the corked bottle given to him by Mr Pyke. Besides this slow rotation of glass the man-spirit made no move and just sat as though waiting in deep contemplation.

A clamour of voices issued to disrupt the silent night. In the street far below, boisterous forms staggered from the judge's doorway. His guests were departing and making merry still as they hailed their fine friend Lord Remington. Dutiful servants fussed along a line of parked carriages and worked in guiding drunken passengers to the correct vehicles for their journeys home.

Dismissing the activity, Benjamin turned back to the lofty chimney, only to find the stack empty. The brief interruption had allowed the Baron to slip away once more undetected.

6

Ignorant of the race and chase above his head, Lord Remington waved to the last departing guest before retreating quickly to his house.

Pausing in the hallway, he watched impatiently as a servant secured the door, fighting a burning temptation to double-check the man's work himself. He jumped to a crashing of bolts and shuddered to the echo rolling far off to the empty spaces of the building.

'Is the rest of the house shut up?' he demanded then of the servant.

'Yes, my Lord,' the servant said with a bow.

'Good, good,' Remington said, barely reassured. 'I will retire to the library for a time, I think. Bring me wine.' With a quick turn he added, 'And the box, bring the box.'

As the servant again bowed and moved quietly to follow his instructions, the judge climbed the stairs, grunting in the effort to carry a bellyful of food and drink up and on towards the library. There, among high shelves laden with books, and by a flickering fire, Lord Remington cast off his heavy wig and flopped into a comfortable chair with a relieved sigh for aching feet. After his long day marking the end of Billy Buckler, the judge felt tired to his bones. Yet he also felt sure the sleep he so desired would not come tonight. Hoping to gain some small comfort from the fire, the judge reached out to the warming flames and was alarmed to see his hands tremble despite the heat that played over them. The library door swung open and the judge snatched his hands back, hiding shaking digits from the servant who entered. The man carried a silver tray to his master's side. Upon it, a large glass of red wine sat by a rectangular box of finest wood and silver lock.

'Ah, capital,' Lord Remington said, steadying his voice as the items were set down. With a wave he dismissed the servant and said, 'That will be all for tonight. I will breakfast late tomorrow, very late.'

'As you wish, sir,' came the reply, and the door was pulled behind.

Remington waited until he heard the door click firmly. Then, in a flash, he grabbed eagerly for the box. With those same shaking fingers he worked to slip its catch and threw back the lid to behold two pistols of elegant design within, lying by powder and shot. Snatching one up, he began to prepare it with breathless urgency.

The heavy weapon felt good in his hands, the cold weight of its metal chasing away the tremors his fire could not. Its form offered the promise of strength, a strength he did not feel despite his bravado earlier when friends had crowded his table.

Lord Remington was alone now, and afraid, very afraid.

Oh, Billy Buckler was in his grave true enough, and the pirate's reign of terror ended with the rope's sudden drop and sharp stop, but what of his dastardly crew? Not a man extra of the Ghostmaker had been snared in the trap that delivered Buckler to justice. And navy claims of buccaneers scattered to the winds by their captain's loss did not sit well with Lord Remington as he fidgeted with his pistol. But no vengeful pirate would find him unprepared this night.

Rubbing a cloth vigorously over the second, empty weapon, the judge tested its action, thumbing the hammer before pulling the trigger to send it down with a sharp, efficient click. Grunting his satisfaction, he hauled back the mechanism once more and peered along the weapon's length, focussing on imaginary targets about the room. He tracked ornaments along the mantel, and shadows dancing and weaving by firelight across bookshelves before settling finally on a bead of light atop a long candle. With a grin for his flickering quarry, Lord Remington steadied himself, and squeezed. The hammer snapped loudly down.

And the candle snuffed out.

The judge sat, startled by the occurrence, and sought some logical explanation with his tired mind. In the midst of pondering, a gentle tickle of air on his neck turned him towards the windows, and through the gloom he spied curtains slowly shifting on the breeze.

Is the rest of the house shut up?

Yes, my Lord.

Unconsciously the judge's fingers tightened on the pistol as he stared at the dreamy shifting of material, playing back and forth, back and forth, until it seemed the very gloom there moved in similar fashion, almost as though that black shadow...the one in the farthest, darkest corner of the library...was itself made up of strips of fabric to be pushed and pulled by the night breeze. Only when the shadow began to grow and spill into the patch of moonlight across the carpet did the judge accept the night played no tricks and what he beheld was unbelievable yet maddeningly real, and far worse than any pirate.

Frozen in his seat, the terrified man opened his mouth to scream, but no sound came from a throat stilled and dry as graveyard bones. Pinned there, he watched as the form of a man slowly emerged to grow terribly huge by the light of the fire, a man whose face under his feathered top hat was half-painted over white to a vision of living death. The judge found strength enough somehow to raise his useless pistol to the hellish shape, and the movement was met by the dark man's own. A skeletal hand lifted to present that which the demon carried, and the judge beheld a bottle, empty and uncorked.

The voice of the Baron came, deep and dreadful.

'By stick and stone, and root and bone, I am sent. For YOU!'

7

ool! Benjamin cursed himself for having been distracted so easily.

Upon reaching the place where the Baron last sat, he had hunted round empty chimney pots for any trace of the demon, but there was no sign anywhere, and the only visible movement at the pots that had been his perch were lazy curls of smoke from fires in homes beneath his feet.

Benjamin stood, alone and confused, trying desperately to pick up the trail again. But there was nothing near or far, until, on turning fully around for the umpteenth time, his gaze fell on the façade of the judge's home. And there he watched the spirit emerge from an upper window into the night. Like a mammoth spider, the Baron oozed from the opening, the rags of his living cloak spreading to find sure holds in the brickwork for his short journey towards the roof. Gaining that place he paused, and Benjamin perceived how the figure drew out his precious bottle again. The Baron held it high as though to examine by the light of the moon what it now contained. Within the corked glass a soft glow of dancing emerald light washed the spirit's face with its hue and lit a terrible, gratified smile. It caught too his nod of satisfaction before he tucked his prize away and swept quickly from sight.

Benjamin sprang into the pursuit. His leap across the watching moon easily cleared the street, and his landing was sure and soft on the judge's roof. Casting all about at once he looked for his slippery opponent's escape route or a movement to draw him on and into the chase again. But even though his arrival was barely an instant behind the Baron's departure, the night shrouded the phantom completely and there was not a sign of the demon's passing. Desperately rushing to every corner of the roof, Benjamin searched through the darkness across city rooftops stretching empty from St Paul's to the Thames and beyond. Moonlight offered nothing but a rising river mist. With fists clenching in frustration, Benjamin watched routes become obscured by its thickening wisps and reluctantly accepted the chase was ended, for tonight at least.

Exasperated at the loss of the Baron, and all the more at a lack of answers, Benjamin strode back to the leading edge of the judge's house, retracing the spirit's path from the open window. Determining to uncover what had occurred inside, he leaned without hesitation for dizzying height and reached past the edge of outermost tiles, there to dig his nails into the brickwork. Fully inverted yet firmly supported, Benjamin edged into space and began to crawl hand over hand down the building's side. With no blood to rush to his vampire head, he travelled effortlessly until the opening was gained. Suspended there at the window's upper frame, he halted just long enough to probe inside with night senses attuned. Discovering no threat, he kicked free and swung noiselessly in.

The sound of fireplace embers crumbling was louder than his soft landing on the library floor, their dying flare more than sufficient to reveal the scene to him. Directly opposite stood the judge's empty chair. About it lay objects scattered by an apparent toppling of a side-table. Here a pair of pistols had tipped from an open box, and a glass had shattered to allow its contents spread a dark stain on the rug. And beside all, prone by the hearth, lay the sprawled figure of Lord Remington. The lack of heartbeat to Benjamin's ears told all he needed to know of the judge's condition even as he approached the fallen man.

Turned upward to the ceiling, the judge's face contained a look of such wide-eyed fear there could be no doubt he had peered on the Baron's ghostly features, an action too much for this mortal man to endure. But abruptly, Benjamin sensed that was not all to the dead man's fate.

In kneeling close by the body, a vague and uncertain feeling rose to nip the edge of vampire senses. It hinted at something other than life gone amiss from this dead man's frame, and Benjamin struggled to identify it. There was an emptiness in the man, an absence from him, something not there that should be. Confused by the feeling, Benjamin passed a hand above the body, as though to bring into sharper focus that which crept just past the reach of full understanding.

There came a rush of activity beyond the library door, sudden and urgent, and it pulled Benjamin sharply from his examination. He caught the sound of footsteps racing along the corridor.

The vampire moved in a blinking.

The door burst open and Lord Remington's servant entered to raise a candle high in search of the disturbance he had detected by the crashing of his master's table. A cry of fright issued for the body on the carpet and the servant staggered, a hand flung to his mouth in drowning the fearful sound. He circled the terrible scene and turned all about, stabbing the light to all parts of the room in search of the judge's killer. Finding no-one besides, he plunged to the open window and thrust out his head.

'Murder!' he howled to the night. 'Murder!' Driven by growing panic, he retreated and fled the room to seek help.

Not for a moment in his confused state did the servant think to look up to where a silver-eyed boy clung firmly to the ceiling plaster-work, watching his hysterical departure.

With a last glance to the judge staring mutely up at him, Benjamin slipped through the window and into the grey pre-dawn.

8

Sunrise caught London teeming with news and wild rumour.

Murder!

Lured by reports of Lord Remington's fate, crowds poured to his house at first light. Soldiers posted before the building held the crush at bay and forced order on the unruly as the Chief Justice arrived to investigate. Setting his face sternly ahead, the man held to grim silence for questions hurled from the fray and quickly mounted the steps to the death house. In place of answers, the crowds made up their own. Fanciful theories and gossip began to jump from lip to ear to feed the craving for information and gory details.

The judge was judged by a midnight court of criminals.

Hanged with his own rope, he was.

Executed by pirates!

Pirates. By nine of the clock the word was repeating everywhere. Billy Buckler's men had been in the city all along, it was said. They carried with them the 'revenge' promised by the man sent to the gallows, others insisted, a reign of terror to be visited on London! Mistaken for a buccaneer in his feathered hat at half past the hour, the ever fashionable Lord Dudley Darnley was chased and badly accosted by hysterical citizens. By ten in the morning a tradesman hinted at sightings of armed men watching the judge's house during the trial, setting tongues wagging all the more. By eleven, rich gentlemen in coffee houses were speaking with unshakeable conviction of assassins, shipped into England aboard the Ghostmaker, killers from the darkest jungles of the Indies with orders to dispatch the judge with a dart of tribal poison. At midday little Dora Charleston, whose family neighboured the unfortunate Lord Remington, declared at lunch how she had watched in the night from her bed chamber as a dark figure flew in at the judge's window. How her parents laughed at such a silly dream. Then, as clocks struck one, all speculation was swept aside by fresh intelligence to dumbfound everyone. A most dreadful report came racing from the river. The mortal remains of Billy Buckler were missing, vanished in the night from Blackwall Reach. Stories of revenge from beyond the grave shivered to life and multiplied rapidly to become ever more frightful as the clock wound on.

By the stroke of two all the rum was gone and the

Ghostmaker pirates grumbled with curses for the world of everyday people.

Brooding in shadow as surely as any vampire in London, the buccaneers held fast to their hiding place while the gossiping tongues in the city made it a nervous and watchful place. In the dim interior of the Gravediggers tavern, they griped and waited for the return of their host and spy, Mr Robinson. In pursuit of information, he had set out early to look and listen on the streets about.

At the centre of all sat Mr Pyke, alone in silence as he too searched. At a table set aside from the rest he bent to a rough-cut document beneath his hands and considered its many scrawled drawings. He followed lines that ran in jagged circles to represent islands, with zig-zag mountain tops and single-line rivers coursing to a sea of squiggles. An octopus sat ridiculously above the waves to peek between inked arrows running to and fro across the map, these the recorded voyages of the Ghostmaker to hidden coves and beaches. And though a compass marker had been included on the page, no names to identify locations were set down – Pyke knew all by keen memory. But likewise, not a single sign, no badly drawn dagger, no childish skull, not even a slashed 'X' was visible to identify that which Pyke needed to know as he sought again and again through the daylight hours.

'Still no closer to our treasure, I see.'

Pyke started from his research to find the speaker, Mr Davy, standing over him. The man was accompanied by the Ghostmaker's other officers, its pirate council of scarred Mr Estoban and one-eyed Mr Stubbs.

'Keep your voice down,' Pyke hissed for Davy's words and with a wary glance to the crew. Assured that none besides had heard his comrade's dangerous talk, he sank back in his chair. 'It could be in any one of a hundred places...a thousand.'

Davy sighed and pulled up a chair opposite the first mate. Idly lifting the document, he allowed his eyes to wander across its amateur geography.

'A fine to-do,' he mused as he travelled beyond the map to the depths of his own imagination. 'There can't be no small island as could contain the Ghostmaker's treasure, that's one thing for certain.'

'Aye,' Pyke agreed, 'but that offers no clearer heading.'

Mr Stubbs narrowed his good eye.

'Well there's a fine pickle gifted by our bold captain,' he said, displeased. 'He lies in one place beyond our reckoning, and our treasure lies in another no less mysterious. Fine band of cut-throats we are, I must say.' He splayed a tattooed hand over the map. 'And Billy never shared a hint with you, his own first mate, not even once? A remark he let slip in passing, maybe, a loose phrase to set us on a course?'

Pyke shook his head.

'Billy offered but two things whenever pressed on the subject of treasure. "Our reward," he used to say with that gleam in his eye, "our treasure, leaves every man of the Ghostmaker rich beyond reckoning."'

'And the other?' Estoban prompted.

Pyke aimed a finger to his temple and affected a playful tone.

'"The map secured in ol' Billy's head keeps a pirate from getting dead."'

Davy gritted his teeth in frustration.

'Well he be sure dead now.'

'Aye, for sure,' Pyke admitted. 'For now.'

'That's right,' Stubbs grumbled. 'But there was never no plan for the captain to up and disappear like this. That was not part of anyone's figuring.'

'What of it?' Pyke challenged him sharply. 'It's a minor obstacle on the course we travel. We have a trail to follow and we will. All will be well when we have our captain back, have no doubt.'

'But will the slave's magic still work when we do?' Estoban asked. 'It's been many more hours than we thought first…perhaps too many.'

Bounding from his chair, Pyke held up his map, first for the officers and then for all to see, thrusting it furiously towards each man in turn.

'See here! Do you see? I have wracked my brain and retraced the Ghostmaker's path to bays and ports and coves and islands, and still the same fog descends on the truth of it. A treasure beyond all measure lies waiting, just as Captain Buckler promised us if we do as we promised him. We regain our captain, we help him in his final revenge on merry old England and we see our fortunes made. That's it and nothing more, you all agreed. There is no other plan.'

Calming himself, Pyke retook his seat to stare hard at the men as he went on.

'You have already seen our magician's work, and more than once. Through all the voyages of the Ghostmaker have you ever seen magic more potent? Our trickster has power enough to pass the gates of death and return. You know it, you've seen it. We stick to the plan.'

The men exchanged doubtful glances but did not challenge the strange truth they recognised in the first mate's words.

'Look,' Mr Davy said with a gesture to the tavern's shuttered windows. All turned to spy the last rays of daylight ebbing to black night between the slats.

'To work,' Mr Pyke ordered.

Jumping to action, the pirates made ready their weapons and filed out quickly. Men followed one another in silence, a rag-tag army tramping past the bar to a door at the rear exiting to a walled yard. There they assembled and maintained a keen look-out in waiting further orders. Suspicious eyes probed for uninvited guests through gloomy corners and recesses between barrels, but none with vision keen enough to spy the dark boy figure crouching in deepest chimney shadow on the roof. As the pirates kept watch, so too did Benjamin Blake.

Mr Pyke emerged after his men, yet barely had he done so when sounds beyond the yard's twin gates announced another arrival. Pirate hands travelled to pistols and swords in preparation for the noisy visitor. The barriers parted, and tavern keeper Robinson came upon the scene, labouring under the weight of two small casks in his meaty arms and with a third rolling before his foot.

'Gentlemen,' he said, startled by the ranks of stern faces regarding him. Giving over to a mischievous grin, he kicked the rolling barrel among the crew. 'Rum, anyone?'

The delighted pirates moved to relieve their host of his remaining barrels, freeing him to approach Pyke and Davy.

'Well?' Pyke demanded as the man fought to catch his breath.

'Well,' Robinson began and took a kerchief to his

sweating brow, 'you boys are the talk of the town with all that harum-scarum at the judge's house. Gentle folk be packing pistols and swords fit enough to start a war. I declare, I lost count of the soldiers out and about.'

'That's not the information you're being paid to bring,' Pyke said, drumming irritable fingers on a pistol grip.

'No, no,' Robinson agreed, becoming more serious at the pirate's actions. 'There is something else.'

'Go on,' the buccaneer said, leaning forward to listen to the tavern keeper's words.

In the shadow of a chimney above, Benjamin did likewise.

'The bodysnatchers you seek? I found them.'

9

'Did you 'ear something?'

In their man-sized hole dug into the cold earth, William Hackett stopped shovelling and cocked an attentive ear. When his partner's continuing efforts disturbed his listening, he nudged him impatiently with a bony elbow.

'I said, did you 'ear something?'

'What?' Jack Butcher snapped in reply. Pausing to rest on his spade, he too listened. 'I don't 'ear nothing.'

Hackett straightened from the job at hand and with a wince for his aching back he pushed his head slowly above ground to scan the world about. From this low vantage point the surrounding headstones and monuments towered to the starry sky, the spaces between them made ominous by the night. Turning slowly, he peered across the graves to the wheels of the cart standing hard by, waiting for the cargo he and Butcher laboured to fetch up from its final resting place.

'Oi!' The harsh whisper from Butcher drew Hackett down to his work and he set about digging once again.

'Blow me down, I think they buries 'em deeper every week,' he cursed with a grunt and cast another load of dirt over the edge of the pit.

'That's 'cos you and me are so 'pre-eminent', innit?' Butcher said with a smirk. 'The powers that be have to dig down to China-land to keep the dead from ol' Butcher 'n' Hackett.'

'We're what?' Hackett once more halted his labours and took to staring in dubious wonder at his accomplice. 'Pre- what?'

Butcher straightened and cracked his back, delighted at the opportunity to explain.

'Pre-eminent,' he repeated, savouring the word like a morsel of fine food. 'It means existing over and above others in terms of the quality of our labours, that is, we are distinguished beyond them in some skill or talent, which in our case means being better in the field of grave robbing than all the rest of the bodysnatchers in London. We are…pre-eminent.'

'Blow me down,' Hackett said, more than a little perplexed by his friend's behaviour. 'Did you go and fall on your 'ead?' His face screwed up in distaste as a thought struck him. ''ere, you didn't spend your last wages on a book of reading, did ya?'

''course not,' Butcher chuckled as he laid into another pile of earth. 'I can't read anyways. No, Doctor Wheatley said it, didn't 'e? That time we run 'im up three stiffs in a single night.' Here he paused again and, with a dramatic shift of his shoulders, he took on the character of their client Wheatley. '"One must declare, one simply must, that you fine gentlemen are beyond question pre-eminent in the supply of fresh specimens for one's examinations."' He added a curt sniff for effect.

Hackett eyed him critically.

'Well,' he said, 'be that as it may, and pre-whatsit as we may be, this tub of guts below ain't gonna be that fresh unless you get back to work.'

'Just sayin',' Butcher replied with a shrug before resuming his spade-work.

Thunk.

The sound of metal striking wood drew smiles from the two men. Reaching for the lantern illuminating their task, Hackett drew close to the partially exposed coffin lid. Wiping away a layer of clay, he rapped his knuckles softly against the soiled wood.

'Knock knock, sleepy head,' he said with a chortle.

Butcher threw a cupped hand to his mouth to muffle his words of reply.

'No, no, let me sleep,' he said in mock alarm and laughed along with his companion.

The bodysnatchers sniggered together and doubled their efforts, shifting the last scoops of clay from the casket and brushing the lid clear.

'I'll fetch the gear,' Butcher offered and he clambered quickly from the hole.

Picking his way carefully through the dark, he approached the cart, casting glances here and there for any sign of soldiers lying in wait to catch grave robbers in the act. For an instant his eyes locked onto an inky patch off between the markers and he paused to better focus his eyes and sudden suspicion. At a distant point, framed by a clump of gnarled trees, he thought he had spotted movement, of a shape resembling a man in a tall hat, flitting among the shadows. Yet when he looked directly at the spot there was nothing. He dismissed it, a trick of the night invading his mind, and he pressed on.

Arriving at the cart, he sought over the tailgate for the tools necessary to complete the night's endeavours. Fingers closed on a crowbar for forcing access to the casket, and a length of rope for "resurrecting" the body from its chilly place of rest. As he gathered the tools, Butcher's eyes travelled to the splintered hole in the tailgate, a consequence of the previous night's adventure with the pirate captain. Some of tonight's pay would have to go in fixing the damage, he decided, in case someone drew dangerous conclusions from it. Determining that Hackett would share the expense for repairs, he made his way back to the hole.

'Careful below,' he whispered and dropped the crowbar to his colleague's waiting hands. While Hackett set to work teasing the nailed lid from its fixings, he prepared the rope. Dropping an end into the grave, he draped the coil across his shoulders and braced his knees for the effort to come.

'Right ya be,' a breathless Hackett said at last, scrambling from the grave while Butcher began to haul on the secured load.

''e's an 'eavy one sure enough,' Butcher grunted. He made room on the line for his accomplice to add his strength to the final phase of hauling. Together they heaved back, step after wheezing step, until finally, the shrouded head and shoulders of the corpse came into view.

'Come on, mate,' Hackett groaned through his teeth, 'the doc's waitin'.'

With a final puff and pull, the partners dragged their prize free to a thump of dead weight. Happily ditching the rope, they rested a moment ahead of the next part.

Drawing a deep breath through his nostrils, Butcher slapped a weary hand to Hackett's shoulder.

'All right, then, grab 'is legs.'

The men took firm holds at either end of their dreadful package. Groaning again in unison they drew the body up on their trembling legs and came fully upright in time to see pirate faces emerging from the night on all sides.

Rooted to the spot, Hackett and Butcher watched the ring of buccaneers slowly tighten round in an array of glowering features adorned with scars and gold teeth. Swords winked dangerously in the moonlight as pistols clicked harshly. Within yards of the trembling bodysnatchers, the pirates halted as one and without a word. And they glared.

The bodysnatchers sought desperately for a sign as to the villains' intentions, as well as any blessed hope of escape from it. They found nothing in the scowls but the cruellest promises. Finally turning unsteadily towards their transport, Hackett and Butcher caught in a shared moment the sharp-bearded pirate leaning there, standing apart from the others and staring back. Unlike his compatriots, this man's weapons remained secured, allowing a hand to rest on the hilt of his sword while another tapped slowly and accusingly on the damaged tailgate.

'Questions,' Mr Pyke said. 'I have questions.'

10

From deepest cover nearby, Benjamin watched the graveyard.

And he listened.

With ears attuned to events within the dour circle behind him, he turned his vampire vision to the inky night, scanning to the very limits of sight for that figure who had not yet shown himself, but who waited, he was sure, out there in the dark somewhere. Whatever transpired between bodysnatchers and pirates, the Baron would be the final actor to play a part in the drama unfolding here.

Benjamin sensed him even now.

'Questions,' he heard Pyke say in breaking the silence. 'I have questions.'

''appy to 'elp,' Butcher grunted as he fought a losing battle with his end of the heavy corpse.

'Good,' Pyke replied, and he peered at each man in turn. 'Where is Billy Buckler?'

'And who might that be, sir?' Hackett tried with a weak smile.

A thunderous explosion of dust at the feet of the bodysnatchers drove both to leap back with cries of fear. Whipping hands to ears stung by the pistol shot, they released their grip on the corpse, and it fell to earth with another meaty thump.

'What is wrong wiv you?' Butcher demanded of his colleague, astounded by the stupidity of his words.

Hackett shrugged awkwardly and remained quiet.

Gazing into the night still, Benjamin watched bats whirl in panic from the gunshot, and he tracked their progress where they raced across the brooding tombs. Thus it was he saw, among the black curtain of trees, the shifting of a figure who was no ordinary night creature.

Benjamin darted through the gloom towards a row of tall monuments in search of the Baron.

Furious at the evasive bodysnatchers, Pyke turned his smoking pistol to the cart and rapped its barrel loudly against the damaged tailgate.

'This porthole was gifted you last night and damns you to worse than Hell if you do not answer me now!' he barked.

To reinforce their leader's words, the other pirates raised weapons and stepped ever closer.

'All right, all right,' Butcher said, casting his hands out in hasty surrender. 'We took 'ol Billy…er… Captain Buckler.'

'Took him where?' Pyke demanded, moving forward to jab his pistol under Butcher's chin.

'Will you let us go if I tell?' the trembling bodysnatcher asked.

'Give me the information I seek and we won't kill you,' Pyke agreed. 'Talk.'

'All those we...uh...resurrect we bring to Doctor Wheatley,' Butcher admitted.

Far off, where Benjamin crept along the cold stone wall of a tomb, he paused and listened to the ongoing conversation. Ears sought details as his eyes sought the Baron.

'Dr Wheatley,' he whispered and burned the name into memory.

At a place where mausoleums crowded together in oppressive silence, Benjamin faced innumerable narrow paths between them stemming from his own, an impossible choice both left and right in locating his elusive quarry.

It was the shadows that made the choice for him, or rather one shadow among the rest. Across the unmoving night before him, Benjamin's eyes fell to the tiniest of movements at the low corner of a tomb. There, where the stone marked the junction between paths, a tiny shapeless mass snaked away across the ground, drawn away around the corner between markers. He recognised at once the tattered end of a flowing robe, tugged like a devil's tail by a figure unseen who strolled among the dead. Benjamin plunged for the spot.

Pyke sought more from his captives with another thrust of his pistol.

'Doctor Wheatley?' he prompted.

'That's right,' Butcher agreed eagerly, 'the surgeon at St Bartholomew's 'ospital.'

''e asked for us to fetch Billy Buckler special,' Hackett cut in, as keen as his companion to please the dangerous audience. 'Special delivery, 'e called it, and paid double the rate.'

Benjamin halted, pulled up by the information. Focussing intently, he waited for the resurrection men to offer yet more details. And as he waited he continued his scan of the sightless paths, probing junction to junction and to each black recess marking the doorway of one tomb after another stretching away.

Where are you, Baron? he asked silently in preparing to move deeper among the graves. Just as he made to take a step, his gaze travelled upwards and he froze, held by what he saw over the mausoleum rooftops.

On the very pinnacle of a high granite column, erected to the memory of some rich Londoner as dead as his neighbours, a portion of the night sky shifted and drifted lazily where a dark form perched, his cloak billowing slowly on the air. The dreamlike flow had obscured the light of a distant star for just a second and betrayed the location of the Baron. There he sat under his black top hat, enshrouded in night-marish cape while keeping a vulture's watch on the land of the dead, watching and waiting, a dark spec-tre ready to pounce on unwary souls.

'Special delivery, why special?' Pyke demanded, whipping his gun from Butcher's neck to jab it between Hackett's wide eyes.

'Well, obvious innit?' Hackett squeaked, and he shrugged awkwardly his reluctance to offer more until the pistol against his head clicked and forced it from him. 'Souvenirs! The doc said 'e 'ad custom-ers ready to pay 'andsome like for the bones of Billy Buckler.'

Souvenirs.

Pyke's face twisted to a mask of rage and he spun to the pirate crew in a flash.

'Find him!' he bellowed, 'find Wheatley tonight! Get moving!'

The circle of pirates sundered as men charged away to all points of the compass, spurred on by angry commands and the terrible knowledge of their captain's fate.

Pyke whirled back to the grave robbers, his teeth

grinding as he turned the pistol furiously between one and the other in struggling to decide which deserved better the shot it contained.

'We meant no 'arm,' Hackett pleaded from behind his hands. 'It's just business, innit?'

'You said you wouldn't kill us!' Butcher wailed pitifully.

The words seemed to reach Pyke through the red fog of anger behind his eyes, and with great effort he drew back from lethal action against the shaking captives. For their part, the bodysnatchers watched his movements closely, seeking hope in his hesitation and the easing of his finger from the trigger.

'I did promise, didn't I?' Pyke said distantly, and a cruel and knowing smile grew on his face. Nodding with satisfaction for the plan in his mind, he turned as if to go but took no steps to leave. Instead he inclined his face to the night sky. 'BARON! Come! I summon you!'

The monstrous form blotting the sky above Benjamin sprang forth instantly to the call, and the moon was swallowed in the Baron's passing. His shade swam across the earth like a spirit loosed from its grave on some fiendish errand. It followed the Baron's course and rejoined his form where the spirit landed to scuttle among headstones to the pirate's voice.

Benjamin hurled himself after. Vaulting markers, he sprinted towards Pyke and the grave robbers, arriving in secret on the edge of the scene as Pyke once again turned his attention to the men. Benjamin paused to stare in wonder.

'Gents,' Pyke said, his teeth gleaming in a wicked smile, 'please say hello to the Baron.'

The confused grave robbers looked from Pyke to one another and next into the empty night behind the pirate. For a brief spell, besides the stones and silent trees, there was nothing to demand their attention. But all at once, and with the barest movement of black on black, there was something. It came on as a creeping growth across the ground, a seeping advance towards the pair as they watched its steady increase. Spreading forth, the drifting, shapeless thing reared above the bodysnatchers to devour the very night until they could see nothing else. And at last, from the midst of its swirling, the torso of the skull-painted Baron appeared and hovered over the gawping men.

Minds became lost in terror at the demonic vision. The bodysnatchers retreated with no more than shrill cries to hurl at the dreadful form in its feathered hat. Unable to look from the nightmare as they fled backwards, their feet struck a forgotten obstacle, the shrouded corpse they had dropped. The men flailed and grabbed at one another for support and so toppled together, screaming into the open grave. There they thrashed about in blind panic while the Baron's form grew above the edge of the hole and peered down on their desperate attempts to untangle twisted limbs.

Regarding his prey with a cold indifference, the Baron reached to the folds of his cloak and drew out twin corked bottles. He closed fingers over the containers to open both with the softest pops before presenting the vessels for the men's glassy-eyed consideration. And his own eyes surged with focus as his booming voice filled the air.

'By stick and stone, and root and bone, I am sent. For YOU!'

Cloak ends spilled into the grave like poisoned water, like flowing tentacles stretching to coil about the feet of the trapped men even as they clawed tearfully at the walls of the earthen trap containing them. Black tendrils swam about kicking legs and squeezed to heaving chests, encircled necks and plucked at quivering lips and flaring nostrils. And as blackness drew up, the Baron went down, into the grave where he and his cape became one and filled the hole to the brim.

Deep and smothered within the earth, a pitiful screaming began.

11

S taring on in horror, Benjamin witnessed the bodysnatchers' end.

The dreadful mass within the grave surged and heaved, giving witness to the awful struggles below until, and by slow degrees, the turbulence began to ease like the ocean after a violent storm and at last turned flat calm against the edges of the hole to become a motionless oily pool.

In the brief interlude, Benjamin looked to where Pyke stood, overseeing the Baron's terrible work with a measure of evil amusement on his face. He leaned idly against the cart's frame and stroked his beard while looking on, having about him the air of one pleased by some street entertainment and not a grotesque act of murder. The man's attitude prompted Benjamin to ponder how many times this rapscallion had unleashed such pain on others as to leave him so unmoved and pitiless.

The question was chased from Benjamin's thinking as fresh activity within the grave signalled the rising of the Baron. Drawing up through his cloak, the terrible form of the demon emerged from the pit to glide before his pirate master, his dour features a direct contrast to the pirate's grin. One large hand extended to offer the corked bottles which held the results of his work, that same green light Benjamin had spied after the assault on Lord Remington.

Pyke's face, caught by surprise in the eerie glow, shifted at last from pleasure to one of distaste in eyeing the Baron's offering. Perturbed, he took an involuntary step away from the shimmering bottles and steadied himself.

'Not to me,' he ordered sharply, and Benjamin noted the measure of shivering fear in his tone. Turning instead to the night, the buccaneer issued a shrill whistle and stood aside to the sound of approaching hooves from the graveyard's edge. The pirate carriage trundled into view, a phantom coach snaking between tombstones. Stepping to meet the vehicle where it halted, Pyke opened its door and gestured quickly within. 'Give them to her.'

The passenger appeared in the open doorway, and Benjamin saw again the features of the little serving girl. Without a word, she reached to receive the Baron's gifts and looked directly into the face of the demon. Watching the scene, Benjamin was intrigued to see how the girl demonstrated none of the fear

Pyke had displayed as the bottles were pressed to her, nor any apparent dread for the fearfully painted spirit. For the longest time, as her tiny hand met his, girl and Baron peered into one another's eyes as though engaged in silent and secret communication until the meeting was abruptly cut short as Pyke slammed the door in the girl's face.

'Get along,' he barked, and the coach driver whipped up the horses to speed them into the night.

For his part, the Baron watched its departure, and his gaze, it seemed so clear to Benjamin, was drawn to deepest sadness.

'Baron,' Pyke said with a rude snap of fingers to regain his attention. 'Get yourself to St Bartholomew's double quick. I want a word with the good Doctor Wheatley before dawn.'

The Baron bowed slowly in reply, yet in so doing Benjamin followed how the demon did not for an instant take his piercing stare from Mr Pyke, and in those dark orbs sadness was replaced by a barely concealed hatred for the pirate. He would obey, Benjamin understood, but would far happier choke the life from Mr Pyke with his mighty hands.

In return, the pirate offered a sneering grin for the supernatural power he controlled before turning to stride away between the graves.

The Baron remained alone, floating beneath

twisted trees. That portion of his body visible amid the flowing of his cloak turned slowly about as though pushed by a soft breeze of indecision. His instructions were clear but he made no move to follow them just yet. Within his caped circle he remained, and looked after Pyke's departure and again to the path taken by the carriage. Next he allowed his eyes to fall to the open grave where the lifeless bodysnatchers sprawled in the pit. Returning then to the starting point of his watching turn, he halted, though his cloak continued to weave and shift lazily about him. After a considered pause, during which he appeared to listen closely, to his own thoughts or to the night itself, he moved once more, shifting just his head this time, the slightest motion betrayed by the inclining of his top hat. Bringing his chin towards his left shoulder, he spoke deeply to the dark.

'Who follows the Baron?' he demanded.

12

Benjamin froze in his hiding place.

Was it to him the Baron addressed the question? Had demonic senses perceived his presence now that all others had departed the graveyard?

Surely this was a bluff, Benjamin told himself, and he remained perfectly unmoving in the shadows. No creature, natural or supernatural could so positively sense the presence of a stealthy vampire. And yet, how confidently the Baron now turned his frame towards his place and narrowed blackened eyes to peer the harder into its enveloping darkness.

'You have followed me two nights now,' he accused the gloom. 'Two nights trying to learn the Baron's business. Show yourself!' As he made his demand, the Baron's caped flared and he lunged towards Benjamin's spot.

Vampire reactions were instinctive. Springing on his toes, Benjamin executed a skyward leap, rolling high over the demon's head to land at his rear, there to brace for another rushing advance.

Following the boy's flight, the Baron spun about to consider the young figure in the crescent moon's light, and floated near for a keener inspection.

'That's close enough!' Benjamin warned. He snapped fingers to a warning sparkle of light and flexed in preparation for a witch's spell.

Intriguingly, the Baron's own fingers appeared immediately to mirror the boy's as he continued his examination, as though the very act of imitating Benjamin's motions would offer some better understanding of him and his abilities.

Spying the phantom's action, Benjamin tested it, slowly moving his right thumb to the tip of its neighbouring forefinger, giving no clue in his features as to the purpose of a motion that dripped sparks.

The Baron's reaction was instant. Clearly fascinated, he mimicked again with his own fingers and drew back rapidly to rise on his cloak for a broader view of the threat he sensed.

'Secrets and spells learned by moonlight magic,' he concluded, his tone carrying a measure of wonder for the truth. 'Who are you, boy spirit?'

'I am Benjamin Blake.'

He watched the Baron repeat the words softly, trying them on his lips.

'A strange name,' the Baron concluded and, with a flick of his eyes towards the boy, added, 'for a witch.'

Benjamin understood at once the Baron's intention. He too was testing, seeking strengths and the true nature of the opponent he faced.

'Not so strange as the title of Baron for a murdering demon,' Benjamin offered boldly.

Angered, the phantom plunged to thrust his face dangerously close to Benjamin's.

'No mere demon am I!' he snarled. He withdrew and drove high on flaring strands to proclaim to the world, 'I am Baron Samedi, guide and gatekeeper to the world of spirits.'

'Yes,' Benjamin replied, 'you keep them in your little bottles, I know that.'

'Pah!' the Baron scoffed. 'You know nothing of my business, Benjamin Blake.'

'I know more than you think. I know you come to a pirate's call and kill at his command. And you will kill again unless I stop you.'

The Baron glared.

'You will not stop me. You will not dare!'

'I won't stand by and allow you to kill innocent people.'

'How little you know.' The Baron sighed and for just a moment it seemed to Benjamin the gatekeeper was burdened by some knowledge he desired to share. But as he looked on Benjamin's determined features, his own quickly tightened to some understanding which sent a knowing smile to those white-painted lips. 'Oh, but I see,' he whispered to himself. 'How sharp your teeth and with silver eyes, you are no witch, vampire boy.' The knowledge appeared to amuse him greatly and he sped into a trailing circle, the better to re-examine his opponent from every angle, laughing as he flew.

Unsettled as Benjamin was to be fully circled by the Baron's cloak, he held his nerve and gave no hint of fear while the chortling spectre floated once more round and called loudly to him.

'How long, Master Blake, have you been a child of the night? Long enough to learn a witch's trade, but not so long to challenge me, I think.' Here he chuckled and flicked fingers in mock spell-weaving.

'I have magic enough for you,' Benjamin assured him. He rubbed thumbs along fingers to add weight to the threat.

Amused still, though cautious enough to draw back on the air, the Baron laughed and sailed off to flit between trees and headstones as black mist.

And in an instant, he was gone.

The gatekeeper's sudden passing gave over to the graveyard's former stillness, and Benjamin blinked at the unexpected shift as he peered in search of the elusive spirit. Every sense heightened but he found no trace, neither sight nor sound. The graveyard's atmosphere grew heavy and Benjamin readied himself, not believing for a moment that his words had chased the Baron away.

The attack came from his right, a burst of shadow from deepest black. The Baron's cloak erupted from the tree line, rolling like an explosion of ink through water. Peeling back it revealed the speeding form of the phantom, his clawing hands stretching for Benjamin ahead of a half-skull twisted to a mask of fury.

With a vampire's roar Benjamin spun to face the challenge, hands forming a spell of devastating power. But his conjuring was too slow, and the racing Baron reached in time to swat the boy's arms aside and he lifted him from his feet with a triumphant cry. Travelling skywards from a spell that blasted nothing but earth, he stared hard on his captive and then, without warning, released him. Benjamin watched the world turn beneath as he fell headlong, and he passed into the open grave to land among dead bodysnatchers. Scrambling to his feet, he braced and sprang upwards to escape the pit, only for the Baron waiting at the graveside to grasp his ankle and fire him below ground once again.

The Baron's ghostly face peered down on his captive and the hole he lay in.

'It fits you well,' he decided aloud and threw back

his head to laugh ferociously at his own joke. Lifted as though by the power of his mirth, his cloak swam high about him and blocked out the stars. 'Hear me, Benjamin Blake,' he boomed at last, descending to squat on the grave's edge, and now with a finger pointed in daggered warning, 'we are not enemies, you and I. This caution once and this one time, do not block my business in this great city. Whom I serve must soon be saved, lest forever we are both enslaved. Farewell, vampire boy.'

Coursing high on his dreadful garment, the Baron sped like a storm cloud across the moon.

Benjamin sprang furiously from the earth and searched for a parting glimpse of his dark opponent. Graveyard mist drifted, and Benjamin found himself alone but for the countless dead and as many questions crowding his mind.

13

Whom I serve must soon be saved, lest forever we are both enslaved.

The Baron's words echoed in Benjamin's ears as he sped west in pursuit of the elusive phantom.

Saved or enslaved?

What was the mystery those tantalising words hinted at? Was the Baron's service to Mr Pyke designed to save the dread pirate? Surely not. Then who? Save who, and from what? Slavery? And under whose control?

Benjamin pushed the wave of questions away as he worked to calculate the fastest route over the tiles to his destination. Delayed by the showdown with the phantom gatekeeper, he realised the crew of the Ghostmaker must already be gathering in alleys and dark doorways around the hospital of St Bartholomew.

There to await Baron Samedi's arrival.

He quickened his pace to the maximum a vampire's

powers allow, becoming less than a shadow where he sped between chimney stacks and through lines of washing slung across the way. He cleared streets in a bound and sent terrified birds skyward from their nesting as he raced headlong.

To his left, rising huge and proud, the hulking dome of St Paul's Cathedral loomed against the sky. It towered over homes and lesser churches around, dominating Benjamin's eyeline towards the curving black line of the Thames. His compass point these many years past, he took his bearing now from the cross-topped dome and altered his course north-west.

The first indication of his nearing St Bartholomew's came not from any visual recognition of the structure but from a fetid stench that assailed his nostrils, thrown up by the cattle pens of Smithfield market located hard by the hospital itself. Even were he blindfolded, Benjamin could follow that stinking path on the air right to his target. Finally, through funk and dim light, St Bartholomew's came into view.

A patch of deepest shade by a chimney provided the ideal resting place from which to view matters, and Benjamin eased quickly into its concealing safety to examine the hospital and the access roads surrounding.

The building itself, a grand four-sided construction around a central square, was a slumbering giant at this late hour. Only a single point of light glimmered across the entire structure to offer a hint of life within its walls. Set into the rooftop farthest from Benjamin's position, a raised sun-roof gleamed to the burning of a lantern in a room beneath. Benjamin pictured the occupant, an impatient Dr Wheatley sitting by the source of that light in waiting for the coming of a pair of bodysnatchers now as dead as the cargo they had promised him.

Mindful of what was coming instead for the unsuspecting doctor, Benjamin shifted attention to the rooftops about. Was the Baron already out there somewhere, lying in wait? Benjamin scanned and caught nothing but the sight of a solitary house cat on high, indifferent to the night and lazily grooming its paws.

The apparently deserted streets were more rewarding to a vampire's searching. A first probing quickly revealed a skulking pair of buccaneers using the blackness of a doorway to conceal their presence near the hospital's eastern side. A peek over the edge of his hiding spot uncovered two more, directly below and holding close to an alley wall which traced south towards the river. Benjamin guessed that the streets north and west of the hospital concealed similar groups of furtive scallywags.

An echoing clatter of horses hooves far off signalled

an approach. Turning to the sound, Benjamin had barely a minute to wait before the source was revealed, and he watched the pirate carriage roll towards St Bartholomew's. Its driver reined in steaming horses to draw up just short of the hospital's grand entrance.

The scene was set.

Come along, Baron, Benjamin urged, I'm here.

London seemed to hold a breath. When the moon gave in to fear and plunged to a thick veil of cloud, the night paused in waiting around that single light within St Bartholomew's, a lonely beacon in a sea of crushing blackness. Save for the uncaring feline, now creeping to the edge of Benjamin's vision on its way to some new perch, the world had stopped.

But the cat was not creeping towards anything, Benjamin realised with a start. It was slinking back, retreating from some dark emergence which caused the fur on its back to spike in alarm. The cat offered a frightful hiss and fled into the night. Benjamin watched the night grow darker with the coming of the Baron.

The phantom seeped between pitched roofs to hold momentarily within their depths. Eyes glistened beneath his hat-brim in a cautious searching before allowing for an advance on serpent tongues of cloak. Cautiously sliding to the building's edge, the spectre inclined to the light beyond, the sheen weakly illuminating a hunger in his painted features. After a final wary search, he rose up to terrible height and sprang forth to become in a moment a great burst of jagged pitch hacking the sky, effortlessly crossing space to the hospital roof. His cape billowed then in slowing his descent and scurried into the glow from the window where he halted to peer on the scene within.

With no less supernatural skill, Benjamin proceeded to follow his opponent. He eased from the chimney's cover to select his own safer route, safer because it was a path to the rear of the Baron. With careful timing he sailed to the next rooftop, passing high and unobserved over sneaking buccaneers. Quickly he skipped from shadow to shadow in approaching the hospital. One final leap would place him directly behind the Baron on the same rooftop. But, recalling the gatekeeper's uncanny perception for hidden vampires, Benjamin delayed his jump and instead crouched low as he waited for the spirit's next move before making his own.

The motion that came was not the Baron's, however, and Benjamin stilled to listen as the night gave over to a new arrival. Along the street, tramping in his boots, came a solitary walker hastening towards the hospital. Benjamin looked to catch Mr Pyke's face through the gloom as the man made his way to its steps, his casual stride betraying nothing of dangerous intentions. Upon reaching the entrance, the buccaneer stopped, there to turn a slow circle as though examining the neighbourhood for threats or unwanted witnesses. Assured he went unseen, he eased a pistol from his belt and slipped inside.

Benjamin returned his attention to the roof in search of the Baron's awareness of his master's arrival. But with a curse he found only the empty window and its soft interior shine.

The Baron so stealthy had vanished once again.

14

Dr Ebenezer Wheatley shot another bitter glance at the table clock and grumbled for the inefficiency of bodysnatchers.

Pacing back and forth between dissecting tables, where sheeted corpses lay cold to his foul mood, the doctor ground his teeth in vowing to deal harshly with Hackett and Butcher whenever the hapless pair finally arrived.

That pair of no-good layabouts.

By twelve of the clock, they had assured him, midnight exactly, they would deliver a fresh specimen on which he could work and experiment through the night hours in his private chamber. And yet at…he glanced for the umpteenth time at the clock… at ten minutes till two there was neither body nor snatchers before him.

A sudden thought struck and he paused to drum a tinny beat with fingernails on a receiving cradle. Perhaps, he mused, the grave robbers had been discovered, perhaps in the very act of resurrecting their latest corpse, his specimen, and they languished even now in the hands of the night-watch. Good, he concluded, they would hang for both the crime and their incompetence. The notion was scant consolation, though, and in a flash of agitation for lost work he thumped the cradle to set its silvered support chains jangling.

Snatching up a short bone saw from a table laden with frightful-looking dissecting tools, Wheatley satisfied his vengeful imaginings by playing the serrated blade against the lamplight, delighting in its purpose and metallic gleam.

'Bumbling fools,' he mumbled and dropped the saw back in its place. The metallic chime of its landing was enough to briefly drown the clock's ticking and the fitful snoring of his medical assistant Kirkby who had long since dozed in a corner.

With a dejected sigh, Wheatley mulled over those specimens laid out on his dissecting tables, previous 'guests' as Hackett so often quipped and always with a wink for Butcher's amusement. The doctor strolled among them, revisiting each covered figure in turn and considering their suitability for inclusion in his life's work, the incomplete manuscript of anatomy waiting by pen and ink on his desk. But he irritably dismissed one body after another; no, no, and no. He had probed what secrets they held in death with little result. These poorest Londoners offered no great discovery and added nothing to his knowledge. They were all wretched specimens, unworthy of his talents.

Not all, though, he reminded himself quickly, no, not all. Among the mortal remains conveyed by the resurrection men this past week, last night's guest had truly been a prize specimen.

The pirate Billy Buckler.

Ah! What a catch and wondrous examination he had been. Wheatley relished the memory of it, the body's physical dimensions on the slab with that face so terrible even in death. He marvelled again at the strength evidenced in those powerful arms and legs, the history of battles recorded in the criss-cross of scars across the whole of the corpse, and the wealth of detail to be read in that brow, with a thickness and breadth to match the earliest savages to stalk the earth.

And the heart, don't forget that heart.

Dr Wheatley shuddered in recalling it. Through all his many midnight studies, never had the doctor exposed such a vessel as Billy Buckler's heart. Larger than any he had previously encountered, it was a blackened organ so unyielding to the knife that he devoted hours of examination to it. In any lesser man, he had concluded in wonder, such a muscle should have sickened and surely killed the rest of the organs and limbs, yet in Buckler it fuelled a thriving in the man and his unending crimes. Amazed still by the frightful organ, Dr Wheatley turned to peer once more on the monstrous heart where he had stored it in a preserving jar upon a shelf where it now bulged foul and poisonous, demanding its own chapter in his manuscript.

Yes indeed, he decided with a smile, Billy Buckler had proven a great reward to medical science, to say nothing of the financial rewards to be gained in dividing the rest of the late pirate among rich trophy seekers who were keen to possess even part of the legendary figure for posterity and delicious thrills.

In his chair nearby, Kirkby snorted and jerked as he was chased through the corridors of an unsettling dream.

Looking on his assistant, Dr Wheatley took to wondering about the young man's slumbers as he continued his pacing, an interesting diversion from the torture of the clock. What, he contemplated, was the content of Kirkby's dream just now? By no means the cleverest student, Kirkby yet displayed in his sleeping motions the workings of some inner world only he was privileged to see, not that the fool would recall his night visions on waking. Oh, to understand dreaming, Wheatley thought, now there was a subject to put to the knife. Never in his work had he extracted a clue to explain the visions that came uninvited to a man's skull after dark. How famous he would be if he could tap that source, why, he would become the most famous explorer of man's internal workings. Certainly he possessed the education and tools necessary for such a discovery. Yes indeed, with his years of schooling, his researches and secret night experiments, he could be the one to make the greatest discovery.

If only bodysnatchers delivered on time as required!

Angered again, the doctor snatched up another shiny cutting tool and slashed the air. Science delayed by dimwits!

Yet, he caught himself, dead men tell no tales. Nor do they dream. Only the living, like Kirkby there, dreamed dreams in that "little death" of sleep. Just feet away, and beneath the thinnest layer of skin and bone, a drama unfolded behind his assistant's eyelids, waiting for a man of science to perceive them, to reveal them.

Taking a step towards the sleeping man, Dr Wheatley slipped his dissecting tool back and forth in gentle motions as he pictured the necessary incision by which to expose the workings of a man's head. Done quickly enough, he deduced, the brain might still be pulsing and firing with dreams even as he beheld it in the lamplight.

A wink of illumination flared on the blade's passing and played to Kirkby's eyelids, bringing the man awake with an explosive snort. Through sluggish waking he started at the unexpected sight of Dr Wheatley standing over him, and the gleaming knife he held so dangerously.

'I fear there will be no examination tonight, Kirkby,' the doctor informed his startled assistant sadly. 'You may go.'

Unable in his moment of fright to form a verbal response, Kirkby nodded mutely and eased from his chair towards the door, offering careful glances as the doctor replaced the knife among its fellows and stroked the blade fondly.

Tomorrow night, Dr Wheatley promised his fine collection of tools as he listened to Kirkby's fading footsteps, tomorrow night we will try again.

A harsh disturbance in the corridor brought the doctor's frowning attention to the door. What sounded like a muffled struggle had interrupted his assistant's padding footsteps and brought a deep, unsettling quiet in their place.

'Kirkby?' Wheatley called. 'I say, Kirkby, are you quite all right?'

Mr Pyke filled the doorway.

'He'll be all right when he wakes up,' he promised grimly and cocked his pistol to take aim at the astonished doctor.

15

'What is the meaning of this?' Dr Wheatley spluttered.

Mr Pyke caught the edge of fear behind the man's indignant tone and smiled for it as he stepped into the room. Circling the examining tables and their ghost-like occupants, he took time in perusing the many shelves of jarred specimens.

'Well I never,' the buccaneer said, eyeing one discoloured mass submerged in preserving fluid. He tapped his pistol softly against the glass container. 'Is that what I think it is, my good doctor?'

'That is the stomach of a man whose diet consisted mainly of pudding,' Wheatley informed him.

'Nice,' Pyke replied, his curled lip indicating he considered the specimen to be anything but.

'I take it you have not come so late for lessons in anatomy,' Wheatley prompted.

'Correct,' Pyke confirmed, and he faced the doctor once more. 'I have come to collect my captain.' He levelled his pistol again.

Dr Wheatley took an uneasy step back from the weapon and bumped his table of dissecting tools to a clamour of metal. Reaching with a hand to steady himself – and work hidden fingers – he held out the other as though to halt the pirate's shot.

'Billy Buckler,' he said, 'it's Billy Buckler you speak of.'

Pyke rolled his eyes.

'Get many pirate captains through every week, do you?' He waved his pistol over the covered tables. 'Which one is Captain Buckler?'

The colour drained from Dr Wheatley's face as he slowly shook his head.

'None.'

Pyke stormed forward and pressed his weapon hard against the doctor's forehead.

'You'd best choose your next words carefully, saw-bones,' he hissed through gritted teeth. 'But choose them quickly.'

'He's here, he's here,' Wheatley shrilled desperately, 'he's just...not...on a slab.'

Confused, Pyke stepped back and looked around the room again, seeking a place where a man so large as his leader could be deposited. He glared at the doctor, the anger in his face demanding a speedy answer.

'The drawers,' Wheatley explained in a breathless

tone. He pointed towards the row of long drawers set below a specimen shelf.

'Show me,' Pyke ordered. He jabbed the physician in the ribs to get him moving.

Following the sweating doctor, the pirate glanced to the table of dissecting tools, spying at once the slim, vacant place left in the line of instruments. With a wry smile, he proceeded after the medical man and watched his hands carefully.

Dr Wheatley arrived at the wooden drawers and hesitated, suddenly reluctant to expose to the angered Pyke what had become of his leader. A threatening flick of pistol spurred him to action, and he drew a deep breath in sliding open a slim rectangular drawer with trembling fingers.

The gleaming white bones of Billy Buckler emerged into the lamplight.

The sight brought Pyke's rage to boiling and he whirled towards Dr Wheatley, striking him hard across the jaw with his free hand. The question that surged to his mind fought a crushing disbelief to reach his lips, and through a red cloud of fury he struck the sawbones, driving the man back until he stumbled whimpering against a dissecting table, there to sob pitifully over a covered corpse.

Pyke drowned thoughts of murder through snarling effort and shifted his pistol off target as he worked to give voice to the question bursting within.

'Where is the skull?' he spat through grinding teeth. 'What have you done with the rest of Billy Buckler?'

Still sobbing pathetically, Dr Wheatley tried to explain through tears and quivering lips. When words failed, he flapped a hand towards his desk.

'A notebook,' he blubbered, 'I keep my list of trophy buyers there, all recorded.'

Pyke hauled the man to his feet and shoved him to the desk. Eager to please, the doctor rummaged through a drawer to produce a small notebook which he held as a blessed offering to the pirate.

'How many have bought the captain's bones?' Pyke demanded as he snatched the little book away.

'Four have placed orders,' the doctor admitted. In the face of the pirate's renewed fury he offered more behind wringing hands. 'But only one has collected, only one.' Here he indicated an entry in the notebook. 'He purchased three pieces. Two leg bones and…the skull. Everything else is still here, I swear it. All of the bones and, of course….' Wheatley threw a hand to his runaway mouth and stifled the unguarded comment so nearly uttered.

'Of course what?' Pyke's eyes flashed up from the notebook. 'Speak, you butchering dog, or yours will be the next body cut up in this filthy room. While you're still alive.'

Dr Wheatley swayed weakly at the thought, and his vision swam until Pyke grabbed his shirt collar and hauled him close with a scowl.

'The heart,' Wheatley confessed. He pointed limply to a shelf. 'Your captain's heart.'

Astounded, Pyke shoved the doctor from him and stepped to the collection of jars, his brain unable to take in what he beheld within one foul container. Only when his fingers reached unconsciously to brush the glass did he accept the unbelievable. Blood surged hot beneath the pirate's skin, fuelled by the vision of tortures he would inflict on the physician who had sundered his good captain so. But then, even as Dr Wheatley sought with terrified eyes for the buccaneer's cruel intentions, the storm in Pyke's face fell to an abrupt calm, and a knowing smile eased the furious grimace that had held there. Rounding on his captive, he stepped deliberately towards the man, causing Wheatley to jerk back from that smile and the torments it promised. Yet when Pyke reached out, it was not to seize the man, but rather the lamp beside him which he carried to the window, there to raise the light once, twice to the pressing night.

'I'll tell you something, doc,' he said, leaning against the glass even as the corridors of St Bartholomew's filled with a tumult of charging feet, 'I've done things in my pirate life, terrible things. I could turn you hair white with stories. And the law in merry England says I should swing for those terrible things. But, I declare, I never did anything to compare with your labours here. And yet there's no hangman's rope for someone as important as you, is there? So who's to punish you for what you've done?'

Sobbing through fear and pain, Dr Wheatley trembled at the arrival of the Ghostmaker's crew. He watched the dreadful gathering fan out across his dissecting room and feared the worst until Pyke waved directions and the men set about bagging their captain's bones, though not without numerous hateful glances to the doctor. When it came to the matter of Billy Buckler's heart, a brief jostling argument settled things and one reluctant scallywag was selected to take charge of the jar and its grisly contents. As quickly as they had come, and without a word, the buccaneers departed.

Pyke made his own slow way after them, holding aloft the notebook for the doctor's consideration.

'You have caused us much pain and inconvenience, sawbones,' he said, holding his back to the snivelling Wheatley but knowing full well how the doctor was already drawing up that razor-sharp knife snatched earlier from the table. 'For that, you deserve a fitting punishment.'

The knife reached its highest point above

Wheatley's head, and its stabbing descent towards Pyke's back had just begun when a massive hand flashed to stay the doctor's wrist in a crushing grip. Pyke continued on his smiling way while Dr Wheatley looked fully into a half-skull nightmare swelling to fill the room with consuming cape and booming voice.

'By stick and stone and root and bone, I am come. For YOU!'

16

The Baron transfixed Wheatley with his pitiless gaze and drew forth his bottle.

With a thumb-flick he uncorked the tiny imitation of the doctor's own jars and held it for the terrified man's consideration, passing the glass hypnotically to and fro before him.

'Look, witchdoctor, look,' the spirit commanded, turning the bottle over in his fingers, 'look into my specimen bottle.'

Despite his wilting terror, Dr Wheatley gazed on to behold the coming of the Baron's magic. He saw the first of a sickly green light pulse between them, and his blood turned to ice when he recognised how the light came not from the demon fingers grasping him, but from within himself! It flowered beneath his shirt, an emerald hue spreading from the cuffs to his fingers and from collar to the ends of his hair. The light grew in strength and seeped forward, drawn towards the open neck of the bottle and, Dr Wheatley knew in a silent scream of understanding, it pulled his life force with it. He felt it as surely as he felt the cold flowing into his body, an icy seep moving up from his toes to replace the warmth that now abandoned him by slow degrees. A thousand miles away he heard the knife in his hand tumble uselessly to the floor, and with failing sight, he watched the face of the Baron shimmer as the bottle began to fill.

'BARON! ENOUGH!'

Shouted from between the corpses, Benjamin's barked command brought the spirit angrily about. In his movement, the Baron retained a firm grip on the wilting doctor, but not so the bottle. The container escaped his fingers and tumbled to the floor where it shattered across the tiles. Baron Samedi was for an instant bathed in green light swirling past his face towards Dr Wheatley.

'You,' the Baron hissed. 'You dare interrupt my work. Defiant one!'

'I dare,' Benjamin agreed, readying for the fight. 'I will not let you murder.'

'Foolish vampire.' The Baron cursed and he flung off the weakened doctor. 'It is not your place to stop me. I am the keeper of who lives and dies, I see them fall…and I see them rise!'

Benjamin at once felt his senses tingle for the magic that came at the Baron's words. He perceived too the shifting of space between him and the phantom, an invisible pulse wrought by the conjuration. Benjamin's fingers tightened against the gatekeeper's attack. And in time with the motion came the full realisation of what the spirit had done. With slow dread, Benjamin shifted his attention to the tables of the dissecting room and to the stained sheets gathered in folds on those resting there. Folds that were suddenly moving.

To a shuddering beneath one cloth, the first rising came. A concealed body eased up to sitting and paused a moment in its place, turning to Benjamin as though capable of sight through the fabric draping its head. Benjamin held fast as the remaining corpses followed the lead of the first to rise one by one until all six sat on the edge of their slabs, a group of sheeted ghosts as white as the Baron's glowering face.

The first reanimated form again gave a lead to the others. Bringing a mottled and diseased arm into sight, it dragged the sheet aside and revealed its hideous zombie features. Foggy orbs regarded Benjamin spitefully while dead partners threw off their own coverings and joined in staring the vampire down.

The Baron passed a hand high over his dead army.

'Perhaps, Master Blake, you should depart. For how do you kill what is already dead?'

The Baron snapped fingers for obedience.

Banshee screeches filled the room. Jars rattled

to the undead chorus, and zombies clattered from tables and rushed forwards. Blackened fingers and scabrous hands lashed out for Benjamin as he moved and conjured in a single instant.

Leaping high over the shambling attackers, he twisted perfectly in the air to land on a slab so recently vacated. The force of his landing set dissecting tools clanging. Fingers came together in a lightning flash and Benjamin cast out.

'Levitas!'

As one to his command, the sharpened tools became airborne, and to a flick of fingers they sped on their way. Darts of reflected light hurtled to find six lumbering targets, slashing through ragged clothes and dead flesh with force enough to pass on and embed themselves in the wall behind.

The monstrous assailants jerked with poisoned gasps as they were struck. With slow brains they examined wounds and considered matters with furrowed brows even as Benjamin looked on in astonishment. At last, judging the occurrence to be at once confusing but harmless, and quite forgetting how to die, the unaffected beasts shrieked with fresh rage and hurtled on.

The zombie rank had almost gained Benjamin's place when he again moved. This time he launched backwards for the safety of the doctor's desk, there to unleash his next assault. Thrusting arms forward, he issued his incantation.

'Pulvis!'

Targeted by the destructive spell, the specimen shelf exploded to hurling splinters and glass. Released from collapsing jars, hideous parts slopped to the floor while preserving fluids sprayed the room to drench zombies in a reeking shower. The creatures came once more to a dumb stop, now to peer through matted hair at their own dripping hands as they struggled for an understanding of events. When one blinked and issued a slobbering giggle for the soaking it had received, its accomplices acted likewise and filled the dissecting room with hellish laughter.

Benjamin did not laugh. He understood far better than dull zombies what had been done, and he hesitated just long enough to confirm by smell the potent mix of alcohol and preserving fluid he had set free. The lantern flew at his whispered command and it tumbled to shatter among the distracted zombies, its explosion turning all to flames in an instant.

Laugher became shrieks of torment in the inferno. Zombies thrashed against raging fire, their efforts becoming a freakish dance as they crashed against tables and shelves and each other until, one after another, they toppled, dead at last between the slabs.

Benjamin spun to deal with the Baron, but the

spirit had already reacted to the loss of his undead servants. In a blinking he seized Benjamin's throat and that fearful skull-face pulled close. Vampire fingers worked rapidly to create a spell but the spirit was quicker. Raising his powerful arm as though it held no more than a handful of feathers, the Baron flung Benjamin upwards.

The burning room, the Baron, the unconscious Dr Wheatley, all sailed away as Benjamin travelled helplessly up. There came an eruption of glass and wood at his back as he crashed through the roof window. Diamond shards glittered to the light of the growing fire and peppered Benjamin in his racing ascent. At an immeasurable height above the destruction, beyond the hospital roof itself, gravity played its inevitable part and he was dragged speeding back.

Vampire senses gathered mid-fall, pivoting Benjamin just enough for his feet to gain roof-tiles but not to achieve full balance. He toppled dangerously, the momentum of his descent pulling him backwards and he passed across the edge of the building. Through a desperate scramble for purchase one flailing hand found the gutter at the very lip of the roof and prevented a crashing plummet to the courtyard far below.

Pulling up, he regained the roof in time to meet the arrival of the Baron. The gatekeeper surged through the ruptured skylight and poured across the roof in a dark flood. He came on and carried with him the weeping Dr Wheatley whom he cast roughly to slide across the tiles. Benjamin watched the doctor crash down, realising too late that the Baron's action was not one of cruelty, but one of distraction. Too late he saw what spirit carried in his other hand.

Benjamin sprang back to avoid the Baron's range but his adversary was still one move ahead. The caped one threw out a hand, and the silver chains which had held the receiving stretcher whipped to find Benjamin. Guided by the spirit's power, one of the chains found a trailing ankle and snaked hun-grily about. A wrist was snared in similar fashion and Benjamin was pulled cruelly down, cracking tiles where he fell.

The curse of silver ran hot and vampire strength was useless against it. Benjamin kicked fiercely but helplessly while Baron Samedi began to reel him in, smiling at his victory.

17

Benjamin was hauled up in chains to the stern face of Baron Samedi.

With a predator's sniff for its prey, the spirit addressed him through snarling lips.

'Fair warning was given, Benjamin Blake, to clear my way and avoid my sight. And yet you persist.'

'Why are you doing this?' Benjamin demanded. 'You have the bones you came for. The doctor does not need his spirit bottled up.'

'How little you know,' the Baron replied, his face becoming sad for the boy's lack of knowing. 'How clumsy your actions have been. And how dangerous to the one I serve.'

Benjamin fought crushing bonds.

'Tell me, then, and I might understand your service to a murdering pirate.'

Again that previous look of willingness came into Baron Samedi's face, that spark of desire to unburden himself, to share some information yet hidden. It passed quickly, and with a sudden glare of determination he flung the boy harshly from him.

Benjamin crashed along the roof amid tuneless ringing links. His body met a chimney's brickwork in a shuddering collision and the Baron's fingers splayed instantly with power. The chains obeyed the magical instruction, and metal serpents tightened to wrists and feet and encircled the brickwork. In a moment's panic Benjamin realised the formation taken by the chains also crushed his hands flat to his body, rendering all defensive spells impossible.

Baron Samedi floated near to inspect his work. He reached to confirm the strength of twinkling bonds holding his adversary and, satisfied with all, he thrust the same hand beneath his cloak. A new bottle was produced for Benjamin's brief consideration as he turned once more in search of Dr Wheatley.

'Don't do this,' Benjamin urged him. 'Defy Pyke and show your mercy.'

Stung again by the boy's words, the Baron gave over to a frustrated rage.

'I cannot!' he insisted. 'I do what must be done.' Offering no more than this vague explanation, he bore down on the doctor.

Wheatley issued a feeble cry as cloak strands pulled him to his feet. His eyes flared, mesmerised once more by the devilish container thrust to his face. And again the ghostly emerald hue came as the dreadful transference recommenced. Wrestling uselessly against his chains, Benjamin was a powerless witness to the spirit light drifting from man to bottle, and all under the sombre gaze of the Baron whose painted face basked in sickly green illumination. He held fast to his victim, supporting the doctor as the man's legs gave over from struggling and buckled. The last of Dr Wheatley's life force fled him and ebbed into the little glass prison.

It ended. The doctor tumbled lifelessly down, his rigid features turning towards Benjamin in unanswered pleading. Hovering above, the Baron carefully re-corked the bottle and tucked it away.

'Another life claimed,' Benjamin mocked, 'you must be so proud of your work.'

'There is no pride in what I do,' he replied, clearly wounded by the accusation, 'only necessity.'

'I have power, and never served pirate or witch,' Benjamin said. 'I used mine to win my freedom, why can't you?'

'You are lucky to have a choice, Benjamin Blake,' Samedi replied. 'I have none.'

'There is always a choice in magic, always a way.'

The spirit scanned the night as though in search of Benjamin's truth, but in vain.

'No, there is no other way for the Baron now,' he sighed, 'I am a slave with no choice but to serve.'

He drew close to consider Benjamin's imprisoning chains a final time. 'So I must go and leave you alone to greet the rising of the day.'

The words shook Benjamin to the core and jerked his eyes to the east. A growing shade of grey on the lip of the earth challenged the night sky. He struggled against the chains to no effect as the Baron floated off.

'Why run away, Baron?' he challenged. 'Are you too ashamed to watch me die?'

Receding with the night beyond the roof, Samedi cast back his sad words.

'I told you, Benjamin Blake. I take no pride in what I do. Held by silver, bound in stone, you must face your end alone.'

'Curse you, Baron,' Benjamin cried defiantly. 'There is always a way!'

If the spirit heard, he offered no indication from the whitened face that vanished last into the surrounding dark, and Benjamin's call echoed unheard across the city.

Alone, watched only by Dr Wheatley's lifeless eyes, Benjamin wrestled furiously with his bonds. The cursed gatekeeper had done his work well, and Benjamin's exertions proved useless against the might of enfolding chains. Fighting the impulse to give in to rising panic, he focused all attention on his predicament and what possibilities might exist for escape. Squirming this way and that, thoughts of freeing even a single hand quickly proved futile. Links of chain held fast to prevent fingers and thumbs from all conjuring, while the silvery coils pressed his elbows close, reducing movement further and crushing him to the brickwork.

Could he stand, he wondered next, perhaps to bring the circle of chains up and over the chimney pots? Pressing on his heels, he tested the method, only to fail as metal bit hard into the structure.

Frustrated, he stole another urgent glance east, where the greying sky was suffused with the first hints of blue, and where the stars already dimmed.

A crash from beneath signalled the dissecting room's ongoing destruction. Flames rose through the shattered roof window, drawn to lick hungrily at the outside air. Benjamin heard snapping wood, and with the sound another possibility came to him. Burning away, the fire would soon consume the roof beams, and the resulting collapse might take him down with it, towards a salvation of sorts. But how could he rely on such an uncertain method? The flames did not race to beat the dawn, and even if the roof should give way, the chimney might not. Benjamin pictured himself dangling helplessly against the sun's merciless blast.

The image set him struggling fiercely again, bringing all his strength to bear on the chains but only to feel once more the futility of the approach, even as the eastern horizon began to glimmer.

Held by silver, bound in stone, you must face your end alone.

The Baron's words came back to taunt Benjamin as fear prickled his skin and demanded an answer from a flood of racing thoughts, any answer that would…

Bound in stone!

He was secured by silver, loathsome and potent to a vampire, but bound in stone, a substance as weak to him as silver was strong!

With renewed hope – and a promise to curse himself a slow-thinking fool later – Benjamin concentrated all his strength and flexed hard, pulling forward, bunching fists against the links. He hauled on lengths of chain unseen, those biting to the sides and rear of the chimney. Through the limiting effects of silver the effort took all his might, causing muscles to strain and tremble in the attempt. Metal squealed against rough corners and held fast, but now he heard stone grinding under the pressure of the tightening bonds and, to a dusty puff and spill, the first bricks began to sunder.

The morning's glow spread farther along the

horizon in heralding the sun's imminent appearance over the rim of the world.

More stone crunched and burst to powder, and Benjamin hauled on, not ceasing in his efforts for a moment. An extra inch of space gained by his work gave more room to drag deeper against his confinement, and though layers of brick resisted yet, the battle was turning in his favour.

A spark flared in the east. Dawn raced across the earth.

Benjamin saw and offered his vampire roar against the distant light. The furious sound reverberated across rooftops and echoed down streets between. The chimney vibrated to the very sound and, to a sudden deafening implosion of stone and soot, the stack collapsed to the void within.

Benjamin tore chains away, releasing himself in a frantic scramble to rise and seek the quickest path from the advancing light. The curse of silver was giving way fast to that of sunlight.

West! At least to the edge of the roof, he reasoned, there to calculate further escape from the new threat hurtling closer. He plunged across a blur of tiles, chasing night shadows retreating before him as they melted and died with the dawn. He stepped to the chasm falling away to the street and he peered into a pool of darkness yet unaffected, the hospital's shadow still defiant. Perceiving the few seconds it would afford, Benjamin stepped into space.

The light of day, blinding, piercing, blasted overhead and dashed against upper windows of the building facing his descent. Reflected daggers pricked vampire skin and eyes. Benjamin struck pavement on St Bartholemew's western edge as sunlight tore from streets to his left and right. Behind, the dawn began its rapid crawl down the hospital's facade in pursuit of him.

Trapped in the dwindling pool of shadow, Benjamin sought for a path to safety. Almost too late he saw it, directly opposite. It was a small rectangular opening cut into a pavement kerb, a drain offering a last hope, holding as it did a darkness that would remain unaffected through the burning day. He raced for the spot, his back burning in the pursuit of heat and flaming light. With a final diving effort through the surging day, he passed with a splash into the dark, merciful depths.

18

enjamin spent his day grumbling in a sewer.

Ankle deep in foul liquid, he sat in squalor while the mortal world roused and pursued its business. Silently he cursed Baron Samedi from the dripping dark as the sun's slow passage held him to a hole no bigger than a Newgate cell. He cursed the gatekeeper for the previous night of chaos and death, and cursed him all the more for questions left unanswered in his wake.

A slave with no choice but to serve.

What did a spirit so powerful mean by such a vague statement? Benjamin felt certain he had come close to an answer, close as his own burning destruction, but the mystery had remained just out of reach behind the spirit's painted mask. He mumbled fresh curses in recalling it, that spark of truth displayed twice in the Baron's unpainted eyes. It had flickered there so clearly, a desire to free himself of it until something greater had caused the phantom to keep his...

What? Admission, a confession?

Was it held by fear? Could the supernatural creature the Baron was know real fear?

Abruptly from the world above, cries of 'murder!' came with the sound of rushing feet and broke through Benjamin's musing. He did not need to see in order to understand. The disturbance spoke of the night's violent events. He pictured mortal men scratching their heads in confusion having discovered the carnage in Dr Wheatley's scorched room, and their increased bafflement upon finding the doctor's body splayed on the roof, and with such a look of maddened fear etched on his dead face. The men would seek answers the daytime world could never provide.

Benjamin offered a frustrated kick to the surrounding water for the answers he sought but could not gain. Rats drawn to the curious trespasser scurried away in squealing fright and pressed into slimy recesses as the vampire's grumbling echoed after. At this very moment, despite being more determined than ever to gain the truth in things, he was held to a standstill, confined until the passing of the day – a whole day! – while pirates could scheme and act on whatever information they had forced from Dr Wheatley. And their murderous plot with the bones of Billy Buckler could proceed unchallenged towards its end. All because of the Baron.

Adding then to the passing sounds of the sunlit world, the wheels of a heavy cart rumbled close to the drain. Pulling up to a clip of hooves, the vehicle stopped directly above, and Benjamin detected the sound of workmen clambering to the roadside amid bitter mutterings for their task. Barely a moment later the disgusting cargo they transported cascaded into the drain, a vile flood of newly collected waste gushing to drench everything within.

Benjamin ground his teeth to contain fresh curses for Baron Samedi.

The day slipped on, and Benjamin's anger gave way to the more logical search for a plan for after dark. If the Ghostmaker's crew was indeed making progress, picking up the pirate trail again was vital. But what chance of that, he wondered. Even if the Baron thought him dead and dealt with, surely he would trust to caution and advise Mr Pyke to seek a new hiding place far from the Gravediggers tavern. And whatever possibility remained of rediscovering the buccaneers, there was none in attempting to trace the Baron himself where the spirit slipped to and from his own supernatural realm.

Oh, do you forget your learning so easily, young vampire?

That whispering voice, so persistently familiar,

came to straighten his back and to still all pondering. Sounding at once within and without him, but not of him, he heard it in the gloom of his cell and the corridors of his mind in the same instant. It bubbled up from the depths of his imagination and through the narrow sewer pipe beside him that fed a rotten course from the drain to the river.

It was the sound of a witch's grimoire forever calling.

Yes, you remember, don't you? What I taught you, with mirrors and the moon, the moon and with mirrors. Say you remember.

'Yes,' he answered unconsciously.

Benjamin did remember. One spell among the coded many that had been burned into his mind by white-hot moonlight all those years ago, one sufficient to reveal what was sought. He pictured without effort the required symbols, they flared behind eyes that had seen them etched on pages now turning and turning back to the river's gliding touch. It was complex magic, long in preparation, but strong enough get him back into the chase. He bunched a fist as though to catch the truth of it.

'Yes!'

The symbols blazed in his brain just as they had that first frightened night in the woods. They dazzled as then, bright as the swords that flashed against a supernatural beast on the hunt for moonstruck pages. He laughed aloud at the memory so powerful, and next laughed into a stifling hand as nervous footsteps increased their pace past the chuckling drain.

Day crept on to evening. New shadows rose to avenge the old and at last drove the sun away. Fading to grey in its low place between buildings, the drain gave up its final weak sliver of light by slow degrees and swallowed fresh darkness.

Released at last, Benjamin touched the night and crept from the pit, a dripping vile creature of the supernatural underworld. Moving swiftly to an alley devoid of travellers, he clambered on filthy nails beyond the streetscape to recover his place above the city. On the opposing roof of St Bartholomew's he caught lingering wisps of smoke, the last remaining evidence of the previous night's rampage.

Benjamin turned south-east towards the river and his path home.

The city seemed quieter beneath his passing and he paused to draw clues from it. He saw no strollers as on that first evening when making his eager way to the gibbet of Billy Buckler. Daytime jubilation at the villain's execution and feelings of restored order had seemingly vanished during his confinement. Good citizens had retreated behind doors and windows locked tightly against murder and foul acts to be found on the streets of London after dark.

It was not until Benjamin passed into the shadow of St Paul's that he saw the first indications of mortal life. From on high he caught and watched a long procession of carriages snaking west, and he recognised in their adornments the vehicles of the rich and privileged as they trundled on their way. Passengers bedecked in wigs and finery sat visible within, lords and ladies, politicians and ambassadors who laughed and conversed happily towards some night of merry-making. Their route and final destination were just as clear to Benjamin. Beyond the great cathedral, the convoy would shortly reach the tree-lined Mall and progress from there to Buckingham House, where King George III was no doubt waiting to greet all for colourful festivities.

Benjamin dismissed revellers and their fun and raced homeward.

19

'My lords and ladies! Pray welcome their Royal Majesties, King George the Third, and Queen Charlotte!'

The herald's officious announcement, appropriately haughty, carried across the candlelit assembly and demanded a reply of silence. Throughout the sparkling ballroom, beautifully attired guests turned to the call in rustles of taffeta and faced a broad marbled staircase to offer their dutiful hush. The orchestra likewise stilled as musicians rose in unison to wait in attendance as servants bearing trays of food and wine halted on their rounds and dignitaries interrupted their most important conversations. And no less expectant in one distant corner, giggling young debutantes hid behind hand-fans and waited, though not like the others for king or queen. No, together they waited in heart-racing anticipation...for him.

After a suitable delay of precise seconds, the royal couple appeared. Sweeping into view, they stepped in time to the head of the stairs and acknowledged the bows and curtsies flowing from front to rear of the throng like a wave. With his fair wife on hand, King George led the way down, waving regally to favoured courtiers and nodding imperiously to princes and politicians as he drew near. The resplendent crowd parted ahead of the royal pair as they strolled to take the centre of the room, and here the king paused, looking about him with a frown, as though for something amiss. Joyous faces darkened at his majesty's apparent displeasure until the ruler, with a wry smile on his lips, signalled with bejewelled fingers for the orchestra to proceed. Music filled the air and the king's guests eagerly applauded his royal humour.

'My lords and ladies!' the herald declared over rising music. 'The children of the royal household. Their Highnesses Charlotte, Edward and Elizabeth.'

The siblings appeared in a flurry of robes and ribbons to the gathering's applause and renewed salutes. Three wide and practised smiles gleamed on the party-goers while eager ladies-in-waiting pursued and fussed over Charlotte in descending the steps.

'Booooring,' the princess whispered behind her smile.

'Don't let Papa hear you say that,' Edward warned through his own frozen beaming.

'I hope there's cake,' little Elizabeth said.

'My lords and ladies...!' the herald began once more.

A collective squeal erupted from the debutantes' corner. Fans fluttered excitedly to a heaving thrill of anticipation.

'My lords and ladies!' the herald was forced to repeat. 'Pray welcome the Prince of Wales, heir to the throne of Great Britain and all her dominions, his Highness Prince George!'

Girlish shrieks pitched higher than the orchestra's strains and, to Charlotte's despairing eye-roll, the debutantes stared in wide wonder over their fans for the first glimpse of...him.

Smiling and striding, Prince George met his cue and appeared boldly at the head of the stairs. In his waistcoat of finest silk and cuffs of lace touching glittering rings, he spread his arms to receive the loudest greeting from his father's guests.

'What a peacock,' Prince Edward's smile grumbled.

'Now, now,' Charlotte scolded the little boy playfully as she offered a nodded greeting to the Spanish ambassador, 'be nice.'

George progressed towards the ballroom, step by stockinged step down the marbled stairs. Halfway, he paused, all at once and with a mischievous smile, knowing how his actions extended the applause. The young royal, at seventeen a most eligible suitor for any of the quivering ladies nearby, drew up to his full height and allowed the light of a thousand candles play against the gold stitching of his tailed coat, the collar of which he had turned up strategically to parallel the bold lines of his cheekbones. Easing a kerchief of finest embroidery from his sleeve, he dabbed briefly the corners of his mouth as though finalising his appearance and, with a look of mock surprise, dropped the square to flutter towards the boards. The effect was immediate, and to the prince most amusing. In a burst of activity, the eager ladies of court bustled to a race of lace, competing thunderously across the dance floor to gain the drifting prize, all the while striving valiantly to maintain grace and poise in the tussle. Debutantes elbowed and eyed their opponents jealously while Charlotte observed with a weary sigh for fools.

The smiling George advanced again, his every shining-buckled step tracked by feverish gazes. The beating of fans reached an intensity to threaten the lights of a nearby candelabra. Lady Matilda of Warwick, quite abruptly overcome by a fit of nervous hiccups, had to be led away by her mother. Almost to the last step now, and the prince flashed his perfect smile. Lady Gertrude of Falmouth shattered the wine glass she had fought wilfully to hold steady throughout the beauteous display. And finally, the moment, the signature moment all waited trembling for was but a heartbeat away. In a unified instant of stillness, fans ceased fluttering. Debutantes chorused an inward breath, held, and braced.

George knew well to play his part now. With a final wave to some fawning dignitary he stepped lightly from the stairs, tugged briefly at a risen cuff…and tossed locks of golden hair from his smiling face with a flick.

Amid the ensuing gasp of unbridled joy, Lady Sara Caitlyn of Blenheim fainted and kicked up her bloomers to the absolute mortification of her parents.

Greatly entertained, but with grace enough to conceal it from the adoring ladies, George began to circulate, deliberately taking the longest route around the ballroom towards the debutantes. One would not wish to appear too keen. Tush, that would never do.

'I'm so glad that's over,' Edward whispered as his brother was swallowed up in the crowd.

'Can I have some cake now?' Elizabeth groaned.

Charlotte offered a distant 'Yes' to both utterances and stepped away from the younger children. With eyes narrow in scanning the room for a face as yet unseen, she moved on the hunt through a forest of wigs and finery.

Attentive to the king's instructions before the

party, she acknowledged deep bows and good graces from all she passed in coursing the ballroom. Papa's command had been clear. His guests from near and far were to receive plentiful royal smiles and blessings, the better to maintain loyalty in a kingdom troubled by rebels and pirates. That recollection caused a more natural smile, one of private amusement, to break at her lips. How her father would explode to learn she was seeking audience with a pirate even now. His Majesty would surely match the crimson shade of a grenadier's tunic if he knew. The thought of infuriating Papa forced Charlotte to hide a chuckle behind her hand fan.

And why should she not have her wicked entertainment, she mused through her continuing search. She noted how George had not yet shaken off his entourage of giggling girls to do his duty, while Elizabeth was doing far more for the kingdom by drawing smiles from a foreign admiral with her new dance steps and having fun in the process.

Impatient for her own jolly measure, Charlotte drew a lady-in-waiting to her side with a secretive flick of fan.

'Highness,' the young lady said with a precise curtsey.

'Did you deliver my note?'

'Yes, your Highness.' Curtsey. 'Before six o'clock

as you said, and from my hand into his alone, as directed.' Curtsey.

Excellent, Charlotte thrilled inwardly. Somewhere nearby, a dead man waited to keep his appointment with her.

'Where is my subject?' she asked of the servant.

'I direct your attention to the orchestra, Highness,' was the lady's reply.

Spying at last her target, her go-between in the matter, the princess made her way towards him, deftly skirting her parents, three dukes, a peer and a simpering viscount. For his part in waiting for her, Mr Percival Fox lingered discreetly by the orchestra as required. He was, however, suddenly surrounded by a cluster of businessmen eager for his close attention. Charlotte understood. As governor of the Bank of England, Mr Fox was the key to new fortunes for many, and therefore was as honey to buzzing bees. At her approach, the banker distracted the rest in greeting the princess with a plunging bow.

'Mr Fox,' she acknowledged him curtly. Eyeing his action, she wondered if he was trying to kiss his own shoes.

'Your Highness,' Fox drawled, 'your entrance was, as ever, momentous. Oh, to be so young and pretty.'

'Thank you,' Charlotte replied, struggling to mean it. In truth, she did not like one bit of the man, seeing in his leering smile the very sneaky animal he was named for. And she would have told him as much, but Papa had tutored his children well in the art of good relations with prominent men like Percival Fox.

'If I may be so bold to add,' the banker went on, 'your Highness looks enchanting tonight, truly a feast for the eyes.'

Charlotte felt her skin crawl. Fox was old enough to be grandfather to the royal children. Luckily, just then a servant drew near with a tray of wine, and the princess snatched a glass to fill her mouth with something other than abusive words for the man.

'Tell me, Mr Fox,' she said quietly, collecting herself to acknowledge the courteous nod of a passing lady, 'did you bring him?'

'Him?' Fox asked absently as he cast sideward interest in the same lady. His wordless greeting for her was met by one of distaste as she fled.

'Him, sir, him!' the princess repeated sharply, locking eyes with the man. 'Do you toy with me?'

Startled, Mr Fox worked every angle of his smile to regain the royal's good graces.

'Him,' he repeated, 'him, of course, how foolish of me, your Highness. I did, I do…have him, possess him, I mean. The one you desire to meet…view, to see, is to hand, quite close by and nearby, in fact. My man awaits a signal even now.'

'Then give your signal and let us see,' Charlotte instructed. Remaining stern of face, she hid her amusement at Mr Fox's attempts to oblige in frantically seeking all about for his servant. She watched him finally catch sight of the man and receive a confirming nod in reply.

'Aha, perfect,' Fox gushed, 'the library. This way, Highness. Your secret guest awaits.'

20

The library was blissfully quiet after the tumult of the ballroom.

Charlotte led the way, followed by the still nervous Mr Fox who bowed and smiled repeatedly as the princess swept towards a comfortable chair. Sitting – firm back, no slouching – she faced the banker and opened her hands expectantly.

'My servant is on his way at this very moment,' Mr Fox assured, his features squirming to a bloodless hope he was correct.

'Good,' Charlotte said. She brushed at her gown to disguise an excited tremble she felt in her hands.

'If I dare to say, your Highness,' the banker ventured, 'I believe you will be struck dumb. What comes is quite the most amazing sight.'

'A princess must never be dumb,' Charlotte shot back, 'and certainly not one who will be a queen one day.'

Mr Fox paled.

'Quite, your Highness, quite. Such wisdom in one

so young. England will one day have a great and wise regent.' He choked on the words as Charlotte flashed him a questioning look. 'Oh, eh, another great and wise regent, I meant of course, one to match your father's great greatness and wise wisdom.'

Charlotte rolled her eyes, though, in truth, she was rather enjoying Fox's discomfort.

A knock on the door announced Mr Fox's servant, his arrival sparing the banker any further embarrassment. The man entered, and carried with him a rectangular chest fashioned from oak and iron, its lock and the studs across its frame winking to the candles' dance. Charlotte unconsciously pressed back in her chair as the box was set before her.

'Leave us,' she instructed, oblivious to the manservant's bow in her fascinated staring at the container of grim promise.

'Prepare yourself, Highness,' Mr Fox warned, and he reached to undo lock and lid. To a groan of hinges he stepped back in allowing Charlotte her eager view. 'Behold the skull of Billy Buckler.'

Empty sockets of bone stared to transfix the princess. The pirate's snarling gaze, even now communicating the bottomless hate she had witnessed at the gallows, met Charlotte's eyes over leg bones crossed on a setting of blood-red velvet. Even in death, she realised with a shudder, the merciless brow and gritted teeth made the head a fearsome sight. She heard her own dread whisper fill the space between the living and the dead.

'There is such cruelty in that face.'

'Oh, indeed,' Mr Fox agreed readily. 'Dr Wheatley, ah, the late and much lamented Dr Wheatley, spoke of the pirate's brain being of a form to make impossible any hint of kindness or compassion. You will have seen evidence of that for yourself when the wretch was brought for execution. What a shameful display to the royal family that was.'

Gingerly, Charlotte extended her hand, meaning to touch the skull, daring herself to, just between the eyes, but after a moment's consideration she withdrew from bared teeth threatening to snap dainty fingers.

'I have heard it wildly told,' she said, 'that the doctor was killed when Billy Buckler's phantom came in search of his head.' She did not believe such fantastic tales, but was there not a thrill in allowing for them, by candlelight, and with the dead so close?

'That is just one of many uncanny stories linked to Billy Buckler's name these days past,' Mr Fox informed her. 'I heard a tall tale myself just this evening, one of grave robbers in Stepney. In the midst of their despicable enterprise, it is said they came upon Buckler's ghost searching among the graves for a new head. Both thieves died of fright on the spot, apparently. Stuff and nonsense, of course.'

'Of course,' Charlotte repeated weakly. 'And what of the fantastical tale that Billy Buckler cannot die?'

Percival Fox looked puzzled a moment before recalling with a smile.

'Oh, your Highness alludes to the disturbance at Billy's execution. The assault by the old navy captain with the pistol...what was his name...Captain Faulkner, yes! What a sad case, a man so eager for glory he sank his own reputation in falsely claiming Billy's head last year. But as you see, your Highness, I possess it now.'

'What on earth do you intend to do with it?'

Mr Fox mirrored the skull's hungry smile.

'Beyond entertaining my guests at parties,' he said, 'I haven't quite decided. But it seems to me that having cost England so much in lost treasure, it might be fitting for Billy to earn something back for his country, as a paid exhibit perhaps. Until then I shall hold him under wraps.'

'Do you keep this in your home?' the girl exclaimed, aghast. Her eyes remained locked on those of the skull.

'My my, no,' Mr Fox assured her, 'I should never sleep with that devilish countenance peering down from my bookshelf. No, I have secured a deep vault to hold Captain Buckler for now.'

Charlotte looked deep into the pirate's dead features and then deeper still, her gaze slipping down into those eyes, those bony pits that swallowed light and offered nothing but darkness in return. And despite herself she followed the darkness, and in the dark reached out again, this time to finger-tip the polished space between eyes that sat vacant and yet, somehow, watching.

The crash that came to shake the library brought a startled cry from the princess. Snapping back her hand, for a second she was at a loss for the source until she turned to see the door thrust forcefully open by a soldier of the Royal Guard. The man made way for others of his rank, and at last for their leader, handsome Captain Madigan, tall and determined in his dress uniform as he scanned the room and with a ready hand to his sword.

Charlotte smiled for her champion, tried not to, and swallowed hard to steady her voice.

'Captain Madigan, what is the meaning of this?'

'Highness,' the young officer said with obvious relief. 'You were missed at the party. And in such times...' He let his words hang as he spied Percival Fox's discreet motions in closing the box of profane contents.

'I had business with Mr Fox,' the princess cut in.

She waited for Madigan's nodded understanding that her words meant an end to all interrogations.

'You should return to the party, your Highness,' the officer gently suggested. 'There is cake.'

Charlotte bristled visibly.

'And dancing,' Madigan promptly added. He bowed to avoid the girl's withering gaze.

Better, she decided.

'And would you dance with me if I return, Captain?' she teased and tested him.

'Your father would surely imprison me in the Tower for that, your Highness.'

Charlotte noted how expertly Madigan dodged the question for fear of her power, and secretly she was pleased. Papa had schooled her well in observing the truth lying between the words of his subjects. But, she decided, that was enough fun for this evening. She dismissed bankers and buccaneers with a wave.

'Goodnight, Mr Fox,' she pronounced and swept between the soldiers.

21

At last the spell was ready.

In the dark chamber of his hiding place at the Tower, Benjamin stepped back to assess his preparations. All items unnecessary to the work – his books, furniture, candlesticks – had been pushed aside to make way for the magic to come. His reading chair and book table, his fine rug lying as a thick roll across a pair of chairs, all stood now along one wall, with the largest piece, the grand study table, upended at the head of the line. Pausing to overlook the wide space left behind, he swept clouds from chalky hands and rechecked the drawing at his feet, seeking keenly for the tiniest of flaws that would render the magic design useless.

White-lined symbols ran from him across the boards. From a memory still brimming with the spells of a witch's lost book, he had traced overlapping forms on the wood, twin lines zigzagging towards the fireplace, crossing to form at their intersections a number of diamond-shaped enclosures. In and about these lay all manner of magical signs, swirling and curving in contrast to the sharpness of the frame containing them. Each unearthly symbol was a vital part in what he was about to conjure, and each had to be just right.

Finally, and completely encircling this floor-map to power, Benjamin had arranged the outermost layer of the spell. Lying equally spaced to form a broad ring were mirrors of all shapes and sizes. The simplest hand glasses lay by larger framed pieces, some square, some oval, all peering up blindly to the darkened ceiling in waiting.

Waiting for the moon.

Benjamin stepped into the circle of glass and carefully positioned his feet at the first of the chalk marks. Satisfied with his work, he turned towards the fireplace and another cluster of mirrors he had set there, these smaller glasses precisely angled within the hearth to reflect the gaping black portal of the chimney rising above.

The first hour of night chimed distantly.

With tingling skin, he sensed the moon's approach. He pictured the Tower walls outside paling to its stealthy advance, and in his mind saw the moon's surface blaze forth in triumph over the night.

It was time to begin.

Holding flat his right palm, Benjamin raised it to his lips and blew softly to send an undead whisper of 'Incipe' across the items on the floor. His timing was perfect. Looking on, he saw the mirrors in the hearth glimmer in catching the first weak lunar rays tumbling down the chimney.

The portal admitted the light directly to the polished surfaces, and thin streams of moonlight flowed into the room from the hearth.

With fingers and hands set in proper order, he proceeded.

'Levitas.'

There came a soft sound, an irregular pecking as of midnight birds seeking to intrude on events, and Benjamin glanced knowingly to the floorboards for it. It grew steadily to a harsher beat, and he watched mirrors wobble as though driven by it. But he knew the truth. Under his control, it was the mirrors themselves creating the noise as their frames vibrated on the wood in answer to the whispered incantation. At last, abruptly seized by power and cast upwards, the glasses left the floor to hang on the air in a perfectly suspended circle about him, there to await his further command.

Now for the difficult part.

Benjamin's left hand moved from his body, the palm turning carefully down as he extended his first and second fingers. These he drew to a gentle stirring until each mirror obeyed and began to rotate about itself in answer to his motion. Slowly at first, and then faster they spun, until all whirled beyond the capacity of even supernatural eyes to follow.

His right hand travelled slowly to a distance matching the left. Its fingers did not extend this time but came bent in readiness. Benjamin chose his moment. He quickly turned up his hand and flicked.

The circle of spinning mirrors began to move, turning counter clockwise to accelerate in a wide wheel of speeding glass. Benjamin saw at once his measurements had been precise and true to memory. A mirror swept through reflected moonbeams in a flash of disrupted light and passed rapidly on to make way for a repetition of the process by the next glass, and in turn each mirror after, faster and faster until beams flickered in sequence at terrific pace.

Maintaining firm control, Benjamin eased a foot to the right and stepped onto the first symbol in the first quadrant.

'Show me what was.'

The already rapid turning of the mirrors increased even more to the words. Polished surfaces whipped by, thrumming on the air and catching the light so fast that individual flashes blended to become a single throbbing orb.

Peering into the light, Benjamin saw the spell's offering.

Like a painting given life and motion, the mirrors gave up their captured images. Streets and houses appeared, and carts, and a bustling multitude of people. From the depths of magic, London was exposed to his gaze. But gone was the moon of now, and gone all shadows as the spell revealed London as it had been in the daylight of hours past. The vision shifted and pulsed, sweeping through avenues and sunlit alleyways to find people gathered at St Bartholomew's hospital, lured by news of the dreadful fate visited upon Dr Wheatley. Benjamin's gaze sped past all, pulled at lightning speed across the city to that which he sought. Sight plunged to darkness in passing down a tunnel, no, a chimney, this one to the hearth and hall of the Gravediggers tavern. Here Robinson stood alone in sweeping up the mess left by pirates long departed. On the vision travelled, on at breakneck pace to the river, there to fly between sails of merchant ships waiting for the tide. Faces flashed by, men in their hundreds working to load and unload cargoes for the mammoth warehouses lining the docks.

'Why here?' Benjamin demanded. 'Show me.'

Images wobbled, refocusing on a single warehouse standing at odds with the day's hustle and bustle. At odds because, unlike its neighbours, this building was closed up and locked tight against all business and trade. Just one small window, set high above the swarming workers stood partially ajar, and in the opening, a grizzled, sea-worn face maintained a sombre watch.

Passing unnoticed by the guard, the spell of sight flew into the building's dim interior and raced down to its wide floor where the assembled crew of the Ghostmaker stood, secure in this new hiding place. At the head of the gathering was Mr Pyke. He walked slowly back and forth, the late Doctor Wheatley's notebook in his hand which he held for all to see as he instructed them.

'Tonight, lads,' he said, his voice a ghostly echo through the magic portal, 'tonight the last pieces fall into place.' The crew growled its assent and Pyke opened a page of the notebook and held it high. 'The man we seek, this Percival Fox, friend to the King of England, is the rogue who holds our captain. He needs visiting, this thief of bones. Every man here will meet him tonight. Every man here will search his home until we have what we want. Are we agreed?' The crew roared in unison.

Percival Fox! Benjamin seized on the name, a clue to be followed!

Stepping on, Benjamin advance quickly into the second quadrant.

'Show me what is.'

The scene at the warehouse became indistinct and was lost, washed over by flashing light until a fresh image bloomed from whistling mirrors.

The place and the way lay deep underground. Here in permanent night was a passageway fashioned by the work of men. The walls and ceiling of the corridor Benjamin perceived were lined with polished tiles where they travelled to reach an iron gate. Beyond stout bars a second obstacle held, this one an imposing metal door. The twin layers of security, gate and door alike, were secured by the mightiest of locks, each demanding some huge key to grant access.

Even as Benjamin studied, voices echoed to him along the passageway. A single lantern passed, raised in the hand of a young man who nervously guided two others, one a youthful man who conveyed a studded chest, the second a much older figure than his companions, and having a sly look to his features.

The man with the lantern hurriedly produced a large ring of keys and worked to release the gate and afterwards the stout door. Stepping aside, he admitted the bearer of the chest who ducked within and shortly re-emerged empty-handed. The courier nodded eagerly to the watching older man, keen to please.

'Will there be anything else, Mr Fox?' he asked.

Percival Fox reached to demand lantern and keys.

'You may both go,' he instructed coldly, eyeing his

two juniors until they bowed obediently and scurried from him. With their footsteps echoing away, Fox proceeded into the vault.

Setting the lamp and keys on one of many chests crowding the room, Fox unlatched his own to reveal to Benjamin's unheard gasp the skull and crossed bones of Billy Buckler. Taking up the skull, Fox turned it over in his hands in the flickering light and brought the bony face close to his own to stare hard into those empty eyes. Finding nothing to fear in the dead gaze, he walked to a small table bearing a velvet cushion and set the grinning skull upon it.

Would the vault protect Billy or would Billy protect the vault?

Fox seemed amused as he worked to set leg bones in crossed formation before the skull. His sly smile glinted one last time over his prize as he nimbly recovered keys and lantern and exited the room, the boom of door and gate unnaturally loud in the dungeon-like atmosphere.

Benjamin moved without delay to the third quadrant. If he hoped to reach this vault beneath Fox's home and the prize it held, he needed the location, and quickly.

'Show me.'

Falling backwards, racing into retreat, the vision fled the tiled corridor where Fox walked, and it sped up a long flight of steps to pass the bars of yet another metal gate. The light of the moon filled the scene but, to Benjamin's astonishment, it was not one of a domestic setting in some comfortable private home. No, here he looked on a vast marbled space containing rows of desks, upon which sat ledgers and account papers. The desks were hemmed in on three sides by a long serving counter running around the space. Clearly this was a place of transaction between businessmen and staff who would stand at intervals along the counter. Travelling rapidly, magic sight found tall doors and easy passage through a keyhole to the street beyond. There, under the very moon that offered vision, a broad flight of steps descended to the waiting carriage of Percival Fox where it parked beneath a nameplate of polished brass proclaiming the title of this place of business.

The Bank of England.

Benjamin gasped aloud as his eyes filled with the gleaming image from the mirrors.

Percival Fox was not at home! He had delayed his journey, and diverted to secure in his own bank that which the pirates and their voodoo slave sought at his house!

Benjamin trembled as a dazzling understanding blazed brighter than all magic.

He was ahead of the hunt at last!

22

'Come along, Mr Smith, place a bet or quit the game.'

Having issued his challenge, Mr Turner drew deeply on his clay pipe and eyed his colleague across the table. He offered a wry smile to display his confidence to Mr Smith who continued yet to agonise over the playing cards he held. Between the pair, a pile of coins lay scattered across the rough gaming table, glinting in the lamplight as a promise for the winning hand.

'Well?' Turner prompted once more. For added effect, he drummed thick fingers on his own neatly stacked cards.

Smith's face twisted under pressure, and he desperately sought, but did not find a more pleasing combination of cards in his hands.

'Blast you!' he cursed at last and flung down the useless deal.

'Oh, hard luck,' Turner simpered. With a grin he reached to gather the winnings to himself.

'Another round?' he suggested then.

Smith shook his head and rose.

'It's time for me tour of the premises,' he grumbled, though secretly he was thankful for the opportunity to escape losing any more money to his workmate.

'I'll keep the cards warm,' Turner promised with a wink, 'in case you changes your mind, like.'

Muttering bitterly, Smith collected his keys and lantern and turned his back on lost money to leave the office.

The unlit interior of the Bank of England loomed vast and silent as the watchman pulled the door behind. After the confines of the little accounting office, the space was overwhelming to the senses, cathedral-like in its scale. Indeed, Mr Smith considered and not for the first time, his place of work was of a size and design to rival even nearby St Paul's. But he had seen it all a thousand times during his lonely watches of the night, and had long ago lost admiration for the building's imposing columns and graceful decoration, now so ghostly in these quiet hours of night. And so he walked uncaring across a floor of black and white tiles between empty desks, his tuneless whistle floating to echo far off in vaulted heights. At the edges of lamplight, shadows which had come in their thousands to replace the people of day danced to his lonely tune and followed the rhythm of his tapping heels.

Playing the light across the desks he passed, he found everything ordered and arranged for the coming day's business. Ink pots were secured, thick recording books stacked neatly and chairs set in precise fashion as required by management. Mr Fox insisted on tidiness above all in the bank's dealings. With a contemptuous grunt for old Fussy Fox as he was known, but safely behind his back, mind, Mr Smith angled right and to the first stop on his hourly rounds.

Shadows fled between stout bars at his approach, and Mr Smith was satisfied to find all as it should be. The sturdy iron gate he checked held to its frame, and with a testing rattle for good measure, he found the lock properly secured against trespass to the vaults below.

His task complete, the watchman took a moment of pause – as so often he did when alone at this particular gate – and he peered into deepest black between the bars. He raised his lamp as though expecting the result to be different to any other night, a pricking of that wall of blackness for a glimpse, just a pleasing glimpse, of the untold riches of the world stored in this place, forbidden to all but a chosen few of the bank's staff. But just as on every other night, the light revealed nothing to his gaze but the flight of marbled steps descending to the inky blackness flooding the vaults.

In place of sight, Mr Smith's imagination happily offered rooms of gold and jewels waiting to sparkle to his lamp. He envisioned treasure chests buried beneath avalanches of coins, together with rubies and diamonds and emeralds in such numbers they erupted from the containers like, why, just like the Arabian caves or castle keeps in his stories from childhood. The dream made him sigh and he drew fingers to touch the single lock standing between him and all the wealth of England. He did not bear its key and, in truth, here in the lonely gloom, part of him was glad of it. He had walked those marbled steps just once to visit the passageways down there, and once was enough. Escorted by a guide when first employed as a night watchman, he had undertaken a journey through an underworld of dripping echoes, where iron doors lined the way, and his imagination then had whispered not of treasures within, but of condemned souls piled high, and the watchman over them the very Devil himself. He had been grateful to return at last to the light, grateful more not to have met Lucifer at the end of those turning corridors. Recalling the visit with a shudder, he decided no measure of riches could lure him back, not alone, not at night. Smith rattled the massive gate again, this time to ward off bad dreams and devils with a noisy echo.

Abruptly sensing those same devils behind, Smith swung from the gate with a gasp. Had he just heard, no felt, some hint of motion off there in the dark? He thrust his light towards a corner of the building. And though he found nothing but shelves of ledgers, the watchman threw all his senses into explaining the source of a cold tickle suddenly rising at the back of his neck.

There are those mortals, though very few, who are attuned to the presence of the supernatural. Even fewer recognise what they detect with that internal sense. Smith was such a man, possessing the gift but lacking the understanding to make it potent. And so, as Benjamin paused in shadow above the watchman, he perceived Smith's search for a rational, daytime answer to the suspicions needling him. It was easier, perhaps, to accept the presence of mice in the walls rather than the reality, a vampire holding fast to a column over his head. Clearly happier to accept the explanation of scurrying rodents, Smith continued on his rounds, though Benjamin smiled at how the man moved a little faster to a whistled tune that was shakier now.

A moment's further pause and Benjamin dropped softly by the gate. With a final glance to confirm the watchman's departure, he slipped as easily as smoke through the bars. The lock here did not need to be disturbed until the return leg of his journey, when he would carry along the solid form of Billy Buckler's head. Down he went, gliding effortlessly between tiled walls through crushing blackness. Doors appeared at intervals on left and right as he travelled, forbidding portals lining the way to farthest reaches and the gate of his vision and the door it shielded. Crouching at last by the lock securing the barrier, he offered a keen and cautious scan of the space about before caressing fingertips to the keyhole.

'Levare,' was the whispered incantation, and it brought the softest of clicks in reply. Benjamin watched the lock pop and he progressed quickly on to the final obstacle. As easily sprung as the gate, the vault door ground open at his command to present the yawning void it contained. Thickest night swam to greet his arrival with a cold breath against his face.

He plunged within, knowing already through mirrored vision the final path to take between stacked chests. He drew out a canvas bag as he moved, ready to receive and convey bony contents. A sharp corner appeared, and he sensed the end of his search in navigating it. Ahead lay the farthest extent of the vault, where the deepest pools of shadow lay stored. And where, on a cushioned shelf, through sockets filled up with inky death, Billy Buckler stared back.

Benjamin paused in spite of himself for those bottomless eyes. Here at last, later than planned, he stood in private audience with the notorious pirate. He looked studiously on the buccaneer's skull, taking in the smooth sweep of the crown, the fierce prominence of the brow, and the smile that leered defiantly at the trespasser.

'Hello, Billy,' Benjamin said as he peered even deeper into those unseeing…

Senses flared in warning! Benjamin cast attention about in seeking the cause of his alarm, and up to the tiled ceiling, and past that to the city streets far above. Movement urgent and noisy came to him, betraying a rampaging approach towards the bank. He strained harder to perceive, to identify the disturbance which was a sound of…feet… charging feet bearing a weight of jangling swords and clacking pistols.

The crew of the Ghostmaker was at hand.

Skull and leg bones clattered into the bag, and Benjamin exited rapidly. The slamming of door and gate reverberated as he raced back along the maze of passages. Through the muffling earth he tracked the pirates' ongoing charge, struggling to guess how far or near they were in their unknowing pursuit of him. He pressed on, driven by the clamour and racing to beat the impending attack.

Sprinting the final length of corridor, he spied at

last the ascending steps, only to sense in that same instant an urgent advance on them from within the bank. Benjamin came to a sliding stop and retreated to deepest cover.

Lamplight betrayed Mr Smith's arrival at the outer gate. It caught the anxiety in his features as he too worked to account for the unnatural storm closing all about the building. Attentive to his duty, he tested the ironwork once more with a firm shake. But even as he did, the growing commotion outside drew him about to raise his lamp high. 'What's this?' Benjamin heard the watchman exclaim as he abandoned the gate.

Benjamin seized the moment's distraction. He raced up, catching sight of Smith just yards off, his back turned where he faced the thunderous advance on the bank's main entrance. The invasion came at last to a sun-bright eruption of gunpowder set to flame, and the doors burst to splinters. As Smith staggered back, and as Benjamin swept fingers to the final lock, smoke and fire announced the pirates' howling invasion, with weapons drawn and eyes maddened for the fight.

'Here now!' Smith barked in alarm, unfortunately calling upon himself the attention of the leading rank of pirates. Pistols levelled and the watchman was caught in a hail of gunfire. His lamp tumbled free to a crash of glass and fire across the tiles.

Benjamin surged through the opened gate. He chose his route rapidly, ducking low to place the bank's long serving counter between him and the buccaneers. He crouched and moved, but had taken just a few steps when his path was suddenly crossed by Mr Turner, roused from his gaming by the deafening raid. The man still clutched a fan of cards in one hand as he took in the unfolding chaos openmouthed. In his panic, the watchman's eyes caught Benjamin's and flared with heightened fear. A scream rose in his throat but was choked off by the fearful sight of pirates leaping onto the counter top. Playing cards were discarded to free hands for whimpering surrender, but the pirates ignored the offer and fired again, and by the light of pistol blasts, the buccaneers found Benjamin.

Fresh pistols were drawn and cocked amid terrible war cries, and Benjamin became the target of ranked weapons coming to bear.

He flung up his arms, but with no thought of surrender.

'Ventus!'

Writing desks erupted. Under the destructive power of Benjamin's magic, paperwork flew to ribbons from slashed ledgers as tables and chairs burst to a whirlwind that hurled daggers of wood in all directions and carried mortal men with all. Benjamin shouldered his bag of bones and raced between the cries of falling pirates as pistols fired wildly after him.

Bounding upwards to clasp brickwork, he scaled balconies and picture frames, clawing higher amid a whistling hail of shots. Plasterwork shattered on all sides where bullets sought to bring him down. One pistol ball, dangerously closer than the rest, zipped past and nicked the bag of bones. The canvas was rent wide, and Benjamin watched dismayed as one leg bone slipped out and fell away. Passing into the storm of firing, it was smashed to tiny, dusty pieces.

He scrambled on, leaping far in reaching for the promise of night beyond a high window. Catching the sill by mere fingertips even as bullets tore at the wood, he hauled up and plunged through a cascade of glass onto the rooftop. In the brief pause of his landing, he listened to profane curses and howls flung after him from below.

Gathering himself, he looked now for onward escape. He spotted it, a route from the bank to a neighbouring building, one easy leap away. With the punctured bag in tow, he made for the place, and was progressing quickly until a dark and terrible shape grew in his way and blocked all hope of flight. Benjamin looked into a painted face enraged, and heard the Baron's voice fill the night.

'Give me that pirate's head!'

23

The Baron swept closer, eyeing his opponent with a keen curiosity slipping through his fury.

'How I misjudged you, Benjamin Blake,' he mused aloud with a wave of one bony finger towards the boy. 'What great witch's magic you must possess.'

'Did you think silver would hold me?' Benjamin replied to confound the spirit's mind.

'Oh yes,' Samedi admitted, 'for the ordinary vampire that should have been enough. Yet here you stand to my surprise, with Buckler's bright skull your stolen prize.' Sounds from the street announced the pirates' hasty departure, accompanied by a fresh round of foul curses for creatures of the night. 'How slow they are,' the Baron lamented with a scornful snort for them all.

'They thought they would find Billy at the home of Percival Fox,' Benjamin said.

The Baron nodded.

'So many pirates in the Ghostmaker's crew, yet not one holds half your wits,' he said. He offered the hint of a smile as he gestured to the bag so cleverly gained by Benjamin.

'And what about Fox,' Benjamin demanded, 'did you bottle him up like the others?'

By way of answer, the Baron reached through the strands of his cloak to reveal a shimmering green bottle.

'And like the others he will play his part,' the spirit assured the boy.

'You speak in riddles and mysteries,' Benjamin said angrily. 'Why will you not speak the truth to me?'

'To what end?' the Baron sighed. 'You cannot help, and lives are endangered because you dabble so in matters you cannot change.'

'The pirates know I have their captain. I can bargain for an end to this, and to your slavery.'

'No,' Samedi replied. 'The selfish men of the Ghostmaker will not stop until they have what they truly seek. Only then might there be freedom. If you wish to help, give the bones to me.'

'More will die if I do.'

'More will die if you do not.'

Folds of cloak slithered in search of the bag, and by slow degrees the Baron hemmed Benjamin in on all sides to encircle the prize.

'Sterno!'

Benjamin's targeted stream of power caught the

Baron off guard and punched him flailing back towards the edge of the roof.

Painted features contorted angrily at the assault and the spirit drew himself up in preparation for a violent reaction. His cloak flared terribly to its many ragged strands and, even as Benjamin sought a fresh escape route, their ends plunged to the roof. Slates exploded under the impact and the building itself trembled beneath Benjamin's feet. Maintaining his balance, he looked on as shattered tiles were plucked up by the ensnaring cloak and turned as edged weapons for the fight.

Benjamin tightened his grip on the bag and watched crude blades cut the air on every side. Too numerous and too fast for him to counter, he retreated in search of a strategy, and in a flash of daring he found one.

Benjamin charged straight at the Baron.

Ducking past his opponent's slashing attacks, he raced towards the startled spirit, locking eyes with him in a furious challenge. Phantom arms reached to meet the charge, but Benjamin sidestepped and drove on, headlong and through the inky cloak itself. The clear rooftop waited just behind the spirit curtain.

But Benjamin fell. Where the solid roof had been an instant before, emptiness met his first step through the supernatural garment of night. The path to freedom turned to a sucking abyss beneath, and

Benjamin tumbled with a cry, flailing as London was replaced by a ceaseless pit of nothing.

In utter confusion he fell, snatching for purchase where there was none, seeking in vain through limitless space for some understanding of a place that defied all reason. Down through unending and starless night he fell, helpless to control his spill through buffeting winds. And in his plummet farther and farther, round and round, he realised he was suddenly not alone in this void. From the outer reaches of the chasm came shapes that were in the same instant shapeless, colourless forms drifting and indistinct, tracking his wild descent. They floated closer, these swarming wisps, circling his tumble as though intrigued by him, so strange a presence in a space that was theirs. The forms increased in number and spiralled in chasing him down, and all peered on him in wonder, awe-struck by his intrusion. And Benjamin looked back no less astounded into the smoky faces of the restless dead.

He had passed through the Baron's cloak into a realm of death.

On he sped, forever it seemed, pursued by phantoms, and all the while still clutching the canvas bag. Even when his descent became a bewildering spin he maintained that fierce grip. And even when a mighty hand thrust from the dark to seize the canvas, still he refused to let go and held firmly against the stronger hand of an unseen challenger.

The fall was slowed now by that pulling hand, and Benjamin was hauled back, drawn upwards by it, away from the pit and its nightmare inhabitants. In a flash, the mortal night world returned and the Baron shook Benjamin off to send him crashing to the broken roof, there to gasp as he was assailed by the shock of a long forgotten sensation.

Cold.

For the first time in his vampire life, Benjamin felt a stab of ice through his body. Limbs were seized by the cruelty of it, fingers locked in protest and mortal memory shrilled at it. He shook uncontrollably and cried out against the pain. Made powerless, he lost his hold on the bag and fell back to find the Baron towering over him, framed by jagged tiles as he poised for the finish.

A single sharp edge came to rasp against Benjamin's throat, holding him while cloak tendrils slid over his legs towards the fallen bag. To an unspoken command they struck, snatching away the canvas between bladed rows that closed like jaws.

'It is over, Benjamin Blake,' Samedi declared sadly. 'My contest with you is fought and won.'

Blades clicked like hungry teeth and Benjamin's frozen mind despaired.

'Stop!' a tiny voice commanded, sharp and bold. 'Baron, no more!'

Deadly cloak strands halted immediately in answer to the call, holding in space bare inches from Benjamin. Shivering yet, he probed for signs of the speaker and through the slow parting of strands he beheld the one whose voice held power enough to stop the spirit's attack.

In the Baron's shadow, Mr Pyke's little slave girl looked on Benjamin and smiled.

24

Her actions spoke louder than words.

At the girl's slightest glance, the Baron bowed respectfully and drifted from her path. And when the child reached casually to remove a tile from his floating cloak, the phantom responded by dropping all others to a great clatter and shatter.

Eyeing the girl through torturing cold, Benjamin understood at last the truth Samedi had kept hidden, even in his words.

Whom I serve must soon be saved, lest forever we are both enslaved.

'I am Lara,' she said, anticipating one of the many questions he could not yet give voice to. 'You are Benjamin Blake. The Baron told me about you. You can do magic, like me.' She smiled for his confusion and gently stretched to touch a hand before giving over to a frown. 'You are colder than a vampire should be.'

'He slipped to the other side,' the Baron explained simply.

Lara nodded her understanding.

'Yes, it's cold there. But don't worry,' she assured Benjamin, 'it will pass.'

'I don't...understand,' he managed.

'Then I will explain.' Lara smiled again, pleased at the opportunity for a story. She sat cross-legged on the roof and screwed up her face in pondering the appropriate beginning for her tale. The perfect opening suggested itself and brought delight to her eyes.

'Twelve summers ago I was born, at sea. Not on the Ghostmaker, mind, that comes later. My mother was enslaved, taken from our home to the West Indies. There she worked in the big house of a man who grew fields of sugar cane. The fields needed many slaves for the harvest. The adults worked hard while the children spent the long hot days with Mama Gaston. She was grandmother to all the children on the estate. But she had special eyes for me. She would whisper to my mother, "Lara has the gift" and she would wink and point. Once, when I heard her say it, I looked for the gift. I looked under my bed, and under the shack and behind the herb bottles on Mama Gaston's shelf!'

Lara chuckled into her hands at the memory.

'When I asked her about it, Mama said I would know the gift right well when I saw it and said no more. Well, long after that, on a night so very hot, there came a cry for Mama Gaston and her healing. A man had fallen down by the fields, they said, sick and dying, and Mama was needed double-quick. My mother was working so Mama took me along. She grabbed me up with her bags of herbs and marched us along under a moon so bright it made the road ahead white as the sugar we made. And when we reached the edge of the fields where the man lay, and everyone there weeping over him, Mama Gaston stopped stiff as a cane, right in the road, and she took to shaking with fear. And her eyes were as wide as that shiny moon. But I wasn't afraid. "Do you see, child?" she asked me then. "Do you see?" And I said, "Yes, Mama, I see." "What do you see, tell me now," Mama said. She was testing me. So I said, "I see the man, the floating man in his tall hat and big cloak." When no-one else but Mama could see, I saw the Baron too, come to collect the dead.'

'The gift,' the Baron whispered reverently. 'For a child of the gods.'

Lara shrugged.

'Don't know where it came from, don't know why, but I had it, and that made me a friend to the Baron. I made the gift stronger with spells I learned from Mama Gaston, and secrets the Baron shared with me. I helped many people, cured many. I always used my gift for good. I learned that from my mother.'

'And then the pirates came,' Benjamin guessed,

and the Baron growled at the truth of it.

'The Ghostmaker,' Lara agreed darkly. 'The pirates came and snatched me up. Took my mother too when she wouldn't let go, took us far off. They threw me down in front of Billy Buckler and made demands. They tied heavy chains on my mother and showed her deep water to make me agree. "Keep Captain Buckler from the other side," they ordered with whip and stick, "stop the Baron collecting the captain's spirit till Billy takes his revenge."'

'Pirate devils,' the Baron grumbled, and his fists clenched in rage.

'Over and over I did as they wanted,' Lara went on. 'I took Captain Billy back from the sword and the pistol, from drowning and from fire. I pulled him back many times from the grave that was dug for him long ago. And now I must do it again.'

'The bones,' Benjamin said, 'and the bottles. You need them for your spell.'

'Yes,' Lara agreed. 'Body and spirit are needed for life.'

Benjamin frowned as more questions came through his fading chill.

'But why? With such a gift, the gift you have, why do you not bottle up the pirates and free your mother? Where can she be that the Baron cannot reach her?'

In reply, Samedi swept a hand to gesture over rooftops far off.

'She lies beyond my sight, chained in the belly of the Ghostmaker,' he explained. 'She moves with changing wind and shifting tide beyond even my power to find her.'

'Deep water,' Benjamin said, recalling the pirates' threat to Lara.

The little girl nodded sadly, and with a shrug she rose to leave. She walked under the protective cover of the Baron's cloak and turned to face Benjamin a final time.

'My magic is strong but it can't find my mother,' she said. 'If yours can, Benjamin Blake, help me see her again. But if you can't, you must stay out of my way.' Through the cloak's shifting and drifting, the little girl departed.

'Now you understand all,' the Baron said.

'No,' Benjamin replied, 'not all. Billy Buckler's revenge, what is that? What will happen when he rises?'

The Baron held up empty hands.

'That is a terrible truth yet to be told. Billy hates England and wants to stab her deep, but his foul dark plan he keeps to himself, locked in some hateful chamber of his heart.'

The Baron retreated, carrying with him the canvas

bag, the pirates' prize. Benjamin's gaze lingered on it and feelings of helplessness and frustration crowded him. The bag represented his failed plan to defeat the buccaneers, and was their victory over him. The thought made him angry, and angrier yet for criminals succeeding because of his failure.

'Tell Lara I will find a way!' he shouted after the Baron. 'Tell her!'

Pausing, Samedi examined the rage in Benjamin's face and caught the spark of determination behind it. He turned his gaze to the night sky, and the moon illuminated his painted mask as he pointed to the glittering heavens.

'The life spell works best with the dying of the moon,' he said. 'You have less than two nights, Benjamin Blake. Then Billy rises.'

25

'We have it!'

Mr Pyke thrust the skull high, and the pirates filled the warehouse with their howls of triumph. Pistol shots crashed in celebration and powder sparks glinted on swords raised in tribute to the bones of Billy Buckler.

'The crew of the Ghostmaker wins again!' Pyke shouted above the din and his words brought more cheers from the rabble. 'You all acted together for the good of your captain, acted like a true ship of scallywags! Mark me now, men of the Ghostmaker. When Billy is restored, I'll be sure to tell him how every man here earned his fair portion of treasure stored up for us!'

The mention of riches spurred the crew to even wilder celebrations. Kegs of rum were smashed open without further ceremony, and a night of violent merriment began in honour of the pirate life.

Mr Pyke smiled as he left the men to their fun. Cradling the skull that offered its own jubilant leer, he made his way to a crude construction pitched at the rear of the villains' new hideout, a tented room formed of posts and ship's canvas. He swept the door of rough covering aside to join Lara within where she made ready for her part in events to come.

A lopsided table dominated the centre of the space where the girl worked. On its surface the bones and heart of Billy Buckler had been laid out, their human shape re-assembled with studious care on a bed of shimmering velvet. Through subdued light, Lara moved with slow precision, examining dried root parcels and bottles of coloured powder, each assigned by memory to its place between white limbs and black candles.

Eyeing the scene, Mr Pyke was unsettled by the sight of shadows playing unnaturally against the canvas walls. They weaved and swayed at odds with the candles' guttering light as though to the workings of some spell already underway. The pirate looked uneasily on the magic table and around the dismal room. He started as he beheld a shadow far deeper than the rest in a corner. Shifting dreamily there, Baron Samedi glared back from under the rim of his top hat.

'Is everything ready?' Pyke demanded of the girl.

Lara paused in her work and considered the bones.

'I have done what I can,' she said with a shrug.

'What does that mean?' Pyke challenged her.

'You have worked this spell successfully many times before.'

'I have,' Lara agreed. 'But never when a piece is missing.' She pointed to the captain's legs and drew Pyke's attention to the wooden stump lying in place of one absent limb.

The pirate concealed his doubts with a sneer.

'Work your magic, that's what you're here for.' He crossed to the head of the table, aiming to place the skull with the rest of the skeleton.

'No!' Lara exclaimed, jumping to snatch the head from him. 'It must come from my hands.'

Retreating from the table and the Baron's burning glare, Pyke watched as the girl worked with tender movements to set the skull among the other bones.

'You will not leave this room until the time of the spell,' he informed her. He turned to address Samedi. 'What of the one who tried to steal from us? The spirit boy on the rooftops.'

Easing forward to allow candle gleam catch fully his whitened face, the Baron fixed Pyke with the power of his stare.

'Destroyed.'

'Destroyed how?' Pyke demanded at once as he held the demon's unblinking gaze and searched for lies.

'By claw of rat and bullfrog liver, I watched him drown in London's river.'

Pyke's lip curled uncomfortably at the Baron's words but he kept his slit eyes on the spirit, seeking yet for hints of trickery.

'Very good,' he said at last, though doubtfully. With a final nod he swept from the room.

Moving again amid his riotous comrades, Pyke took time in scanning the vast area of the warehouse, wary of deep shadow patches among the ceiling beams and other potential hiding places along the high walkways above. He was joined in his examination by Mr Davy.

'Is something amiss?' the man asked, concerned by his comrade's upward staring.

'What guards have you posted?' Pyke asked as he continued his searching.

'A man at each of the doors front and back,' Davy reported, 'and more eyes aloft to keep check on the dock and approach roads.'

'I want two men guarding the captain,' Pyke instructed. 'Night and day until this is done, understand?'

'Aye, Mr Pyke, I'll make it so,' Davy said. He hurried off to carry out the mate's order.

Pyke remained, his fingers playing unconsciously across pistols as he continued to probe the dark for lies and interfering spirits.

26

Benjamin brooded in his armchair and glowered on disobedient mirrors.

The instruments of magic lay about his chalked symbols, just as he had set them out. They were useless, and the truth of it infuriated him.

After the rooftop encounter with Samedi, he had sped immediately to his room in the Tower, again to take position at the starting point of the finding spell. Here at his feet, he had assured himself, was the very conjuration needed to help Lara and the Baron. All things were found in the mirrors. Even that moving beyond sight across the vast sea would be visible in the flashing glass.

He had tried so hard.

The mirrors had turned obediently just as before to offer vision in all directions, revealing any subject in any location he chose.

'The Ghostmaker,' was his demand, and the vision had grown accordingly.

Across the rolling current of the Thames his vision

raced, out beyond the last of the city's lights to reach the sea, and farther still to cross the waves of the Channel under the same waning moon that powered his magic in London. Hither and thither it dashed between surf and sky until at last, in deepest night, the Ghostmaker reared, monstrous and dark where it coursed over black waters.

Moving without lights, the ship had all the appearance of a phantom vessel. Its ports and gun hatches held firmly shuttered, cutting any risk of interior lamps betraying its presence so close to England's shores. No sign of life could be discerned upon the deck, or any lantern light in the rigging. Only the softest hue of moonlight against full canvas gave hint to the passage of the forbidding ship.

Deep within the vessel, where Benjamin next sent his vision, a creaking dusk held sway. Just a solitary lamp was permitted here, its weak beams illuminating a passage between groaning, dripping timbers to a place farthest from the world. And it was here, in the core of the vessel, that a bolted cage imprisoned a voice weeping softly and alone for its child.

Benjamin's goal was reached, his quarry found!

But what of it?

He had guided his sight rapidly back out and up, climbing high over the Ghostmaker in search of its bearing. In an instant he peered down where the tips of masts passed below on a wide expanse of featureless water. He turned in all directions across the rolling sea, yet no point of reference presented itself, neither rock nor headland by which to fix the ship's location, nor any star to compete with the moon's glow to offer a heading.

He had driven the vision north, south, east, west, and every view was the same. The Ghostmaker sailed on waves that looked like all others and beneath a moon that was the same here as across the whole of the night world. There was nothing by which his magic could fix the vessel to any degree of accuracy.

The mirrors had tumbled uselessly to the floor, the spell ending swiftly and without result.

Benjamin had retreated to his armchair then, bitterly defeated.

Despite the anger that sparked between his tapping fingers, he felt now the powerless reality for Baron Samedi and Lara against pirates whose planning had been so precise. He bunched fists to tiny lightning storms at the thought of villains laughing in their hideout, forcing Lara to work her magic for them lest they order her mother cast into crushing depths. They would control her until the coming revenge of Billy Buckler, and long after they had summoned the Ghostmaker and sailed away.

The notion prompted a fresh tide of anger in him,

and he almost gave in to its demand for bolts of power to be flung to the ceiling to vent his frustration. But it was the unexpected rising of another unanswered question that stayed his hands and dimmed their lightning. With sharp focus, he set useless emotion aside and fixed squarely on this quiet but persistent query behind his eyes. Fists opened unconsciously and gripped the chair in pulling him forward to examine once more the quadrants of his chalked spell. The growing question drew his eyes across those bordered areas which had already revealed so much but not enough. Individual lines coursed a way to neighbouring spaces, the one giving up the buccaneers in their lair, the other the Ghostmaker's unknown heading. It was here the question held him, between the quadrants. Not in one place or the other, but squarely on the dusty white line separating them. A simple chalked line, so slender to his gaze, yet representing a barrier of unknown measure, formed by land and sea between Lara and her mother. Only when the Ghostmaker was summoned for the final escape from London would the quadrants join, and the thin chalked line would no longer separate mother and child. They would stand together on the deck of the Ghostmaker, hostages yet to Billy Bucker and his crew.

Less than two nights.

He recalled the Baron's words of caution, and they added fuel to the question to make it shine in his mind. Two nights and Billy would come, two nights and the Ghostmaker would turn landward, veering towards its master's call.

The question surged white-hot and obvious to Benjamin and it sent him with a gasp from his chair.

'How will the pirates summon the Ghostmaker?'

He stalked urgently the borders of his spell, peering down from new angles, unable to contain the words as he speculated.

'When the spell is cast, and Billy returns, how will news be sent to a ship so far off the coast? How?'

The pirates must have some means of communicating with their vessel, that was certain, a means by which to signal an emergency or, when the time came, to announce their readiness to escape from London!

Benjamin's fists flexed again, struggling to contain a flow of exciting possibilities. Each one depended on gaining the answer to a new question suddenly presented by the first. If he learned the means of communication, could he be the one to summon the Ghostmaker and draw it into a trap?

Chalk dust swirled to a breath of passing as Benjamin sped once more from the Tower.

27

The buccaneer Tavish spat bitterly and muttered curses against rotten luck.

Maintaining his guard on the warehouse walkway, far above the pirate festivities, he peered enviously on his mates at their rum-swilling and games. Stung by howling laughter and singing, he beat a frustrated hand against the rail and longed to be part of it all. Instead, well, here he was instead, consigned by orders to a windy perch just as the first delicious keg had been spilt open. And from here he now watched the draining of measure after measure without so much as a tankard set aside for him. And why, he silently demanded of no-one. Why had he been the one selected from the whole crew for this thankless duty? For what man jack of the crew was more deserving of rum and song than him, the one who carried the heart of Captain Billy to safety when all others had quivered at the task? Yes, he had done it, not one of the villains he now watched bashing open another keg to toast the life of crime. And yet, he was up here and they were down there. He spat again against ill fortune, for his dry throat and two more hours on watch.

'Mr Pyke be nervous,' he griped, mocking Mr Davy's words as he had assigned him his post. 'Mr Pyke don't think it be the time to relax.' Well the rest of the crew weren't having no trouble relaxing. Why, just look at them, cheering for a barrel race started between Misters Stubbs and Estoban. He watched pirate feet dance for purchase on rolling wood, with Mr Stubbs taking an early lead over that fool Estoban who was trying to balance while holding his mug of rum. 'Come on, matey,' Tavish whispered for Stubbs. But his words were like an ill-wind for the racing pirate. With a cry, Mr Stubbs upended and careened into a group of roaring buccaneers while Mr Estoban somehow raced for the line without spilling a drop to loud cheers from his supporters.

Tavish rolled his eyes and moved on.

With his mood made increasingly foul, the pirate stroked his pistols and longed for a target on which to expend his anger. Any pesky intruder this night would find him ready to inflict a shot from each weapon and a mighty stroke of his sword for good measure. After that, Tavish resolved, he would drink his fill and challenge Mr Estoban to another race.

A scratching sound from the gloom ahead drew

Tavish up from dreams of rum and barrel dancing. Instinctively his hands tightened on pistol butts as he peered into the shadowy veil clinging to the walkway. When the sound came again he drew weapons and cocked both, steeling himself as he aimed towards the sound and prepared.

'Come along,' he whispered through his teeth, 'come and get what I gots for ya.'

The moment of tension was broken by the "scratcher's" arrival, and Tavish tracked a mangy rat where it emerged to scamper along the boards. Abruptly aware of the pirate, the rodent turned and fled.

Muttering curses in its wake, Tavish secured his pistols and walked on.

He reached a shuttered window and stopped to slide its bolt aside for a view of the night. A chill river wind found his neck as he scanned outside where nothing moved besides. The dock far below was an abandoned place at this late hour. During daylight, hundreds had thronged here in pursuing the work of unloading ships and stuffing warehouses, but it stretched ghostly and quiet now, hemmed between shuttered buildings and ships dozing at their moorings. The only sound to break the night air was the irregular tolling of a bell on one of the vessels in marking the lazy rise and fall of the river.

A fresh scratching intruded on the lulling stillness, and Tavish turned from the window to search again for the pesky rat. Finding no sign of the creature on one side, he looked to the other, but failed to detect it. The pirate concentrated harder and frowned for the realisation that the low noise seemed to originate not from a gloomy spot on the walkway but outside the window. Suspicious, but fearing still to come unexpectedly on a disease-carrying rodent, he eased his head out with slow care to examine the area immediately below the opening.

Clawed hands plunged from above to seize his face. Their crushing hold instantly cut off the warning scream that raced to his lips. In a blinking, Tavish was torn bodily through the small window and up towards the roof.

28

Tavish gazed terrified into the face of the demon holding him.

'I want blood!' Benjamin hissed. He bared vampire teeth for full effect.

Speechless with fear, Tavish's hands fluttered about his belt, seeking a weapon, any weapon, to defend against this nightmare made real. But the creature pinned his arms and growled with silvered ferocity.

'Mercy,' Tavish squeaked. He struggled pitifully in the iron embrace of the vampire. 'Have mercy!'

Benjamin maintained his act and took to sniffing at the whimpering pirate's face and hair.

'You're a sinner,' he concluded, 'a thief.' He watched Tavish nod frantically, eager to please. 'A murderer?' Benjamin added, drawing more nodded agreement and a blubbering of fear. 'Excellent!' the vampire declared. 'The blood of murderers tastes sweet!'

With a wail of mortal anguish, the pirate thrashed

against a terrible fate and collapsed to the tiles, there to scramble backwards with watery eyes locked on those of the advancing Hell-creature. Reaching the lip of the roof in his blind retreat, he flailed into space. Only Benjamin's swift hand, whipping to grasp his shirt-front, prevented a fatal plunge to the dock.

'For pity's sake, what do you want?' Tavish pleaded.

'I told you,' the vampire growled. 'I am sent in pursuit of sinners for the eternal fires below. My reward is their living blood!'

Pushed to the brink of fainting by the dreadful information, Tavish seized on a desperate option and offered it with trembling lips.

'I repent!'

Benjamin played along and offered mock confusion.

'What, what's that? You repent?'

'Yes, I repent, I repent,' the pirate wailed. 'I'm heartily sorry for all my sins and beseech my, er, uh, guardian angel and all the, uh, saints in, uh…' With rolling eyes he tried to join his hands in prayer.

'You know your prayers,' Benjamin noted with a fake sneer of distaste.

'Oh yes, yes,' Tavish agreed, 'from my youth. I remember all of my prayers.'

'When did you last attend church?'

Tavish offered a weak shrug.

'I spend a lot of time at sea.'

'Pirate sinner!' Benjamin declared with a lunge for his throat.

'No! No! Please fell spirit, don't. I'll make amends.'

'Pah! Empty promises are easy. Besides, where else will I find a juicy sinner tonight?'

'Below!' Tavish offered instantly, desperately. 'The space below is stocked up with sinners, enough to fill all the rooms in Hell. And much worse than me, mind. Pirates, the lot of 'em.'

'You lie. Pirates work their sins on ships, far from land.'

'We have our ship, the Ghostmaker, ready and waiting.'

Benjamin made a fine show of searching for the vessel, his silver orbs darting about while he sniffed dramatically at the air.

'Where is your ship?'

'Off the coast, plotting a course just beyond sight of land,' Tavish blurted. 'It will come at our calling.'

'How do you call a ship at sea? What foul magic is used for this?' Benjamin snarled, drawing close to the truth at last.

'No magic,' the buccaneer assured. 'Just the simple use of a fishing vessel, one in the pay of our leader. It will carry the signal when the time comes. I heard the name but the once…the, uh, the Lafitte, yes, it's called the Lafitte. Twin lights set across its mainmast call the Ghostmaker to shore, simple like.'

'And?' Benjamin offered the man a bodily shake for more.

'I don't know,' Tavish protested feebly. 'Only Mr Pyke knows all the details…and perhaps Mr Robinson.'

'Robinson?'

'Aye, Mr Robinson, the tavern keeper of the Gravediggers,' the pirate said. 'He does all the running for Mr Pyke, the perfect cover he is. He'll be the one to instruct the Lafitte when Pyke commands. He's a bad sort too, by the way, very bad sins. I think he waters down his rum.'

Benjamin ignored the babbling pirate and let information swirl in his mind. Names to be arranged, leads to follow. But a glance to the eastern sky, and a horizon already touched by the first cold grey of morning told him any course of action must wait another night to proceed.

It was in the brief moment of distraction that Tavish spied his opportunity for salvation from the night creature. With a desperate cry he hauled to break from the grip on his shirt and grabbed for his pistols.

'You'll not take me to Hell, demon!' he shrieked

and loosed crashing explosions with both barrels.

Even as the shots whistled harmlessly past, Benjamin snatched through pistol smoke in a vain attempt to halt the pirate's lethal retreat. Fingers brushed material but failed to catch the man who stepped in blind panic beyond the lip of the roof and tumbled away, screaming to his end on the dock far below.

29

The tumult of pistols and screams brought pirates running.

Charging onto the dockside with weapons made ready, the buccaneers found their fallen comrade sprawled lifelessly at their feet. Oaths of vengeance were uttered in all directions as furious men sought Tavish's killer among recesses along the dock.

'Make way!' Pyke roared, forcing a path through the pack to conduct his quick but close examination of the scene. He cast swiftly upwards towards the window of the dead man's watch and turned to his officers nearby.

'Stubbs, Estoban, to the roof! Report from there!'

With barked 'ayes' the men raced to obey.

'What do you make of it?' Mr Davy asked at his shoulder. 'Too much rum and a drunken step?'

'Don't be a fool,' Pyke snapped. 'His pistols are drawn and smoking. He fired at something.' The pirate let his eyes rove over the whole dock, up to a forest of masts and sails, and along the line between rooftops and sky. At last he returned his gaze to the men surrounding. 'Get the body inside, and yourselves before we're spotted.'

The men jumped to action. Hands grabbed Tavish by the legs and dragged him to the warehouse. The rest of the crew followed in a scowling procession with weapons pointing to all quarters as they retreated. Only Davy remained to watch Mr Pyke where he stared thoughtfully on the dark river.

'What do you think it was?' he prompted.

'Who, not what,' Pyke growled at the smirking moon.

Mr Davy followed the man's reasoning with a start.

'The boy spirit who tried for the captain's bones? I thought he was dealt with.'

'So says Baron Samedi,' Pyke reminded him. 'But who trusts a slave to speak the truth? I feel him scheming against us, plotting an escape with his young magician. I want the guard doubled at once and a close watch on Lara at all times. Make it so.'

'And we're staying here?' Davy asked. 'Is that wise now? If it was the demon boy who done for Tavish, he could give us away, or send soldiers against us.'

Pyke's smile was a knowing leer.

'Then why has he not done it already? Here we stand but I see no troops. I would send the Baron against them anyhow. No, our mysterious enemy creeps about trying to scare the crew because he has no other weapon in the fight.'

'He must know about the girl's mother,' Davy reasoned quickly. He smiled with his fellow pirate.

'Precisely,' Pyke agreed. 'He won't risk her life in tackling us directly.'

A soft whistle from on high drew the men's attention to the warehouse roof where Estoban held out empty hands for nothing found.

'You see?' Pyke said. 'Our interfering spirit has scurried off, frightened by the dawn's light, I shouldn't wonder.'

'He might he have learned something from Tavish before he killed him,' Davy suggested.

Pyke's grin faded as he mused on that dangerous possibility, and he nodded grimly.

'Indeed. Tavish knew little but he knew enough.' He turned the question over in his mind and stared again on the river flowing towards the first rays of day. 'Make ready, Mr Davy,' he barked then, 'we have some loose ends to tie up by sunset.'

30

'Make way for his Majesty the King!'

Captain Madigan's barked order reverberated through the Bank of England. Its commanding echo at once brought a standstill to the work of repair underway on the devastated space. Labourers shovelling wreckage, and clerks gathering torn pages from broken desks halted to look in wonder towards the shattered entry doors. Soldiers there were already jumping smartly to attention while managers supervising on the main floor hurriedly fluffed their cuffs and straightened collars in nervous anticipation of the noble arrival.

Casting a long shadow across the debris-strewn floor as he appeared from the early morning light, King George strode into the building. The heels of his buckled shoes clicked loudly through the hushed interior. Without pause for the bows of those subjects he passed, the monarch moved directly to regard the bank's destruction with a mixture of shock and grave displeasure playing on his face. Behind, flanked by guards and courtiers, Princess Charlotte and Prince George dutifully followed their father.

'What in the wide world happened here?' young George whispered, his mind barely comprehending the scene of utter devastation.

'My question precisely,' his father muttered gravely. He halted to watch the approach of a group of wigged representatives, a bowing troop of fretful bankers. And he looked on with growing impatience as the delegation maintained its stooped posture. No man among them seemed willing to be the first to rise and face their regent's queries. 'Well?' the king demanded irritably at last.

'Your Majesty,' a small rotund man ventured from the assembly, 'I am your humble servant Charles Fotheringay, deputy to Mr Fox. Pained as I am to greet you on such a troubling morning, I am honoured to assist with any pressing questions.' With a faltering smile, Fotheringay bowed again, thrusting his ample belly dangerously hard against the buttons of his embroidered coat.

'My first pressing question is the whereabouts of Mr Fox on a morning such as this,' the king responded. 'Why is he not before me? Surely he is aware of the crime against the bank for which he holds responsibility.'

'Oh dear,' Fotheringay said, wringing his hands

uncomfortably as his colleagues mumbled nervously. 'Your Majesty has not been informed.' The deputy looked in vain for someone else to convey the dreadful news but found all gazes averted from his. 'A messenger was dispatched to the home of Mr Fox as soon as matters were discovered amiss. He is dead, your Majesty, murdered in the night.'

By her father's side, Charlotte felt the skin on her arms prickle at the news. Percival Fox was dead? Just hours ago she had conversed with the man and now he was as dead as – she shuddered at the unintended comparison – dead as the bones he had carried with him for her entertainment.

'My chief banker has been murdered?' the king spluttered furiously. 'And the Bank of England raided, all on the same night? Gadzooks, the world is upside down! Who will answer for this?'

'We are seeking clues this very moment,' Fotheringay hastened to assure the king. With a sweep of his hand about, he added, 'If I may, I will lead your Majesty.'

As the monarch and his bankers moved to tour the wreckage, Charlotte paused and quietly held back. When certain her absence was unnoticed, she quickly sidestepped the group and followed a path of her own choosing through the scene. She weaved slowly and alone through the rubble, meeting the bows of men at their dusty labours while allowing her eyes to travel astonished over piles of stone and wood littering the tiles. Skirting desks covered over with sundered plaster, she was drawn at last towards a wall where the damage appeared worse than elsewhere, apparently caused by what seemed to her to be...pistol shots. Astounded, she scanned a trail of holes leading up and up to where it ended high overhead at a window, the only one shattered among all its neighbours.

The princess stepped for a closer inspection of the brickwork and stretched fingers towards the nearest jagged hole. In so doing, she brought a foot down awkwardly on something that crunched under her shoe. Steadying herself, she looked to an object that was, on first inspection, merely another fragment of plasterwork among the rest. But on gazing more, she realised this fragment was darker than painted plaster, and altogether more familiar to her. Charlotte's blood grew cold as she beheld a rounded joint atop the jagged remains of a leg bone.

'Your Highness!'

His voice turned the princess with a gasp, and she caught Captain Madigan's bow from his place nearby.

'Forgive, Princess,' he said, 'I did not mean to startle you. I noticed you were missing.'

'Oh yes?' she pressed even as she collected her thoughts.

'His Majesty is about to enter the vaults,' he offered with a disarming smile. But Charlotte caught the frown clouding the captain's face as he too followed the trail of bullet holes to that high shattered window.

'I'll be along at once,' she declared and stepped past him, picking her way carefully to maintain a royal poise in crossing the tiles.

Reaching the others, Charlotte was in time to witness the first banker unlock a barred gateway before he descended to the lower reaches of the building, a lantern held to light the way.

'The vaults,' the king explained to his children as they waited to be called forward. 'I am informed that just one item among the many treasures below has been stolen. We shall see for ourselves.'

Just one item. Charlotte's stomach lurched as she chased an image of bony dead sockets from her memory.

With all at last prepared, the royal party moved down. Flanked by lamp bearers, they walked a seemingly endless path until finally the heart of the matter was reached, beyond iron barriers in the cramped space of the bank's most distant vault.

'All areas were ignored by the thieves save for this,' Fotheringay reported, passing his lantern about the room's cold interior to reveal innumerable chests and, strangely, a table bearing only a velvet cushion.

'And all items here were similarly ignored, save one.'

The banker shifted his lamp closer to the object in question. Without looking, the princess knew with a cold unfolding certainty how the light now fell upon the open lid of a studded rectangular chest.

'And the contents?'the king demanded, playing a hand over the empty box.

'That information appears to have been known to Mr Fox alone,' Fotheringay admitted sheepishly.

But Charlotte knew. The skull of Billy Buckler grinned from the depths of recollection, and the dreadful image dragged at her heart.

'I cannot breathe,' she croaked, suddenly retreating. She pushed by the others gathered in the crushing atmosphere of the vault. At the door she collided with Madigan and saw his knowing gaze shift from the chest to meet hers as she elbowed past and into the corridor. There she felt her way back along walls abruptly tilting across her vision and clawed in search of daylight.

Emerging breathlessly into the expansive light, Charlotte became aware of the eyes of workers turning upon her addled state. She gathered herself quickly, wilfully drawing breath and rounding her shoulders to convey youthful strength to all as she remembered her status. She acknowledged those who paused in their tasks to bow courteously and turned once more to the damaged wall. There a group of men had arrived to begin collecting the strewn plaster. She watched with a dizzy shudder as the fallen bone was scooped up among a shovelful of rubble and consigned to a bucket for dumping.

31

Londons morning sunshine was so dazzling after the vaults' murky confinement that Captain Madigan did not at first catch the stern face in the cheering crowd.

As he flanked the royal entourage departing the bank, and as the king paused on its steps to graciously receive an outburst of hurrahs from the multitude drawn by his visit, Madigan looked to ensure his soldiers were assembled in close order about the monarch and his family. Turning then to eye the crowd for sign of troublemakers or protestors, or worse, assassins, he found only joyous well-wishers, with children waving from adult shoulders, until his eyes locked on one who stood out from the rest, a wild form Madigan recognised despite the man's unruly beard and dishevelled uniform.

'God save the king!' the man cried though he neither smiled nor looked from the captain towards King George. 'God save England!'

'Lieutenant Godfrey!' Madigan called for his

second-in-command. His summons drew a thin-framed officer – and Princess Charlotte's close attention – to him.

'Sir,' Godfrey reported with a crisp salute.

'Can I rely on you for his Majesty's safety?' Madigan demanded, though he already knew the man to be a capable and loyal soldier.

'Yes sir!' Godfrey declared with a proud puffing of his chest and an unnecessary second salute.

Madigan nodded in return.

'Very well, you have command until I presently return.' He dismissed his gushing officer with his own salute and turned to descend the steps, watching how the wild man tracked his movements and followed.

'Captain.' Charlotte's voice stopped him halfway down. 'What is going on?'

He saw her frown on the progress of the ragged man through the crowd.

'I must speak with someone who may shine a light on matters here,' Madigan explained even as she continued her examination of the ragged figure.

'From that man?' she asked dubiously.

'His name is Faulkner. He is a man who served faithfully as a captain in your father's navy, and I trust him.'

'Captain Faulkner,' Charlotte said as she

remembered the name uttered by Percival Fox. 'He faced Billy Buckler.'

'And lost his good standing because of the villain-ous pirate,' Madigan confirmed bitterly. He moved to cut off any further questions. 'Please now, Highness, be guided by Lieutenant Godfrey.'

She rolled her eyes despairingly.

'Godfrey trips over his own sword, I have seen it.'

'He will die in protecting you until I return to do so.'

Leaving no moment for argument, he raced down the steps and left her there.

***

He found Faulkner waiting, lurking in a side street.

It did not take any close examination to see the man was a nervous wreck. With darting eyes behind lank hair, the man sought wildly for threats in every direction and took liquid comfort from a concealed hip-flask. The sight pained Madigan.

'Captain,' he greeted the man.

Faulkner jumped for fright despite Madigan's soft tone but he offered a smile for his friend's respect in addressing him.

'I have not been called captain for so very long,' he said. 'How have you been, young James? You have attained a captain's rank yourself, I see.'

'That I owe to your training,' Madigan reminded him, saddened by the man's appearance with a uniform bedraggled by the fall from noble heights to London's gutters.

Faulkner smiled once more for Madigan's kind words and he raised his flask in salute. But as he supped he held a keen eye on the young captain.

'Have you doubled the guard about the king and his family?' he demanded abruptly. 'Do you trust your men?'

Madigan was taken aback.

'Yes, and yes. These are troubling times. What do you know?'

Before he replied, Faulkner looked warily all around as though fearful his answer might be overhead. He even looked up towards spying windows while he steadied himself with another burning sip.

'Pirates.'

A grinning skull flashed to Madigan's startled mind.

'What evidence do you have of this?' he gasped.

'Do you doubt me?' Faulkner demanded, and his teeth clenched in sharp anger. 'Like the rest?'

Now it was Madigan's turn to grow angry.

'You forget yourself, sir. When you stood accused of lies in the killing of Billy Buckler, there was but one voice raised in your defence.'

Faulkner's anger melted as quickly as it had come, and he sagged to the wall, a defeated man weighed down by everything.

'I did kill him,' he insisted in a breath, 'I did.'

Madigan stepped to offer a steadying hand.

'I believed you then and I want to believe you now,' he assured his old teacher. 'Tell me.'

'I have seen them, James, the foul pirates of the Ghostmaker. and more besides.' He blinked against doubtful memories. 'I've seen shadows on rooftops.'

'What?'

'They have come for Billy Buckler! I have seen them, followed them, spied on them. I was here last night, watching as they attacked!' He lunged for Madigan and grasped his arms. 'What did they steal? Not gold or diamonds, I'll wager my faith on that. All the treasure in the Bank of England is nothing compared to the pirates' reward when Billy comes back. What did they steal?'

Madigan's eyes flared in alarm at his friend's words.

'When Billy...comes back?'

'I watched Billy Buckler die twice. The first time on the sea as close as you stand to me now, with a shot from this very pistol. And I ran my sword clean through him for good measure. I felt his last raging breath on my face, James! And yet I watched him hanged three days ago at Tyburn. Oh, I sound mad, but I'm not, I'm not. What did they steal?'

Madigan gave his own hollow voice to Faulkner's madness.

'They took the bones of Billy Buckler.'

Faulkner pulled from the horror of it and found the wall with his back. His tear-stained face twisted in struggling to comprehend all that whirled before and behind his eyes at once, causing him to claw his aching head until, somehow, he found a measure of order in his maddening thoughts.

'When I was a child,' he said in a cold whisper, 'my nursery maid would share candlelit tales with my brother and me. Spook stories at bedtime, of witches and fell sorcery, and she always insisted her stories were true, and of a time when the old people feared a powerful witch with magic enough to call the dead from their graves. What if such a power exists in the world, James? What if the men of the Ghostmaker have found it?'

Madigan shrugged off a tingle of fear along his spine and focussed more on mortal threats.

'You have followed the pirates? Do you know where they have taken Billy's bones?'

Faulkner shook his head.

'Not for certain. They moved their hideout and have grown more cautious. But I know of a man who might be persuaded to steer our search. His name is Robinson.' Before he could offer more, Faulkner stiffened and looked past his friend. 'We are watched.'

Following the man's gaze, Madigan spied Lieutenant Godfrey some way off. The officer snapped to attention as the captain fixed him.

'The king is ready to depart, sir,' he reported and cast a suspicious glance towards Madigan's straggly-haired companion.

'Duty calls,' Faulkner said. 'Can you meet me tonight? Do you know of the Gravediggers tavern, in Deptford?

'I will find it,' Madigan agreed. 'I'll meet you there.'

'We can seek answers together,' Faulkner said, encouraged by his friend's promise and the handshake he offered.

He looked after the young captain's departure and found a measure of comfort in having at least one ally in a hostile world. With a last sip, he took again to seeking about for buccaneers, and finally shifted upwards to peer nervously at the rooftops of London.

32

In the prison of her curtained room where night and day were the same, and a solitary candle offered the barest illumination, the changing of hours for Lara was marked by a pirate's arrival with her evening meal.

Pausing her work with roots and bones, she watched the man deliver her bowl of slopping broth, and was secretly amused by his hasty departure from the 'magic room' with its array of mysterious bottles and hanging curiosities.

For the longest time she fixed on the fluttering door and ignored her bland dinner. She held quite still for she had already sensed the arrival of another visitor. But she knew well this guest did not enter by the way of mortal men, and so she waited until the candle flickered slightly in announcing him before offering a greeting to the thickening gloom.

'I know you're there, Baron,' she said without looking but with a smile.

The creature of the night came on, seeping from

black concealment. His fearsome appearance softened with a smile to crease the whitened mask he wore.

'Ever watchful, magic-schooled, never flustered, never fooled,' he praised her.

Lara giggled at her friend's silly ditty.

'I heard your cloak sliding on a shadow,' she told him.

'I must practise more,' he admitted and offered a bow.

'Do you have news for me? The pirates are uneasy. They have been whispering all day.'

'One of the wicked crew is dead,' Samedi explained, and not without a satisfied sneer. It faded as he caught Lara's glance of suspicion. 'Not by my hand, I swear it. When I kill one, I will kill all, but only when we are free. I know well the rule we survive by.'

'Don't let them hear you,' Lara cautioned urgently. 'What happened to the man?'

'A very long drop to a sharp crashing stop,' the spirit described. 'In the dark of night he tumbled from the roof to his doom.'

Lara eyed her friend closely, spying more than he said with words alone.

'Benjamin Blake,' she half-guessed.

'I do believe it was him.'

Sitting motionless as she did when pondering

deeply, Lara weighed up the Baron's report and what it could mean. Just what was Benjamin Blake playing at?

'Do you think he can help us?' she asked then.

Samedi, whose cape was never without motion, drifted closer.

'He has great magic and years of skill,' the spirit mused, 'and more that that, he has determination. But what are they against the ocean from here to your mother?'

'Maybe he has found a way,' Lara dared guess.

'Maybe you hope for too much,' the Baron cautioned. But he saw in an instant how his words stung the little girl and he lunged to provide comfort, surrounding her with his cloak to keep all hurt at bay, though the best he could offer for now was a strand to wipe a tear glistening on her cheek.

'There is nothing left for us but hope,' she reminded him. 'We have no home, no freedom. No mother.'

'Then let us cling to hope,' he said reassuringly, 'and hope for everything.'

She embraced her faithful friend, barely able to join her arms around his giant neck as she whispered to his ear.

'Find Benjamin Blake.'

33

What's your plan, Benjamin Blake?

That whispering, infuriating, inner voice followed him as he crept over the tiles towards the Gravediggers tavern. Even now, as he stalked his target, it would not be ignored.

Well?

'I don't know yet,' he responded aloud despite his stealth, irritated at the nagging and the sly prompting for an answer he still lacked.

He had spent the sunlit hours in a restless state, turning over again and again in his mind the information gleaned from the pirate Tavish, setting out the parts and exploring the numerous possibilities they offered for action.

Robinson, twin lights, the Lafitte.

Together, somehow, these new elements of knowledge offered hope for a working scheme to outwit the men of the Ghostmaker. And yet, each plan that grew in his imagination from these starting points, each one seemingly brilliant at first, quickly fell apart when tested by matters uncertain and beyond his control.

Twin lights. The signal high in the mast of the Lafitte could bring the Ghostmaker to him. But how would he light those lights? Could he trick the Lafitte into carrying them? And even if he could, where would he intercept the Ghostmaker and snatch Lara's mother from her captors? He did not know the ship's landing point. How could he achieve any of it, and in time to prevent Billy Buckler's return from the grave?

What he could not do with sorcery he could with two lights if only he could find a way.

Well, then, what does that leave?

Robinson, he was the way.

Perhaps.

'Perhaps,' Benjamin was forced to agree as he paused and examined quiet streets converging on the Gravediggers, where the building now stood with a smokeless chimney and shuttered windows. That single word, perhaps, uttered by the pirate on the warehouse roof, promised all and nothing at the same time. Perhaps Mr Robinson possessed enough information to help Benjamin tear down the buccaneers' plot, but perhaps not. Perhaps the tavern keeper could be terrified by a night spirit into telling all just like Tavish, but perhaps he was made of sterner stuff and the ploy would fail. 'Perhaps, perhaps, perhaps,' Benjamin grumbled.

He slipped through inky cover and drew closer to the tavern.

Amid all doubts, two certainties came to offer small comfort as he gained the building's roof. Skipping effortlessly across sloping tiles, he looked across streets winding to their end at the Thames and saw the river's tide had not yet begun to ebb. Good. That in turn meant the Lafitte had not yet sailed this night and might be found even if Robinson proved stubborn.

But in the span of hours left tonight, the dying moon of the Baron's warning would rise, and Lara's work would begin.

The clock was an enemy to add to the rest.

Gliding into the tavern's musty roof space, Benjamin stole across beams to the attic hatch, holding there to probe with senses attuned to the building beneath. Aside from a lone rodent scratching in the walls, all was quiet as the grave. He descended.

He searched quickly, roving through rooms on the upper landing, but found no telling documents or maps, no clues in empty cupboards and beds, and no trace of Robinson. Flitting from shadow to shadow, he gained the stairs and paused again, this time to take in the view his position afforded of the space below. He beheld tables and chairs set out before the bar. Weak, flickering light played over all from the coals of a fire hissing its last in the grate.

Something's not right.

The warning that rose to hold him to his place was no stronger than those softly-glowing embers, but Benjamin knew well to trust it. Unmoving in inky depths, he scanned hard for its origin. What was it he felt? Was he about to catch a hint of cloak swishing in a corner, or the ghostly shine of a white-painted face pushing through the dark? But even in the moment of seeking a solid cause for his vigilance, Benjamin realised he would not find it.

It was not there to be found.

A memory bloomed from the lingering feeling, and he pictured again Lord Remington lying dead on his carpet. The unwanted image of the judge brought with it a chill certainty. Something was missing down there in the dark, and in its place lay a gaping hole in the fabric of the mortal realm. Benjamin sensed it all as he eased towards the bottom step, only to halt sharply once more.

Across the gloomy room, a man was waiting.

He was a night-draped silhouette seated at a table farthest from the stairs. Oblivious to a vampire's presence, the man's unseen face remained firmly set towards the tavern door. His hand upon the table rested next to a long extinguished candle.

Benjamin kept close to the shadows in circling the

motionless form. His path to surprise the man from behind lay along the bar and the wall running to the fireplace. But the nearer he drew, the more aware he became of a familiar creeping sense, one of absence, of something missing from the seated form, and with it came the realisation there was no longer a need for concealing gloom.

'Lumen,' Benjamin commanded with a click of fingers.

The candlewick obeyed and crackled to life. Its flare revealed Mr Robinson's staring face, pale and frozen in death. The tavern keeper's eyes fixed sightlessly on Benjamin's, bulging with a final terrified longing for his bottled spirit.

Benjamin drew back from the unspeakable scene, made unsettled and angry by it. The Baron had struck again, one step ahead, and now mocked him with this gruesome show in posing the dead man for him to find.

Why would he do that?

If not him, it had been the pirates, Benjamin reasoned silently. The heartless buccaneers had propped Robinson in his seat to greet a vampire's arrival. They were probably still laughing somewhere at their sick jest.

But why would they do it?

Benjamin hesitated in his place, caught by a

new alarm that edged his whispering thoughts. He realised at once there was no joke here. He turned sharply, and about again for the trap that must surely be waiting. And at the third time of turning, by the candle's dancing flame, his silvery eyes fell on the pirates' scheme.

It was betrayed by a mere thread, one so fine only supernatural sight could hope to glimpse the reflected light on its tiny fibres. It stretched among table legs between Robinson and the tavern door, and ran taut to the room's dimmest corner where, as Benjamin crouched to better see, it curled to the trigger of a readied pistol wedged among three small barrels. He did not need the faint whiff of charcoal and sulphur to recognise they contained gunpowder.

'Stupid pirates,' he allowed himself, and was just beginning to smile when the door lock clicked.

The candle was snuffed by magic before the latch reached its highest, and Benjamin had concealed himself fully even before the door began its slow opening. From his hiding place he watched the first wary intrusion of another cocked pistol, and flexed his fingers, ready for ambushing pirates.

'Well?' a soft whisper demanded.

'I felt sure there was a light,' Madigan replied as softly. 'I must have been mistaken.'

'Steady, James,' Faulkner advised as the door

swung fully to reveal both men. The pair thrust readied weapons into the tavern's interior and towards the figure waiting in his chair.

'Place your hands where I can see them,' Madigan ordered the man. When the figure made no move to comply, Madigan took a bold step forward with his weapon. 'Do it!' But the step was sufficient to reveal staring dead features, and he gasped.

At his shoulder, Faulkner released a grim breath.

'Dead a while,' he judged.

'I did see a light,' Madigan said with a gesture. 'Look how the candle still smokes.'

The men grew instantly alert and swept their guns to every corner of the room in search of hidden enemies.

'Show yourself!' Faulkner commanded in a voice of rising disquiet. 'Show yourself, Billy!'

Madigan glanced to his friend with concern for his growing agitation.

'What are you saying?'

'It must be him, James!' Faulkner exclaimed. 'He's here! He's come back already!'

Overcome, the ragged sea captain lunged forward, the pistol he held just for Billy Buckler seeking its mark.

A step behind, Madigan cast a restraining hand to Faulkner, aiming to pull him back from the trap that might yet be waiting. But even as he found the captain's shoulder, he felt Faulkner stop, and so sharply he nearly collided with the man. He felt the jerk of alarm that passed through Faulkner's frame and saw him look down, down to where his leg made contact with a nearly invisible thread that drew a harsh snap of metal from a distant corner.

Madigan understood and whispered a soft prayer for his end.

Then, astonishingly, in a blinking, there was a boy, young and pale and with black hair and...and silver eyes! In the instant of snapping metal, Madigan saw him burst up from the shadows, and watched his bizarre action in offering a violent punch to the space between them. 'Sterno!' the boy cried, and next Madigan was flying through the room, thrown back to roll uncontrollably over the tavern floor. On his way he collided with Faulkner as he too was carried on a wind of power that rose from nowhere to sweep them from the tavern and into the street.

Landing heavily on his back, Madigan heaved for the air driven from him by the blow. Across Faulkner's groaning form he looked towards the Gravediggers and saw the boy for an instant again where he was framed in the doorway. And even as he met those impossibly silver eyes, the frame dissolved to a bursting wave of fire within the tavern. It spilled over the boy, obscuring him as it spread through the building. A moment later, though it felt an age to the stunned officer, the gunpowder's eruption tore the structure to its parts of wood and stone and shook the ground beneath Madigan's back. His vision was blocked by Faulkner as the man scrambled to throw himself protectively across him, and together they huddled until the rain of fire passed by.

When next Madigan looked, the boy was gone, lost to the storm of flame and wreckage.

34

'What on earth was that?'

To an avalanche of papers from her lap to the playroom floor, Princess Charlotte jumped from reading and ran to the window. No less startled, her siblings followed and joined her in tugging urgently at the curtains.

'The lights are shaking!' Elizabeth exclaimed with a gesture to a chandelier's violent clinking.

'It shook the entire building!' Edward declared excitedly. He looked to the decorated walls for signs of cracks or crumbling.

The royal children peered eagerly into the night, spotting together the fiery glow far to the east of Buckingham House, and billowing smoke rolling to the night sky.

'Is it cannons?' Charlotte asked.

'Is it a dragon?' Elizabeth asked breathlessly. 'What is it, George?'

'Perhaps navy ships are firing a salute on the river,' her eldest brother said, trying his best to sound reassuring. The children smiled at the explanation, though Charlotte shot him a doubtful look.

'It must be someone very important for a salute that big,' Edward mused as he stepped from the window.

'Maybe it's the King of America!' Elizabeth gushed. 'With presents!'

'Father is the King of America,' Charlotte sighed with a smile for the little girl's mistake. With nothing more to see from the window, she returned to her armchair by the fire and began retrieving the fallen papers, the city news sheets she had ordered brought to her immediately on her return from the Bank of England. She had spent most of the evening scouring weird and dramatic events that none but she had linked together to a worrying array of thoughts.

So far as she could tell from her studies, the first in the sequence of occurrences was the story of Lord Remington, the judge murdered in his home the very day he passed sentence on Billy Buckler. Despite blame for the crime being laid upon pirates loyal to their dead leader, witnesses attested that the unfortunate judge had not a mark of revenge upon his body when discovered. Rather, they said, he bore the look of a man who had died in the grip of some overwhelming terror.

Demands for justice for the crime gave way to

expressions of regret in later reports of the sudden and tragic death, just one night later, of the much respected physician, Dr Ebenezer Wheatley. In the course of an accidental fire at his surgery, the reports stated with conviction, the unfortunate Dr Wheatley had climbed to the roof of St Bartholomew's in seeking his escape from the flames, only to die there, his heart apparently weakened by the effort. A smaller piece to the rear of one news sheet, meanwhile, attacked a scandalous rumour seeking to link two recently deceased bodysnatchers with the good doctor. The criminals, who were found dead in a grave they had desecrated in the course of their abominable work had, the writer insisted, no relationship whatsoever to the eminent Dr Wheatley, and the very suggestion was a slur on his name. The article concluded the graveyard deaths remained unexplained, though richly deserved.

Outrage was the emotion conveyed when next the papers turned attention to the storming of the Bank of England and the killing of its chief official, the highly regarded Mr Percival Fox. Though described as murder, investigators for the king admitted they remained at a loss to describe the manner of the man's death, as the victim appeared untouched when found. Despite this, the papers joined in a single and disapproving voice to blame revolutionaries and assorted troublemakers in seeking to undermine the nation by assaulting its financial heart.

Charlotte laid the news sheets aside and pinched nervously at her lip as she considered matters.

'Someone is straining her brain,' Prince George cut in, recognising well his sister's habit when concentrating. 'Come, share, I am bored.'

'It's nothing,' she tried, even as he reached to snatch at the news sheets.

'Nothing, eh?' George scoffed before making a grand show of examining her chosen pages. 'Scandalous,' he concluded finally and with a sniff, 'not a single mention of me anywhere.' He chuckled at Charlotte's weary sigh for his vanity. 'All right. Why such grim reading? Is it because you met in secret with Mr Fox on the very night of his death? Oh, yes, I know about that. But does Papa know?' He watched the princess shrug awkwardly both for the question and her own thoughts. 'Or,' he continued darkly, 'is it because each of the three dead men had crossed paths with Billy Buckler and his bones immediately before their ends?'

'Dr Wheatley apparently did not,' she argued, though she suspected a truth the papers denied.

'Come, come,' George scoffed. 'The old rogue was in league with those ruffians who snatched the pirate's remains.'

'You can't know that for certain,' she said.

'Oh, but I can, dear sister.' George winked impishly. 'You read, but I listen.' He leaned closer to whisper. 'I spied on Papa's meeting with his ministers this morning. Dreadfully boring stuff, except for the stories of murder and pirates. Do you know that Mr Fox was found bolt upright in his favourite armchair, wide-eyed and frightened to death by some terrible vision that slipped between the curtains of his room?'

'Don't,' Charlotte protested.

George settled back with a satisfied smile both for his knowledge and the girl's discomfort.

'I'm not just a pretty face,' he pointed out. 'But it looks to me you are on the same track with your papers, clever Charlotte.'

'What in the world does it all mean?' she asked.

George puffed a breath and shrugged as he considered the question.

'Perhaps,' he speculated aloud, 'the crew of the Ghostmaker is keeping to some promise they made their captain, one to carry out his revenge or some such.'

'They attacked the Bank of England and took nothing but his bones,' Charlotte argued. 'What sort of pirates ignore gold and jewels for a pile of bones?'

'That is a puzzling matter,' her brother conceded.

The siblings abruptly became aware of watching eyes and turned to find Elizabeth staring fixedly at them both. The little girl had abandoned her dolls' tea party to step closer with the air of one considering the deepest of questions.

'What is it, young Princess?' George inquired with a smile.

'If it was a dragon on the river just now,' the girl said earnestly, 'will you protect us, like Saint George who you are named for?'

'But of course,' the prince insisted, playing along. 'I would never allow harm to befall my family, even from a fire-breathing dragon.'

Satisfied, Elizabeth faced her sister.

'And you, Charlotte, will you use your fencing skills to protect us too?'

'What's this?' George asked. He sat up sharply with an eager smile.

'Elizabeth,' Charlotte said firmly. Her utterance was a growled warning against further tales.

'Charlotte practises in secret,' Elizabeth said, undaunted, 'with Captain Madigan.' She screwed up her face and made kissy sounds until seized by a fit of giggles.

'Elizabeth!'

'By Jove, the scandal!' George guffawed.

The little girl dodged a swatting of news sheets

and quickly offered Charlotte a toy she carried as a peace offering.

'You might need this for dragons,' she said and turned the handle of a wooden sword towards her sister.

As Charlotte's mood softened again, she smiled for the child's gift and accepted it. She swept it back and forth a number of times in the air as she studiously considered its strength and value.

'A fine weapon,' she acknowledged.

Elizabeth sighed and rolled her eyes.

'It's just a toy, Charlotte,' she reported wearily, 'but it will keep you brave.'

With that, the child returned to play, making kissy sounds on the way, and George and Charlotte grinned after her. But while her brother's smile remained, Charlotte's slipped as she looked to each of her brothers and sister in turn, and spied again the fiery glow through the window to the east.

The princess tugged her lip to a troubling vision of pirates.

35

Benjamin lay in darkness and dust.

His cell was a misshapen space formed in chaos beneath collapsed bricks and roof beams, though it was not these solid materials holding him in place. They were nothing more to a vampire than the simplest maze of cracks and gaps leading to the outside world. No, instead he was made a prisoner by hundreds of eager Londoners standing just yards away.

On all sides of the smouldering remains of the Gravediggers they stood, loudly jabbering and gossiping, busily finger-pointing and gasping. They had arrived within moments of the explosion to marvel at the burning devastation, before Benjamin had gathered himself sufficiently to slip away. He had clambered up from the cellar, where the blast had flung him, only to discover through every stony fissure an impenetrable human barrier already formed. The throngs blocked every street and crammed windows overhead.

So, he waited in darkness and dust, listening to mortal excitement.

'Here,' a cry went up, 'a body!' And when Benjamin peeked, he witnessed a nearby group of men hauling at timbers to reach for the last of keeper Robinson. The man's flopping corpse prompted cries from the crowd before it was covered hastily by a sheet and carted off.

'Here!' Another cry was raised, and heads turned expectantly. But this time the find was met with jubilant cheers and laughter. An undamaged barrel of ale had been salvaged and drawn up to be rolled away by its rescuers.

Benjamin sighed and reclined against blackened bricks. Laughing mortals would get bored after a time, he knew. The smouldering wreck of the Gravediggers would hold them only so long and would eventually cease to entertain as a spectacle. Laughter would give way to yawning, and the witnesses would melt away to return to homes and waiting beds. Then he would be free to gain the rooftops unnoticed. But until then, all he could do was mark time.

'There was a boy!'

The loud voice drew him, and he hunted the cracks for the speaker. Beyond shifting smoke, at a place between the encircling crowd and rescuers, he spotted him. Benjamin instantly recognised the better dressed of the two men he had flung to safety from the gunpowder's fire.

'Search the other side,' the man urged of those scouring the wreckage. Clearly a military officer, the man had taken command of the scene. His companion, by contrast, stood in a uniform that was already tattered before the blast. He rubbed his head gingerly between quick sips from a flask he worked to hide from his companion. Benjamin examined closely this strange pair who had come by night with pistols drawn.

Who are you?

'You saw him, didn't you?' the officer asked the ragged man. 'The boy.'

'It was dark, James,' the man offered with a shrug. He waited until his friend's attention returned to the search before sipping again.

Benjamin's view was abruptly blocked as men picking their way over the ruin came close, too close, to his hiding place and began casting aside a first layer of rubble.

'Maybe here,' a voice suggested, just feet away.

Benjamin pulled back from the sound of many clawing hands as his own worked rapid patterns in the dark.

'Conturbo.'

Deep within itself, the ruin offered a groan for

vampire magic. Wood shifted violently against stone and threw up the mournful noise, like a giant disturbed from its slumber underground. Its rising sent spurts of dust from breaches across the fall and drove alarmed spectators to retreat.

'Get out of there!' a voice roared above a din of imminent collapse, and Benjamin grinned as he listened to the diggers' hasty escape.

He peered through new spy holes, again in search of the officer named James. Unlike the rest, the man had not drawn away from the disturbance Benjamin offered. Steadfast in his place, he dusted himself off as an apologetic civilian explained the dangers of continuing the search.

'Very well,' the one named James reluctantly agreed. 'Disperse this mob and set a watchman. I want that boy found when the sun rises.'

Benjamin chuckled at that.

And so another exciting episode for the London crowd slowly wound down. To ushering hands and appeals for everyone to move along, the hordes melted away, leaving the two military men to whisper between themselves as they waited for their horses to be brought up.

What do you know?

Benjamin added this to his list of questions as he watched the pair converse, noting how the ragged man more than once cast his nervous glance to the rooftops. There was only one way to find out about these men's part in things, he concluded. And, with the pirates' trail beyond Robinson lying as ruined as the Gravediggers, fresh clues were needed. Perhaps these mismatched officers could supply.

The captains took to their saddles and spurred west. Not sparing a backwards glance for the night's devastation, they missed the boyish figure who rose quickly through smoke to follow.

As he climbed aloft and tracked the galloping pair, Benjamin's gaze was caught by that which had been hidden from him in his place underground, but now rose higher than all.

Warming to vampire skin, but chilling to his sight, the dying moon had come.

36

'It's time.'

Mr Pyke pushed from the window and the curving moon it framed against a darkening sky. Gathered about in watchful silence, the crew of the Ghostmaker stood shoulder to shoulder in a brooding rank.

'Make ready,' he instructed them and moved purposefully towards the canvas room. Sweeping past the material, he found Lara at final preparations for the spell. Her work was overseen by two extremely nervous looking pirates who huddled together at the farthest point the tiny room would allow. The bones of Billy Bucker shone white amid surrounding candles. The captain's heart bulged within its jar at the centre of the display and glistened wetly. A trick of flickering light made it seem the organ was pulsing with life already, and Pyke shivered at the image.

For her part, Lara moved slowly, carrying with her a small bowl containing some dark, oozing liquid. Halting at the head of the table, she raised an object from the bowl, and the pirate guards looked on in wide wonder at a dripping chicken's claw she held. This she flicked sharply, once, twice over the bones, splashing damp flecks everywhere. The girl whispered her magic words as liquid ran over dead fingers and teeth. She moved on to repeat the process from each side of the table, only looking to Pyke after she had completed an entire circuit.

'The men must leave,' she said, pointing to the guards who seemed most eager for their leader to agree.

Pyke considered the girl's words, hesitating to play into a trick at this late stage.

'Out,' he snapped at last and the men fled.

Lara turned her head to the ceiling, staring hard there a moment.

'The moon will be at its highest very soon,' she said.

'And then the captain returns,' Pyke added, his words sounding more like an instruction than a hope.

'I sense his spirit moving already in the outer darkness,' Lara assured him, her eyes still peering far off. 'The men must begin the drumming to guide their leader home.'

'I'll tell them,' the pirate said.

Retreating from the room, he found the men standing ready.

Knowing well the ritual, they had arranged themselves to a wide semi-circle at the curtained doorway. At the heart of the enclosure, Captain Buckler's effects had been gathered as required. Thrust into the floor was his long cutlass, its steel blade catching the rays of the moon through the open window on the high walkway. Hanging from the weapon's hilt, leather holsters bore pistols and daggers. And topping off the fearsome display was the captain's battered hat, crimson feathered, black all over and trimmed with blood-red stitching.

Mr Pyke examined the scene, nodding approval for the preparations as he looked across the faces of the crew, meeting each hard stare he found. A movement above betrayed the spectral presence of the Baron, perched in the rafters though barely glimpsed in the lamplight. The spirit's cloak floated like a cloud over the proceedings. With a contemptuous glance to the slave, Pyke signalled for Mr Davy to begin.

'Strike up!' Davy ordered.

From among the ranked men, three pirates emerged carrying large drums. As one they obeyed the command and rapped on their instruments to commence a slow, rhythmic beat. All besides turned in breathless expectation to the curtained doorway.

Within, Lara listened to the drumming as she set down her bowl and stepped to a tray draped in darkest cloth. Plucking aside the covering, she revealed a stout earthen jar surrounded by the Baron's five corked bottles, their misty contents glowing with green fire. The girl reached to set a bottle on either side of the skull and one at the chin before moving to place another by each hand. Lastly she carried the jar to the end of the table and carefully placed it between the skeleton's foot and wooden stump. Removing the lid, she stepped back and breathed.

'We are in the house of souls,' she intoned, speaking as though to the jar itself, 'the candles are lit for the dead and for the god of serpents. Damballah! You are needed. Hear me and come!'

For a time a soft stillness hung in the room. The head of Billy Buckler continued to stare lifelessly at the young sorceress across the opened jar, its smile seeming to mock her magical abilities as the drumbeats continued. The candles shifted for a moment in unison, and shadows danced in hazy response to the rhythm as the first sign of movement came from the earthen container. At its brim, the speckled head of a snake rose with lazy progress, its tongue flicking to test the air. Finding no threat, the creature drew its long oily body to slither down the jar's side until it coiled at the bones of Billy Buckler. After a moment's rest the serpent pressed forward, undulating across root bags and bottles and between whitened ribs towards the pirate's head. Here the creature paused briefly again, appearing to examine the wicked white face it found before sliding on, silently coursing over teeth and bone, and up to slip inside the skull through one hollow eye socket.

The drums outside beat faster and faster.

'Damballah,' Lara continued in her voice small but fierce, 'Damballah, I call on you in your place on the magic island. There is one who must come back, a *gros-bon-ange* to be released. Give back what must not be given, let fly what must surely die!'

The candles surged at her words, and flames that had burned yellow abruptly sparked to uncanny blue, flooding the room with phantom light where the feverish shadows whirled and rampaged like dancers possessed by the pounding music of the drums.

On the table, the skull of Billy Buckler moved. Lara gazed on, watching as the pirate's dead smile seemed to grow before her eyes. But here was no trick of the changing light. The jaws were moving, easing apart where the serpent pressed from within to create enough room to slip free. It exited its confinement to a click of teeth. The creature travelled hypnotically, slithering to the vessel holding Billy's heart, there to entwine it and peer with lidless eyes as it flicked its tongue at the vile contents behind the glass.

The girl moved with urgent speed now, circling the

table to pull corks from green-shining bottles, one after the other. Retaking her position amid the blazing hue, she watched as the ghostly contents drifted into the air, a supernatural mist that crept over the bones and held to them. Green smoke seeped into Billy's nose as though drawn by some interior draught. Eye sockets flared emerald bright, and the skull became a ghost-fire lantern.

Lara reached out to snatch up the earthen jar, holding it high to continue her spell as the drums drove to a fevered pounding.

'I serve with both hands,' she called above the din. 'Damballah, see what I do!' Bringing her arms down, the girl dashed the container against the edge of the table, breaking it into a thousand pieces to the serpent's menacing hiss.

High in the warehouse rafters, Baron Samedi gasped and covered his ears against words that should not be spoken.

Lara cast dusty hands to the shadows that continued to jerk and twist above the ceremony.

'Damballah!' she cried again to the darkness. 'The jar of the dead is broken! Remove the barrier! Give me what I demand! Give me the spirit of Billy Buckler!'

All light was lost. Candles extinguished in a blinking as the drumbeats ceased, and the shadows collapsed exhausted across the room.

Reaching sightlessly about in the heavy silence, Lara found the candle and flint she had stored up for this moment. Sparks cracked until she finally caught the wick and lifted her light high over the table. Across the magic surface, only the snake remained, coiled about the glass container which had shattered in the dark. The creature offered another hiss for Lara's weak flame. Confused by the abandoned table, the girl scanned next the surrounding blackness, pressing it back with her light. Drawn at last by a sound behind, a shuffling movement caused by some dragging form across the floor, she turned to illuminate the place and saw with disbelieving eyes what crouched there.

Lara began to scream.

37

Startled by the shrill cries from the canvas room, the pirates grabbed for weapons.

The men held fast under Mr Pyke's steadying hand but looked nervously to each other, seeking out the one who might prove bold enough to venture forward, someone reckless enough to investigate matters in the room where silence had descended so suddenly again. In the absence of a hardy soul among them, all looked to Mr Pyke where he stood with a hand pressed tightly to his own sword.

Feeling all eyes burning into him, Pyke drew up tall and stepped reluctantly from the assembly. As he did he brought his weapon gleaming into the light and held it firmly. With a deep breath to brace his nerves, he proceeded towards the room.

He was still a few steps short of the doorway when he was driven back as the barrier swept violently aside to free Lara. The girl cried out, dropped the candle in her escape and stumbled towards the pirates. In her frightened haste she tripped, fell, and went crashing down to crawl on until she found her feet again and ran through the circle, her terrified eyes cast back to the magic room. From above, the Baron hurtled down at her appearance, hands clawed and cape flaring in readiness to protect his little mistress.

Baffled and unsettled by the girl's actions, the pirates sought explanation from her, but wide-eyed Lara offered only voiceless breath and a deathly stare for the curtained doorway. The men turned instead to one another and then, amid the confounded quiet, towards fresh noises rising within the room.

Articles crashed about beyond the doorway, and the whole of the canvas structure shook violently. Materials shattered and ripped, and through the clamour of destruction another sound rose. It was at first a low guttural moan of anguish but grew steadily until it was the sustained howl of a tormented beast. And the next, the curtained door itself was attacked, gashed apart by furious hands, and the thing Billy Buckler had become came roaring into the light.

The pirates cried out a chorus of horror and fell back from the monstrous half-formed creature. As one they levelled weapons against it where it advanced on table-leg and bone, a nightmare man-skeleton come to life.

Atop the creature's limping frame, the captain's skull turned this way and that in examining his crew through a single restored and swivelling eye. His once thick mane of hair hung in wispy grey strands, insufficient to disguise missing ears and nose or to hide exposed sinews working the near skinless jaw beneath a straggly beard. Across the body, exposed muscles and tendons flexed, barely clinging to supporting bones. One hand, fully renewed, stood in contrast to the other, a shrivelled claw of clicking white digits. And at the centre of the monstrous figure, slick and veined, the captain's wet heart beat visibly in his chest.

A stunned silence fell upon the gathering, broken only by a grinding rasp sent from Buckler's neck bones as his head continued to turn back and forth. Finally, the captain looked upon himself and considered the chaos of his torso, his mismatched hands, his remaining leg, and he struggled with his dried-up brain to make sense of it all. He faced the crew again to a sickening crunch of spine and snarled through twisted, bloodless lips.

'Where's my leg?'

The words grated like dust to further disturb the men of the Ghostmaker, and all took another half-step back in fright. Pyke alone remained unmoving.

'Captain, sir,' he ventured finally, trying to control the tremble in his voice even as Buckler turned that gruesome face to regard him with a rolling glare.

'Report,' Buckler instructed harshly.

'We met with difficulties regaining you this time, Captain,' Pyke explained, 'but you're here at last.'

With a furious roar, Buckler snatched a pistol from Pyke's belt and thrust it to the man's chest.

'Are you bewildered and blind, man?' the captain roared. 'There's but half of me here!' He cocked the weapon with a click of his skeletal thumb. 'Where's the rest?'

'Captain,' Pyke protested weakly, 'it wasn't like other times. We had opposition, a spirit of some kind working against us.'

But Billy Buckler had stopped listening.

'Where's the girl?' he demanded, turning about until he stared on Lara and the Baron. Uneven strides carried him towards the pair and he aimed his weapon at the young sorceress. 'Tell me how you plan to fix this.'

'I cannot,' Lara said. 'Part of you was missing in death and so part of you is missing in…life.'

Billy's cry and shot came together, thundering towards the roof in pursuit of the pistol ball he loosed to shatter a high beam.

'Don't tell me that!' he howled at the girl. 'There has to be a way! Find a way! Or must I send a signal to the..,' And here he hesitated, just for one awkward and curious moment of eye-rolling bafflement. 'To the…to my ship?'

Pyke alone frowned at the uncertain trip in his captain's words even as the Baron surged forward in response to them.

'You cannot!' the spirit protested. 'The girl has played her part in your dreadful game, you cannot blame her!'

Billy Buckler swept up his arm to deliver a powerful backhanded strike to the Baron's face. It caught the spirit by surprise and sent him hurtling backwards to crash heavily against a wall.

'You have no power over me, slave,' the pirate taunted. He eyed the Baron rising to bloom with a terrible vengeance behind his painted mask.

A pistol click ended Samedi's attack before it could begin, and Mr Pyke sneered as he pressed his weapon to Lara's head.

'Remember who is in charge here, Baron,' was the pirate's stern warning.

'If you kill the girl, you have nothing,' Samedi said quickly.

'And if you move to kill any of us,' Pyke reminded, 'Lara dies, and afterwards her mother. And then what have you got in this living world?' The pirate was quietly pleased at the defeat he caught in Samedi's face. 'We have left nothing to chance, Baron, don't forget that.'

'I do not forget,' the phantom warned all and then

he scowled on Billy Buckler's hateful features, 'and I do not forgive.'

Unimpressed by threats, Billy offered a dismissive grunt for the Baron as he limped to the centre of his encircling crew. Gazing fiercely upon each of the astounded men, he made a show of retrieving his effects and fixing weapons about his wizened body. Seizing last his hat with both hands, he swept it high and lowered it to the ghastly head to cover a brain throbbing visibly through gaps in his skull. The action was that of one crowning himself king, and when next he spoke, his words were a crazed declaration to the world.

'Brace yourself, boys. Out of Hell, and up from the black, shiver me timbers, ol' Billy is back.'

His demented laughter rattled to the rafters.

38

Pyke felt the worried stares of pirate eyes.

Across the hours since the captain's hellish reappearance it had been so. In different parts of the warehouse, concerned groups had formed by warming fires to mutter secretively on the most strange turn of events. Through the flames, pirates cast searching glances towards the first mate where he sat alone, poking at the floor with his sword in trying to find sense in magic gone so badly wrong.

Billy had long since retreated to the canvas room. Limping and laughing hysterically he had gone back into its darkness where he could be heard crashing about in mad merriment for a time afterwards. All had since become quiet again, and the men fretted all the more because of it.

Pyke worried too, though he did not betray his grim thoughts to the crew. When his captain had been a monster in human form, the men of the Ghostmaker had followed him eagerly. Now he was a monster in every sense, and all the glittering treasures and chests of gold could not divert the minds of the pirates from what they had seen. But Pyke worried about what he had heard over what all eyes had beheld. The memory of it played over and over for him, that single moment during Billy's threats to Lara, that moment when the pirate had paused…apparently unable to name his own ship. It was as though, like his incomplete body, the captain's brain…

'Mr Pyke.'

Pyke started, so deeply engaged in thought he had not sensed Mr Davy's arrival at his side.

'What is it?' he asked.

'The men are starting to wonder about our next move,' Davy whispered, 'wondering, like, if orders will follow. If the captain is forgetting that we're ashore too long.'

Forgetting. The very word made Pyke flinch.

'I'll see the captain,' he assured his colleague. 'You just keep the men in line, you hear?'

'As you say, Mr Pyke,' Davy replied.

Pyke rose, his action drawing the close attention of the buccaneers. Raising his sword to re-sheath it, he caught a glimpse of his reflection in the blade's polished metal and shuddered at the thought of the face he was about to peer into. With a moment's pause to brace himself, he walked to the curtained door and rapped knuckles on the frame.

'Come.' The voice of command was a crackling growl and it made the pirate want to *go* instead.

Pyke stepped past the tattered remnants of hanging curtain and allowed his eyes time to adjust to an interior lit by two weak candles. Even then it took some effort to pick out the hulking form of Billy where he sat with his back to the door, but with his one eye on Pyke nonetheless. With the aid of a small mirror, the captain stared coldly at his first mate as monstrous hands worked feverishly with material and scissors.

'How are you, Captain?' Pyke asked, immediately regretting his words.

'Oh,' Billy sighed as he snipped, 'the parts of me here are just dandy. The rest I can't speak for.' His bitter chuckle gurgled like mud in a drain. 'You want to know something funny, though? I ain't got no ears, but I can still hear the men...whispering.'

'It was a shock for them to see you like this,' Pyke offered.

'They've seen worse,' Billy snapped. Facing the mirror, he examined his gruesome features. 'Actually,' he reconsidered, 'perhaps they haven't.' He let slip another bubbling chuckle.

Snip, snip, snip.

Billy cast the scissors aside and worked to set the result of his labour in place. With scrabbling digits he reached to the back of his dried-up skull and tied thin strips of material in a bow, quickly correcting the fit of the portion touching his forehead. Finally he turned about and revealed a newly fashioned eye patch for the empty socket in his face.

'Better?' he asked through a manic smile that creaked like dry leather.

'The men stand ready, Captain,' Pyke said. He worked hard to ignore the cloth addition that did nothing to improve Billy's dreadful features. 'These past days they have done all that was asked of them to get you back. They await your orders.'

'Men hungry for treasure,' Billy scoffed. 'The wretches would kill their own mothers if I ordered it.'

'They'll do what's asked of them,' Pyke said.

'And I will ask it,' Billy assured him, and his remaining eye sparkled hungrily.

'And then you will lead us to our reward so faithfully stored up by you?'

Billy faltered.

'Yes,' he said after an apparent moment of doubt, 'the treasure.' Teeth clicked and finger-bones skittered doubtfully.

Pyke's eyes narrowed, and despite his revulsion he moved to a spot affording him a better view of the captain's wrecked face.

'I can only imagine the size of the hiding place

needed for all we have stolen these past years,' he prompted lightly, so carefully, and he watched tendons and sinews twist uncertainly as Billy worked to respond.

'Indeed,' the captain stammered at last, 'immense beyond reckoning.'

'What is the name of your ship, Captain?' Pyke demanded.

'What manner of fool question is that?' Billy snapped, and the fingers of his skeletal hand clicked uncomfortably as though in pursuit of a thing to be grasped.

'Your ship, Captain,' Pyke pressed him with a note of concern slipping into his voice, 'name your ship.'

Billy laced fingers and cast desperately about with swivelling eye as he was driven by torment so strong he ground his teeth against it. He beat fists against the table and buried his face in his hands.

'I can't remember,' he cried through the bones.

Pyke fell back in cold wonder from the admission. He felt his scalp prickle as his worst fears were confirmed.

'And the treasure…what of the treasure?' he demanded. 'Do you remember its location?'

Billy shook his head, distraught.

'No.'

Pyke reeled from the word, and the room spun

about him. He tried to step towards the door and only the table's edge prevented him from dropping to his knees in a faint.

'We'll have mutiny,' he whispered, struggling frantically to gather his wits. How was he to control the crew in the face of this disastrous truth? There was no plan for this, no magic. No treasure.

The cold steel of Billy's sword drew in a whisper to find the side of Pyke's neck, and it brought the buccaneer sharply to his senses. He looked fearfully to his captain pressing close.

'Stand fast there, Mr Pyke,' Billy warned, his stern tone renewed. 'Don't you go doubting Billy Buckler.'

'What will you do?' Pyke asked.

Billy withdrew his weapon and paced the room in slow contemplation.

'The girl's spell,' he said at last, 'was it the same as before? Did she use the spirits of five mortal men?'

'Aye,' Pyke agreed, 'five men, bottled up as the magic demands.'

'Five grown men, I'll wager, not young, eh, middle-aged and pudgy the lot of them,' Billy mused aloud. 'And by five such men I was returned by half, and half-witted.' He drew his skinless hand dramatically across his face and stroked cobwebs of beard. 'Well, then, Mr Pyke, afore you go spilling your guts to the crew, you listen on to my plan of revenge, altered now for these new circumstances. Mark me, you'll have your treasure yet.'

Whipping his blade to the curtained door, Billy strode from the room and bellowed for attention as he glared on pirates left and right.

'Stand to!' he roared to bring the crew running. 'Around me here, I say! Draw out your swords, men, every one, let me see them shimmer and shine!' Weapons sang free and Billy found himself within a bladed circle. Thrusting forth his own sword he drew it clattering along the line to fill the warehouse with a hellish chime. 'There's a sound I remember well, eh, lads? Swords joining in battle, a sound only bettered by that of steel cutting at English flesh! Am I right?' Voices bellowed in agreement as Billy nodded. 'Aye, well, you'll soon have your chance to hear that merry music again.' The men cheered louder. 'My revenge has been long in the planning, men, growing hard and bitter, impatient to be unleashed. But until now I didn't see the true purpose that lay in my plotting. Now it's clear to me, and you, and you and you will be the agents of a vengeance to burn through history. And when we've done with old England, I swear, we'll sail away on a sea of blood and make a bridge of bones to our treasure!'

The men raged to a frenzy at talk of slaughter and louder at the promise of riches.

Billy turned about the circle, fixing each man with his terrible gaze.

'Are you ready to do as I ask one last time, men, to follow me once more, to see me fully restored as your captain?' Assent came roaring through waving blades. 'Then I need new spirits, do you hear, fresh and tender, unspoilt and young.'

And as the men eagerly awaited the command, Billy flashed his wicked smile at Pyke.

'Bring me the king's children!'

39

Madigan and Faulkner reached Buckingham House at a gallop.

Hauling on reins, the captains drew their horses to a sliding halt before the gates where the beasts snorted and stomped impatiently.

'Officer of the watch!' Madigan barked to the night within. He spied a flurry of movement between the bars as soldiers came into view with their muskets made ready.

'Who goes?'

'Captain Madigan.'

Like some magical password, the uttering of his name caused an instant parting of the barriers, and Madigan led Faulkner to meet the rank of soldiers.

'Captain, sir,' Lieutenant Godfrey called in pressing between the men at arms. Like the rest, he eyed the dishevelled Faulkner with a mixture of suspicion and distaste.

Madigan wasted no time with formalities.

'Increase the guard about the perimeter at once.

Extra shot and powder for each man of the watch, and call the garrison to readiness. Are we clear?'

'Yes sir,' the astounded Godfrey replied with a sharp salute.

'Captain Faulkner is my guest as advisor,' Madigan further instructed. 'Report your preparations to me in fifteen minutes at my quarters, Lieutenant.'

'Preparations for what, sir?' Godfrey asked as the captains spurred their horses on.

'Pirates!' came Madigan's parting reply.

The startling word was greeted with mutterings among the soldiers and an exchange of nervous glances. The moment's agitation was such that none saw the fleet boy-shadow skip across the wall to blend with the night trees of the royal garden.

****

Gaining the rear of the house, Madigan and Faulkner dismounted quickly and passed their steaming horses to waiting guards. They paused there until the soldiers were out of earshot.

'What now, James?' Faulkner pressed his young friend. He scanned the night everywhere for a hint of scallywags concealed in bushes or behind ivy cluttering the rooftops.

For his part, Madigan wrestled with a storm of

thoughts and conflicting strategies.

'How do we get ahead of the pirates' secret game?' he pondered aloud.

'Perhaps we should move the king to a place of better protection. The Tower of London?'

'Don't be ridiculous. Such a course of action would cause panic in the city.'

'Then could you convince the royal family to leave London, even for the shortest time?'

Madigan shrugged doubtfully and continued to consider options in silence.

'And just why should we have to leave?' she asked from nowhere.

The question spun the men to the lighted windows of Buckingham House, and to steps where Princess Charlotte stood overseeing them both.

'Highness,' Madigan exclaimed and moved hastily to the young princess. 'Please go back inside.'

'Captain, you are too bold in endlessly telling me what and what not to do,' Charlotte pointed out with her sharpest stare for him. 'You must learn to tell me why, that I may decide for myself.'

He met her glowering eyes and saw for the first time the full, unblinking measure of determination she possessed. There could be no soft answers to it.

'Billy Buckler did not die on the gallows. He and his crew are in London, plotting the revenge he promised.'

Even the royal bearing of a princess was rocked by the claim.

'But...he did die,' she insisted. 'I saw his bones. I watched him die.'

'As did I, your Highness,' Faulkner said, 'a year since off the Devon coast. He came back then as well.'

'Came...back?' The night was suddenly so very, very cold.

Lord Remington, Dr Wheatley, Percival Fox, bones in the Bank of England.

'The explosion tonight,' she concluded breathlessly.

'That was a trap laid for those who know,' Faulkner said.

'But now that we know, we can act,' Madigan added. 'Your safety, the safety of the royal household, is at the heart of everything we do now.'

Still confounded, but taking assurance from Madigan's words, Charlotte regained her composure and offered a curt nod to her captain.

'I will go inside now,' she informed him of her decision.

'Thank you,' he replied with a smile. He joined with Captain Faulkner in bowing to the princess before both left her.

She waited until the men were out of sight before attempting to turn for the house, fearing her legs would give way beneath the weight of knowledge, the disbelief, pulling at her. You will not swoon, she told herself firmly, you will not be a silly debutante! She drew a steadying breath of night air to drive out all confusion and fear. And in the act of doing so she was seized by the firm certainty she was watched still. Her eyes darted back to the garden for an unseen observer before snapping instinctively upwards to probe ivy and shadows. But there was nothing, nothing save the briefest strange impression to hold her gaze. Looking on, she imagined she had for an instant caught twin pin-pricks of silver light between the leaves, though when she looked directly at the spot, the image was lost.

With a shudder for lingering suspicions, Charlotte returned to the warmth within.

***

Benjamin peered down on the girl's departure, and long after she had vanished inside.

Craning to see her face again as she secured the bay windows, he understood how close he had come to being discovered and was surprised by it. The sharp turning up of the princess's head to his leafy hiding place had identified her as one keenly attuned to the supernatural, but had in the same instant so nearly caught him unprepared. He found himself pondering why that should be so. Mortals were slow, their fastest movements easy to read, kings and queens and their children included. Just not this one. Was there in her, he wondered, some extra gift that made her dangerously difficult to read? Or, more unsettling, was it something in himself that dulled his wits and slowed his reactions?

You were distracted. By her hair, maybe, or her soft neck?

Annoyed by the mischievous suggestion, he tried to push it away only to feel it rebound stronger.

'You are drawn to the girl?' the Baron asked.

Benjamin's fingers were already sparking with power as he whirled in reply to the question. He saw the shadow looming, the whitened face pushing forth, and he looked on the hand of peace the spirit offered as he spoke again.

'I watched closely how closely you watched her,' he said softly, and was it with the hint of a knowing smile?

'She is...aware,' Benjamin offered carefully, awkwardly.

'Ah,' the Baron understood, 'she glimpses through the dark.' He turned a curious look to the vampire boy and studied him up and down. 'What happened to you this night?'

For the first time, Benjamin became conscious of

his appearance, and the layers of tavern soot blemishing his features and clothes.

'The pirates thought gunpowder would kill me,' he explained with a smirk that was met by one from the Baron. 'They are not so clever as they think. That's how I know I can beat them.'

'We certainly will,' the Baron agreed.

'We?'

'By stick and stone, and root and bone, I am sent for you,' the Baron revealed.

Benjamin's eyes flickered momentarily in search of a bottle in the Baron's hand before he guessed the truth.

'Lara sent you?'

'Correct,' Samedi confirmed, settling himself grandly on a seat of ivy. 'I come in peace to you now at her command.'

'She took a great risk by doing that.'

'Billy and his buccaneers rest till day, they did not spy me slipping away.'

'Billy Buckler has returned,' Benjamin concluded, and he watched the Baron's sombre nod of agreement.

'He has, and brings with him a most terrible revenge.'

Benjamin took his own leafy seat.

'Tell me everything.'

The Baron shared all, relating the dark and terrible occurrences of the past few hours, his face twisting in disgust as he described the monstrous creature Billy had become, and turning to sadness at the plight of his mistress, and finally to anger for the pirate captain's dastardly plan.

'I will not take the spirits from children,' the Baron spat bitterly.

'Yet if you do not, Lara's mother will be sent to the bottom of the sea,' Benjamin reminded him.

The Baron's sigh was heavy with a weariness a spirit should not feel.

'Yes,' he said. 'I come to you for help, Benjamin Blake. You said if there is a way, you would find it.'

'I thought I had,' Benjamin sighed in recalling failed mirrors. He in turn explained to the Baron all he had learned from the pirate Tavish, of the vessel Lafitte with its twin lights, and Mr Robinson's role on behalf of the buccaneers. 'We need to know where the Ghostmaker makes land,' he concluded, 'that is vital. I think Robinson knew, and it's why the pirates killed him.'

Samedi nodded.

'A code wicked buccaneers follow above all others,' he said. 'Dead men tell no tales.'

Benjamin looked again to the warm lights of Buckingham House as he took stock of the situation.

'Even in joining forces now we are outnumbered by challenges,' he reasoned. 'To Lara and her mother we must add the king's children. Six lives in the balance, and in three different locations! I have no magic to put me in three places at once, do you?'

'I do not,' the Baron admitted, understanding their predicament. 'To rescue one is to kill the other, sacrifice the children or lose the mother.'

'The Ghostmaker remains the biggest problem,' Benjamin cursed. 'While it sails so far beyond us it foils any plan we might form against the pirates.'

'You thought to trick the ship to land,' the Baron guessed, 'by using Robinson's knowledge and the Lafitte to lure the Ghostmaker near?'

'Something like that. The only way to win this is to rescue all at the same time, Lara, her mother, and the royal children.' In his mind, Benjamin continued to toss about the jigsaw of facts he possessed in search of a plan from the numerous parts.

'All at once and all together,' Samedi mused, his face giving way slowly to a smile. 'Why, Benjamin Blake, the problem we face is the very answer we seek. Ha!' Greatly amused, the Baron clapped his hands and threw back his head to laugh at the night sky.

'Well, what is it?' Benjamin demanded.

Chuckling, Baron Samedi explained.

'The pirates themselves provide us with our best

chance,' he insisted. 'When the next spell to restore Captain Billy takes place, it will be aboard the Ghostmaker itself. It is already decided. Lara will be there, her mother will be there, the children will be there! All at once and all together!'

Spinning skywards from his place, the Baron sent laughter like thunder across the rooftops of Buckingham House, and from starry heights he descended again, plunging with rapid eagerness to hear the vampire's reply.

Benjamin was exhilarated and doubtful in the same moment.

'Our chance only comes if we allow the pirates to take the royal children,' he cautioned. 'It means risking their lives until we have an opportunity to act.'

'To act any sooner means risking the lives of all,' the Baron reminded as he raised a warning finger.

Benjamin considered the words but could find no dispute.

'Then everything must play out on the Ghostmaker,' he agreed. 'And I must find the right time and place to be aboard too.'

'What of the fishing vessel the Lafitte?' Samedi suggested.

'It's the final part to be explored,' Benjamin agreed. 'We can only hope the pirates still need the captain of the Lafitte for their plan and have not treated him like Mr Robinson. Or laid more traps.'

'I will assist in this,' Samedi assured with a decided nod.

'It sounds as though we have a partnership, Baron,' Benjamin said. He offered his hand to seal the deal.

Seizing the boy's grip, the Baron shook and with an air of some amusement chuckled behind his free hand while Benjamin looked on, at a loss to explain his merry behaviour.

'What's so funny?'

The phantom smiled at the vampire's confusion.

'Your face is coloured so black, and mine is painted white. What would a princess think of that?'

Together they laughed.

And together they planned.

40

'I don't like it, I tell you, not a bit of it.'

Wary that his protest might be overheard beyond the confines of the canvas room, Mr Pyke glanced towards the door for signs of eavesdroppers. In the main part of the warehouse the pirates were at breakfast or bent over their work, cleaning pistols and sharpening blades in anticipation of the order to action. Thankfully, none came near the little room and the whisperers within.

'What's not to like?' Davy asked, bringing his colleague's attention back to the table and the large map of London they had been consulting.

'What the captain asks of us brings great risks,' Pyke explained with a sweeping hand across the inked streetscape, 'risks that are unnecessary to our success in this venture.'

Davy smiled at that.

'Captain Billy's never been one to avoid risks.'

'You speak the truth, Mr Davy!'

The pirates turned, alarmed by Billy's sudden

and misshapen appearance in the doorway. The captain's hands rested on Lara's shoulders, holding the frightened girl in place as his glare shifted between the men. He peered hard on each in turn and afterwards to the map on the table as though scouring for treachery.

Pushing the girl along, he moved deeper into the room, his wooden leg thumping with each hobbled step closer to his officers. Taut muscles creaked over whitened bones as he advanced and thrust his torn face to Pyke's. And when next he spoke, he did not shift his deathly stare from the first mate.

'We have nothing to fear in risk,' he hissed, 'and do you know why, Mr Davy?'

'No, Captain,' Davy replied, grateful Billy's attention remained on Pyke and not him.

'Because of what I learned while I was on the other side,' Buckler offered. He let slip a wry chuckle for Mr Pyke's visible discomfort. 'While I dined in the halls of Hell, and supped with the Devil and all his demons, I learned something truly wondrous. Hell has no place for the crew of the Ghostmaker, no matter what we do in this life. And do you know why, Mr Davy?' The captain's eye twinkled madly. 'Because the Devil's afraid we'll take over and kick him out!'

Billy's crazed laughter burst up to fill the room and rattle the very walls. Rocking on his heels, he slapped each pirate shoulder in turn, inviting the unsettled men to share his joke and add to his gales of merriment. Outside, startled pirates turned nervously to the disturbance.

And as quickly as it began, the laughter stopped. Like a candle snuffed out, Buckler's amusement passed and fell silent. His head creaked slowly round to stare furiously.

'Mr Davy,' he said. And that was all he said. Confusion flowed into the captain's face in the place of further words, and he eyed the buccaneer up and down as though for the first time.

'Captain?' Davy croaked respectfully from a throat all at once dried up.

'The girl!' Buckler blurted as one snapping from a deep sleep. 'The girl.' And yet here again, in the very act of parting cracked lips to continue, he hesitated, a lost look washing over him. His wizened tongue fluttered for words he apparently could no longer summon.

'The girl was preparing a document,' Pyke snapped hurriedly to divert Davy's attention from his leader's apparent befuddlement.

'Yes!' Buckler exclaimed, regaining control over his wandering mind. 'Yes, the girl has prepared her requirements for the spell, all spelled out, a spell to be weaved at sea, you see! It lists the...the ingredients, a chart, what goes where, and what you do, I do, we do, what we all do with the voodoo, heh. Have it delivered to the Ghostmaker right away!'

'Aye, Captain,' Davy said with a ripple of uncertainty in his tone. He turned to Lara and reached for the folded paper the girl offered. 'Will there be any other instruction for the ship, Captain?'

'Aye,' Buckler declared. 'Two lights, Mr Davy, our messenger will run two lights and bring the Ghostmaker after dark to the place arranged. Tonight we strike.'

'That cannot be.' The little voice drew all to peer sharply at Lara.

'What are you prattling about, girl?' Pyke demanded.

'The spell cannot happen tonight,' she replied calmly.

Buckler drew himself to full height on his snapping spine and towered over her.

'Explain yourself, girlie.'

'Look to my ingredients,' Lara said, gesturing to the paper in Davy's hand. 'One of them is dust to be gathered from a crossroads.'

'Aye, aye, what of it?' Buckler demanded impatiently as Pyke snatched the paper for close inspection.

'Dust from a crossroads,' Pyke read aloud, 'to be gathered at midnight.' He stared angrily at Lara and sought trickery in her face.

Lara nodded.

'It is the most important item, and I do not have it. I asked Mr Estoban to get some tonight. We can complete the spell tomorrow night, not sooner.'

Billy Buckler snarled for thwarted plans.

'Change the order to the Ghostmaker,' he commanded grimly. 'Deliver my message to the Lafitte. Sail with two lights tomorrow night.' He watched closely as pirate and girl exited the room.

'Do you trust her?' Pyke asked, gesturing after.

Buckler offered a grunt for the question.

'That little pup? Not for an instant. But what can she do now she could not before?'

'I don't know,' Pyke admitted, his suspicions around the girl – and a meddling vampire – not soothed by his captain's words.

'Still fretting over that intruding spirit of yours?' Buckler pressed. 'What was it the Baron called him... Benjamin Blake?' He snorted for his first mate's brooding. 'Pah, you worry too much.' He tapped a skinless finger on the map. 'But tell me now, Mr Pyke, why is it my plan unsettles you so?'

Pyke stared down on the paper cityscape and gained his bearings.

'We are here,' he explained, pointing out the location. 'Our appointment with the Ghostmaker lies here, miles to the east. Yet, under the terms of your scheme, we first move west, to Buckingham House, in order to snatch the king's children. After that we must travel roughly twice the distance back to reach the Ghostmaker at anchor, and with every alarm raised against us.'

Buckler smiled gleefully.

'Exciting, isn't it?'

'Captain,' Pyke exclaimed, 'it is reckless and unnecessary. We should make instead for the ship and dispatch the Baron in our place to bottle up the young spirits we need. By the time his work is discovered, we will be miles out to sea and safely away.'

'No!' Buckler roared in an explosion of fury. With a howl he swept the map aside and smashed his fist into the table top, and again over and over in venting his burst of anger. 'No! No! No! Nonononononononoooo! They have to know it was me! All of England must know it was Billy Buckler returned to take his revenge. I'll not give my place to servants with magic bottles!'

He paused, fighting to control his scorching temper, and turned a careful glance towards the door as he lowered his voice.

'I have forgotten some things, and you have helped me, Mr Pyke, and I am obliged to you for it. But there are things I do not forget, memories that scar more than skin and bone, never to be wiped away. When the time comes to look into the faces of the king's children, I'll seek the very fear I felt the night I was press-ganged from home to serve in His Majesty's navy. Younger than fine Prince George I was, and with a girl prettier than Charlotte promised to me. And England took it all away, everything! And all the floggings and punishments meant to beat me down I'll answer with the spirits I steal to grow strong again. England owes me a debt, Mr Pyke, and it will be repaid in full and to me alone.'

41

Lost to shadow in a far corner of the warehouse, Lara ignored the clamour from the magic room as she huddled at her work. Quietly and quickly, but with keen attention, she focused her mind and laid out ingredients for a new spell, a second, secret conjuration unknown to the men of the Ghostmaker and their wicked captain.

On a square of parchment she arranged bags and wraps and bottles according to the required pattern, all within a neatly drawn circle pierced by the shapes and twisted lines of magic understanding. And, of course, she was mindful to leave space enough at the centre of the drawing for the last vital element. Only when all else was ordered and set did she bring it forth. The doll in her hand was a chubby stuffed thing, a crudely stitched poppet fashioned from a piece of cloth stolen from the pirates' store. It looked on its creator with mismatched button eyes as Lara placed it gently within the circle before whispering over it.

'My *vèvè* is here complete, with dust at head and feathers at feet.' She passed her hands three times over the doll and next reached to produce three long pins in her fist. 'Long as night, sharp as steel, these a bad man's skin will feel.' In a swift motion she stabbed the three pins deeply into the doll's chest.

The spell was done, and just in time. Lara sensed a figure approaching and quickly plucked the needles to conceal them in her clothes.

'What you dabbling with, girl?' Mr Pyke demanded sourly.

Lara shifted her position to allow the pirate a better view of her spell.

'Practice,' she said. 'I want to make sure everything is prepared for the spell.'

'Like dust from a crossroads?' Pyke tested her, and he peered suspiciously from the doll to her open face.

'A midnight crossroads,' Lara reminded and coolly met the pirate's stare.

'I remember,' Pyke growled. 'Just you make sure there are no unexpected surprises this time. Otherwise you'll sink with your mother, I promise you that.' The pirate took cruel satisfaction from the girl's angry scowl for his threat. 'Where's your dark friend the Baron, by the way?' he demanded.

The shadows came to life in an instant, giving up

the Baron where he surged from his hiding place so close to the startled Pyke.

'Here I am, fell buccaneer, close enough to smell your fear.'

With lips pinched thin against a tickling discomfort at his neck, Pyke retreated unsteadily.

'I'll be watching,' he offered as a defiant parting shot and strode away.

The Baron drifted lower, searching for any sign of more pirates nearby as he came to rest by Lara.

'I have gained the extra night required by Benjamin,' Lara informed her protective spirit.

'Well done,' Samedi beamed.

'Will it be enough?' she asked nervously.

'All will be well,' he assured.

Lifting the stuffed doll, Lara offered it to the Baron together with the pins.

'For your work tonight.'

The Baron secreted the items in the folds of his cloak and, with a knowing wink, he smiled again at the girl.

42

'Take up your stance.'

Madigan reinforced his instruction with a stern cutting of the air with his sword before lifting it in readiness. He hesitated when she did not follow suit, and frowned for her glare a moment before understanding reached him. He made his dutiful addition almost wearily.

'Your Highness.'

Charlotte smirked and responded by slashing the space between them with her own training blade.

Better, she decided.

He attacked. Launching at her, he offered an array of thrusts and sweeps to test her, each one chiming musically against her defensive moves, louder and faster as she mirrored his actions and held him back with step and thrust, step and parry. He ended his drive and watched the girl maintain her posture in expectation of trickery.

Better, he judged.

'Remember to keep your free arm up for balance,'

he reminded and returned to his starting point, there to swish his weapon once more in preparation the next part of the lesson.

She attacked the moment he turned. Her cuts and thrusts were deft, precise, lightning fast. Madigan parried expertly, yet he retreated from the flurry of strikes as her energy denied him time to reply. He had nothing until she mistakenly offered it. A rush of alarm to her face signalled the moment, an unseen snagging of her foot in her dress, and her assault became a pitched stumbling past him.

'Damn and blast!' she spat and punished the air with furious cuts. 'Damned skirts!'

'You must learn to cope with the circumstances of the moment,' he said.

'Easy for one wearing breeches,' she hurled back.

'I say it only to prepare you,' he offered gently.

She thrust her blade for the question plaguing her.

'If you wish to prepare me, tell me what you learned from Captain Faulkner.'

'Do not be distracted,' he tried.

'Do not avoid my question!'

He struck back at her anger with his own and offered fresh tests for her sword, only to find she remembered well her training and was not clouded by fury. Despite his flurry of techniques, he made no progress against her and at last gave up, falling back breathless and frustrated.

'Captain Faulkner is obsessed with the memory of Billy Buckler,' he admitted, 'he is maddened by it. He seeks to understand what happened between them, and his mind reaches for outlandish explanations. And yet…' He faltered to visions of a bank destroyed for a prize of bones.

And a boy with silver eyes.

She plunged to cut the answer from him. Her assault became a dizzying series of thrusts, but this time he drove her off to a stalemate of circling and staring as metal echoed to the ceiling.

'What are you not telling me?' she demanded. 'If Billy escaped the noose, whose skull did I see? If not his, why would pirates want to recover it?' Across the length of Madigan's blade, she spied the tightening of his jaw for her reasoning. 'Tell me.'

He lashed forward, this time with power sufficient to draw sparks between them. And this time she held firm, refusing to yield. They collided and stared one another down over crossed blades.

'I cannot tell you things I do not yet believe myself,' he snarled.

'You dare keep secrets from me.'

'I keep secrets to keep you safe.'

Her free hand whipped up and carried to his throat the dagger she had concealed in her skirts.

'Do I seem unsafe to you?' she challenged. Satisfied with the astonishment in Madigan's face, she withdrew her blades. 'There are things a young lady learns for herself in this man's world, Captain.'

She drove her sword into the floor and stormed away.

43

On cautious steps and with hands ready to snatch for the loaded pistols concealed beneath his tunic, Mr Davy moved along the quayside.

Attired in the shabby disguise of a workman, he kept his pace deliberately slow, affecting the walk of an ordinary man at ease in this workday setting of fishermen and traders, a man with nothing to fear and no guilty secrets to hang him.

His heart pounded beneath his shirt as he tried not to think of hanging.

Resisting the temptation to wipe beads of sweat forming under his broad hat, he looked instead at the fishing vessels moored hard by, searching for the boat and captain he had been sent to meet. To the teeming crowds about he was a casual observer, idly interested in the fully rigged vessels bobbing about in the fading light as they waited for the tide's turning.

He avoided the searching eyes of fishermen who paused at repairing nets to watch his passing, and he moved hastily on. He wished he was miles away, hidden from Londoners milling about who would string him up in an instant if they were to recognise him as a pirate of the Ghostmaker. The sooner he delivered Billy's instructions and got away from here the better.

After a few more steps he spied his target, tied up and nestling between larger boats at the quay. Davy made quickly towards the fishing vessel Lafitte and sought for signs of life aboard. Though the craft was clearly loaded and prepared for a night's work, he found no man walking its short deck. Summoning his courage, he approached the Lafitte's neighbour, where crewmen worked at stowing nets and pots.

'Hallo below,' he called out to one, a thickly bearded man. 'I seek Captain Merwin of the Lafitte. He's not aboard.'

In response, the bearded man grinned and turned to his mates.

'Hey, lads,' he called to them, 'man here says he seeks Merwin, but can't find him on his craft.' The comment drew hearty laughs from the other fisherman, leaving Davy much confused.

Another sailor, his face a mask of cracked leather from years of harsh sun and spray, drew near the rail and called up.

'You're no local, I'll wager,' he said as he coiled a rope thoughtfully.

Davy's heart skipped faster.

'No,' he replied, holding his nerve, 'how could you tell?'

'Any man local to this stretch knows there be only two ports of call for Captain Merwin,' the sailor said, and his colleagues guffawed louder. 'If not aboard the Lafitte, he's swamping ale in the Gypsy Rose, yonder.'

Following the direction indicated by the fisherman's knobbed finger, Davy eyed the buildings lining the quayside. He quickly spotted a swinging board above a doorway, a sign bearing the impression of a lady pirate with pistol in hand and one foot on a captured barrel as she advertised the Gypsy Rose inn. With a nod of thanks to the fisherman, he marched… strolled…towards the building.

Easing into the musty interior of the grog house, the pirate felt instantly at home. Partially visible through choking swirls of tobacco smoke, assorted ruffians and cut-throats crowded the bar and rough tables, pausing their whispered conversations and card playing to regard him sullenly. Davy felt narrow, appraising eyes roving over him across tankards of ale. Trusting to his disguise, he drew up boldly and crossed to the bar where he slapped down a coin for service. When the innkeeper limped forward and banged down a sloshing mug in return, he also took to studying Davy.

'Captain Merwin,' Davy said and gulped his ale.

The innkeeper took his time, weighing up the man and his request. Finally, he jabbed his chin with a grunt towards a far corner of the room.

Turning to the spot, Davy spied a pipe's orange flare in the gloom of a booth, and he laid course between tables to approach the tiny beacon.

'Merwin,' he said to the smoker, a red-faced bear of a man who sucked on his pipe through flabby wet lips.

The man's response was to ease one powerful arm into the light and lay a hand flat upon the table.

'You tell me,' he demanded.

'Crossed daggers,' Davy replied, using the code-words whispered earlier by Billy Buckler himself. He watched the smoker turn up his wrist to reveal a rough tattoo of intersecting blades on his sweaty skin.

'And you are Mr Davy of the Ghostmaker,' Merwin said as the pirate slipped into the booth. He chuckled for his guest's urgent glance in search of listening spies. 'I'll bet a month's catch you wish you'd left Mr Robinson alive a bit longer to be your messenger,' he tittered. 'Have no fear, Davy, every man jack in this place has something to hide.'

'I bring instructions from Captain Buckler,' the pirate whispered. He slipped Lara's carefully folded document across the table. 'This paper you are to convey to the Ghostmaker tomorrow night, and you are to run two lights.'

'Lordy be,' Merwin said, issuing a great plume of smoke on a cough, 'the time has come at last. It's true, then. The hangman messed up, and Captain Billy still rules the waves.'

'Yes,' Davy agreed simply. 'And you'd do well to follow his instructions to the letter.'

'I'll see to it myself,' Merwin assured him with a sneaky wink as he pocketed the document. 'Will you share a draught with me in celebration of the captain's good fortune?'

'I must get back,' Davy said. He tossed a handful of coins onto the table. 'Do not celebrate too much.'

'I wouldn't dream of it,' Merwin smirked. He hungrily gathered his reward to himself as Davy slipped away.

Blinking into light made harsh after the murk of the inn, Davy eased into a nearby doorway, there to linger in deepening shadows until, a few minutes later, he watched Merwin exit the Gypsy Rose and clamber aboard his vessel. Satisfied, the unseen pirate mingled with the human traffic and vanished into the dusk.

44

In the hours after sunset, and despite his bellyful of drink, Merwin skipped lightly along the deck of the Lafitte, the final tasks for a night's sailing completed.

Since his meeting with Mr Davy, the river tide had drawn full, and the western wind promised a speedy passage to the fishing grounds. Better yet, Merwin recalled cheerfully, no matter the catch, his pocket of jangling coins would keep him in ale for the days ahead. Serving pirates was indeed a satisfying side-business, he concluded with an uneven grin.

Bypassing the boat's wheel, he strode to the access hatch leading to the lower deck. His crew would not arrive for a little time yet, just long enough for another measure or two from the bottle he kept stashed below. With a pause to examine a blackening sky for signs of foul weather, he gripped the stairwell rope tightly against a swelling tide – and his swimming head – and descended.

He collected a lantern on the way and proceeded

through the low interior of his vessel, navigating bunks and kegs until the farthest point towards the bow was gained. Here, despite being alone, he looked carefully about for unwanted guests before he reached and found his secret flask tucked safely between beams. Happy at discovering the container still half-filled, he popped its cork and licked his ever-thirsty lips. The brandy tasted sweet to his rough tongue and he sighed as liquid fire passed down to warm his innards. Surely this was the one pastime better than serving pirates. He laughed softly in the flickering light and allowed himself another swig.

Such was his loving attention to the bottle's delights that Merwin did not spy the first slow creep of black strands down the stairs behind. Tendrils picked like a spider's legs, testing the surface of the boat in advancing on the lone drinker. It was only when he tilted back his head once more to swallow did the fisherman become aware of a presence, a gigantic form descending within tattered strands of darkness. Startled, he spluttered brandy and wheeled about to find Baron Samedi filling the boat's space.

'Questions I have for you,' Samedi whispered from behind his white mask.

Irritated at the lost liquid soaking his shirt, Merwin faced the Baron.

'What are you doing here?' he demanded. 'You

have no dealings with me, dread spirit, you know that.'

'By stick and stone, and root and bone, I am sent just the same.'

Merwin scoffed at the Baron's theatrics.

'Away with you, slave,' he dismissed him, 'you can do nothing. I know the hold the pirates have on you and your young mistress. What will you do, kill me? Meh! You'll get nothing from me.' He faced Samedi defiantly.

The Baron returned the man's staring and he offered a half-smile for the confidence of silly mortals. He reached beneath his cloak for Lara's sackcloth doll and held it forth for Merwin's consideration as his other hand drew out a single long pin and played its shiny tip in the lamplight. And, with a lightning fast motion, he thrust it deeply into the poppet's eye.

Merwin flung hands to his face and issued a tormented screech. The bottle dropped and burst at his feet, its precious contents forgotten in the sudden explosion of agony behind his eyeball. Shrieking, the fisherman fell back and struck his head on a low beam, bringing yet more pained wailing.

The Baron removed the pin and waited coolly for Merwin to regain his senses. He watched the man blink in fighting to catch breath against fading torment, and he caught the icy fear that crept up to replace it. When the man had sufficiently recovered, the Baron offered again his skull-lined smile. And he stabbed the doll's leg.

With a howl against fresh agonies, Merwin grabbed his tortured limb and toppled to the floor, there to writhe and moan with pitiful tears coursing his flabby cheeks. His clutching knuckles turned white at his knee as he laboured to form words through teeth clamped shut.

'Please,' he whimper-hissed, 'please. No more.'

Samedi again removed the pin but kept it visibly close to the doll while Merwin recovered and dribbled through fits of weeping.

'Look at me,' the Baron demanded. 'Look at me!'

Merwin struggled against the pain in his leg and forced himself to turn to the spirit. His face betrayed the terror hauling at his heart.

'Anything you want,' he promised the Baron desperately, 'I'll tell you anything. Just, no more magic, please.'

The Baron nodded, satisfied.

'Keep a keen eye to this pin,' he cautioned, 'and tell me where the Ghostmaker plans to reach land.'

Wide-eyed despair washed across Merwin's sweating features.

'They'll kill me if I tell,' he blubbered.

The needle plunged into the doll's back and brought

fresh shrieks from the distressed man. Chubby arms reached in vain to quell his suffering and he thrashed madly about, more tears flooding to add to the moisture already beading his face. When the needle was again withdrawn, he collapsed in a heap, breathing hard.

'The location!' Samedi demanded.

'Yes, all right, yes,' Merwin spluttered with a hand held up in pleading against further punishment. 'When the Ghostmaker comes, it will be to London Bridge. Right up the river with all cannons ready.'

'Is this the truth?' the Baron barked, hardly daring to believe the pirates would be so daring. He scratched the needle tip slowly across the surface of the doll's body and watched Merwin squirm against the tearing sensation it offered him.

'Yes, Gospel truth,' Merwin groaned. 'I swear it.'

Tucking the poppet away, Baron Samedi flowed close to his weeping victim. In a rapid movement he grabbed the man's hands in his own and hauled him close.

'Heed me now, fisherman thief,' he snarled. 'You will play your part in the pirates' plan, and that way survive to spend your dirty coins. If you do not, if you betray me, I will return for this and more.' He pressed a small, cold object into Merwin's palm.

Drawing off, the Baron kept his fierce eyes on the

fisherman as his mighty form retreated impossibly through the hatch to fade away like a nightmare on the wind.

Still trembling, Merwin kept a glassy watch on the portal for fear of the phantom's return as his heart eased its bursting rhythm. Only after the longest time, only when he felt certain the Baron was indeed gone, did he dare shift to peer on the spirit's parting gift. Uncurling meaty fingers, he beheld a small bottle, corked and empty but awaiting whatever Baron Samedi chose to place there.

45

Charlotte jerked from sleep and uneasy dreams, disturbed by...what?

She turned her head lazily on the couch where she lay and scanned the half-lit room, seeking the cause of her abrupt waking. The candles had long since burned out, leaving only firelight to chase darting shadows about her curtained chamber. Through patches of shade lying across the room, all appeared normal to her examination. There stood her reading chair, vacant by the fireplace. Likewise her poster-bed with the sheets turned down as though to prove no-one lurked there.

Assured she was alone, she blinked away the sleep which had overtaken her so unexpectedly. In one instant, she recalled, she had been reading, seeking again some understanding of the scheme that so obviously allowed Billy Buckler to trick the hangman, and in the next her eyes had closed, though she could not clearly remember the moment. She did remember visions, unsettling dreams of pirates with hooks and ropes, and a conspiracy made possible with a corpse pulled up by bodysnatchers to confound the law. It came to her then and she smiled. She had simply exhausted herself in pursuing the mystery to its logical solution and dozed off.

Easing up, she scanned again all corners of the room but found nothing amiss. Doors remained secured and the curtains perfectly still. A log in the fireplace collapsed just then to a snapping of sparks, causing her to start. That must have been the reason for her waking, her logical mind again decided, a mere shifting of wood or coals in the hearth, nothing more.

And yet...

She looked through the empty space a third time, prompted by an inner sense dissatisfied with ordinary explanations despite her cool reasoning. All appeared to be in order still, from books on shelves to the contents of the writing desk, and the news sheets she had been studying as sleep crept upon her, all neatly arranged in twin stacks on the low table by her. She stared hard at those news sheets now, so precisely ordered side by side along the table. Her blood turned cold.

She had not set the papers so.

'Please do not be afraid.'

Ice surged through the princess's veins for the

young voice so close.

'Who's there?' she demanded, her own voice sent trembling.

'My name is Benjamin Blake,' the shadows announced, and the firelight danced to the name.

'Who are you to enter the chamber of a princess unannounced?' she exclaimed, angered now.

'I am not of your realm,' his voice replied, 'I come and go as I please.'

'That is outrageous,' Charlotte declared, her rage sufficient to visibly loosen her shoulders and neck. She leapt swiftly to her feet and turned to face down the cheeky visitor.

News sheets fluttered at his invisible passing.

Charlotte faltered before vacant space, stern words stopped at her lips by the vanishing. She blinked against addled senses and a mind demanding a rational explanation where there was none. She looked on all sides for it and finally around to peer fully into the pale face of Benjamin Blake.

'Please sit down,' he said quietly.

Whether compelled by the silver twinkle in piercing eyes or the incisors so sharp as he spoke, Charlotte obeyed without question, her mouth flopping open as she plonked onto the couch.

'What...who are you?' she asked in a voice that was made a mere breath. 'How did you do that?' Her finger flicked in confusion from one part of the room to the other.

'I will answer, I promise,' Benjamin said, 'but there is a far more important matter to deal with first.' He indicated the papers he had examined while the princess had dreamed through the sleep he sent. 'You have been investigating matters.'

'Yes…I have,' the royal girl stammered.

'And tonight you formed a connection between them?'

'I did,' she agreed, 'and I think I have uncovered Billy Buckler's trickery in it.' In speaking, the princess turned eagerly and placed a hand to her papers as though to find her thoughts arranged there, while Benjamin found himself again considering the incline of her neck, and the fall of…

'You have?' he said quickly to refocus his wits.

'Yes,' she confirmed. 'I believe he must have worn a contraption of some kind, with a concealed hook, one that connected to the gallows to stay his fall.'

Benjamin slowly shook his head.

'The real answer is not so easily accepted by mortal eyes,' he interrupted with a sigh.

Charlotte struggled with the words.

'Mortal eyes? What do you mean by mortal eyes?' All at once, uncertainty became full and cold understanding, though she scoffed at the notion. 'Do you mean to suggest the hand of the supernatural is at play here, that some magic force is behind everything? Well, that is a ridiculous notion.'

A harsh grinding rose to catch Charlotte's attention, and she turned to watch, astonished, as her reading chair began to slide across the floor. Dumbfounded, she tracked its incredible approach, transfixed by the invisible power drawing the furniture on until, and only when Benjamin held up a hand to end his spell, it halted, mute and waiting. The boy took his seat and fixed her.

'You asked who I am. Your Highness, I am the vampire Benjamin Blake. I have lived and un-lived for one hundred and forty-nine years. And in that time I've learned how magic is behind so much in the world. Believe me when I tell you, there is dangerous sorcery at play in the story of Billy Buckler.' He gestured to the papers. 'It has already caused mayhem in London and will do worse unless it is stopped.'

'A…a vampire,' she breathed, disbelieving and yet unable to disbelieve her widening eyes as she placed a pale hand unconsciously to her throat. For hadn't he been watching her throat just now?

Benjamin spied the movement and smiled for old beliefs.

'Don't worry,' he soothed, 'I bite only if forced, or commanded by a witch. And I serve no witch.'

'Then why have you come to me?' Charlotte breathed as she added witches to her unsettling store of knowledge.

'I have come to help you defeat a sinister plot,' he added as though to assure her.

'But why?' she asked. She lifted a news sheet. 'Why is all of this happening?'

'Because all of it was necessary to return Billy Buckler from the dead.'

Benjamin watched Charlotte blink and blink again, and for a moment, fearing she might fall back under the weight of information he shared, he prepared to reach and hold...catch...her. But somehow the girl collected herself and drew up with a determined breath.

'There was no trick?' she asked, and watched as again he shook his head.

'No hooks or contraptions,' he finished for her. 'But there was magic.'

As the princess listened, bewildered and growing as pale as the vampire with each new detail shared, Benjamin told all, from the first night of bodysnatching and bottled spirits, the race to recover bones for Lara's spell, to the captain's return, half-formed and hideous.

'Billy Buckler's revenge is coming,' he concluded. Awaiting the girl's inevitable questions, he noted the gentlest shifting of curtains behind her as another trespasser stealthily entered the girl's chamber.

'Revenge,' Charlotte whispered suddenly as she scoured the depths of her memory. 'As the rope went about Buckler's neck he said that. "I'll be revenged on the whole pack of you".' Memory gave way to suspicion and the princess fixed Benjamin with a troubled gaze. 'You know what his revenge is to be, don't you? That's why you've come here tonight.'

Benjamin nodded.

You want to save her, don't you?

'Yes, I do,' Benjamin agreed. 'Billy wants to steal the king's children.'

He heard the skip of Charlotte's heart in receiving the dreadful knowledge and saw the skin on her hand prickle when she threw it against a cry rising at her lips.

'He means to destroy the royal line!' she gasped.

'And he will if we don't stop him,' Benjamin said.

'We must act at once,' the princess said, becoming emboldened in her panic. 'We-we will double the guard about the house, no, triple, and we will ambush these pirate devils when they come.'

'You must let them come.'

Struck voiceless, Charlotte blinked her astonishment, opened her mouth, closed it, and blinked again.

'Are you mad? You would let these men come

unchallenged into the king's home and cause us harm?'

'We must let them think they seize you,' Benjamin insisted gently, 'or an innocent woman will die. No harm will come to any of you until you are on the Ghostmaker. You are too important to Billy's plans. And that's how the pirates will be undone.'

Charlotte scoffed.

'So *you* say. But what if their plan is to murder us in our beds? Why would they trouble themselves to cart us off to the belly of their awful ship?'

Benjamin offered the princess silence by way of reply, allowing her to reach the answer by herself. It came to her imagination as a slow and terrible dawning formed of emerald light as she understood Billy Buckler's intention with bodies and bottles.

'This is unspeakable!' she cried, raising fists against the truth.

'It will not happen,' Benjamin promised, 'it will not be allowed to happen.'

'No!' she exclaimed, jumping to her feet. 'It will not because I will act at once to prevent it!' With fierce purpose, she made for the door.

'There is no mortal power that can save you,' Benjamin called after her. 'If you act now, you destroy our best hope, and Billy Buckler will still come for you.'

'And I suppose only the great vampire Benjamin Blake can stop him,' Charlotte mocked, reaching for the door, 'only you can win the day. Ha!' She half-turned to cast him a cold glance and further spite, but what she saw caused her to whirl fully and crash back against the door, astounded.

Hovering by firelight above Benjamin Blake, and filling half of the room with his rolling black cape, the skull-faced Baron stared down at the princess.

'I can't win the day alone,' Benjamin agreed, 'but we can.'

46

The midnight hour was fast approaching as the lampless carriage drew up to the crossroads.

Reining in black steeds at the head of the vehicle, the pirate Stubbs took time in seeking signs of interruption to the business at hand. Squinting through darkness lying on open fields to his right, he found no movement save for a slow drifting night mist through far-off trees. To his left, where the view was also becoming shrouded in growing fog, a small cemetery stretched away, silent and deserted. Maintaining his close observation, Stubbs stretched an arm to knock softly on the carriage roof.

The vehicle's door swung open in response, and Mr Estoban emerged. Holding to the cover afforded by the carriage, he also took careful time for a visual search of the area, one hand ready at the hilt of his sword. Finally, he stepped aside and motioned sharply for his fellow passenger to come. Lara stepped into the night and Estoban leaned in to offer a whispered warning.

'A false move and I'll put a pistol ball in you.'

Lara considered the pirate's words calmly, and she nodded.

'And then you will cast Captain Buckler's spell instead of me, will you?' she asked defiantly. She caught the buccaneer's uncertain frown.

'Be quick about your work,' he grumbled, displeased by her logic.

Lara walked to regard the spot chosen for her by the pirates. The crossroads was ideal for her needs, she concluded quickly, and the adjoining cemetery made the location perfect. She peered over the low stone wall of the burial ground where ashen headstones were caressed by the quickly growing mist. Slow wisps curled hypnotically and lengthened towards her, giving the impression of being drawn to her magical presence. And when she approached the cemetery's gate hard by the crossroads, the fingers of mist eased through the wooden slats in a cold caress of welcome.

Hearing a crunch of footsteps behind, Lara spied Mr Estoban drawing near and she reached out urgently to halt his progress.

'Do not spoil the earth with your feet,' she warned.

Without waiting for the man to reply, she faced the barrier once more and produced one of Baron Samedi's bottles. Kneeling, she uncorked it. As the night vapours eagerly followed to creep low across the ground and join her, she began to scoop earth into the glass vessel.

Estoban studied the girl's work closely, finding it increasingly difficult to maintain his view through the foggy veil. With each passing minute it increased on left and right, drawing a heavy curtain across his vision. In a short time Lara became an indistinct form behind the thickening trails. And in an instant, Estoban found himself immersed in freezing clouds which cut off all sight of her. So it was with the carriage and its horses, barely feet from where he stood. The obscuring mist left no point of reference by which he could fix his position.

'Mr Estoban!' The whisper from nowhere was harsh and nervous.

'Here!' he replied, recognising his fellow buccaneer's voice. 'This way!'

Stubbs grew from the fog with his pistol drawn.

'Where's the girl?'

'Somewhere there,' Estoban said, waving uncertainly towards the swirling funk. He joined his colleague in peering vainly for Lara.

A shape, huge and dark, whipped past the edge of their vision, startling the men. Estoban frantically unsheathed his blade and stood trembling with his comrade. There came a scuttling movement, behind them, and it spun the men to search anxiously. Next came a beast-like snarling from some unseen throat, prompting pirates to imagine all manner of hellish forms within the soupy clouds. A piercing shriek fell from a long and terrible shadow passing directly overhead and made them gibber, half-mad with fear. Turning to a shifting portion of fog where the cemetery wall marked the border between life and death, the pirates watched as a shapeless figure approached the very edge of the misty curtain. Shifting dreamily, the spectral form was joined by others of its kind, each gliding quietly to peer on the men through the vapour.

'We are done here.'

The pirates cried out and jumped to train their weapons on the voice, only to find Lara looking back at them, her bottle corked and crammed with earth. She eyed them indifferently for a moment until, with a shrug for their mute behaviour, she strolled to re-enter the carriage which had become partially visible again. The men glanced quickly to the wall of the graveyard in search of phantoms and found the place once more silent and dark, with nothing standing there but the same lifeless rows of headstones.

Estoban and Stubbs raced one another to the carriage.

47

The night crept on and kept its secrets.

Through the candlelit corridors of Buckingham House, Princess Charlotte walked alone, kept from her bed by the fearful knowledge she carried. She had long known of the great responsibilities she might one day bear in wearing the crown. But, until tonight, its weight had seemed years away. George was first in line for the throne, and Papa was yet a young man. Royal duties for Charlotte were banquets and parades, not this cursed gambling with the fate of the kingdom and the lives of her brothers and sisters.

Madness. It was all madness. Vampires and giant floating spirits? In London? The creep-stories of bedtime come to a kind of life? Her mind reeled until she was forced to pause and reach a steadying hand to a wall.

And what of this talk of magic?

The spirit boy, Benjamin Blake, he had made assurances and promises of his magical strength and the certainty of his planning, but how easy it must be to speak so when your life is not at stake. Why, Benjamin Blake had no life to lose in any case.

Pushing quietly through high twin doors, Charlotte paused to survey the children's playroom. Here amid their scattered toys, the royal children dozed by the dying fire, the day's playing done. George and Elizabeth clung together on a couch, watched over by a smiling rag doll. Facing an unfinished game of chess, meanwhile, Edward slumped where dreams had overtaken him.

She stepped quietly among them to approach her own chair. In its plump seat she found the little wooden sword that had been Elizabeth's gift.

For courage.

She picked up the toy and turned it over, studying its shape and lines for a measure of that courage she now sought but did not feel. She looked from the false weapon to the slumbering children and for a cold instant, just long enough to tickle the hairs on the back of her neck, she saw how they appeared to be… not sleeping but…

Charlotte fled the room and the torture of imagination, stealing back into the corridor to move as far from the scene in the playroom as possible. She strode on until she felt her head swim, realising only then her breath had caught, forgotten in her chest. Fighting for air to calm a racing heart, she pushed on another great pair of doors and stumbled out to a balcony, grateful for the blast of fresh night air that swept to her. She steadied herself and filled her lungs. And in the moment of pause she looked to the little sword, finding that her grip had tightened enough to splinter the wood and cut her skin.

Looking to the east in vain hope of spying the dawn, Charlotte discovered the thin autumn moon yet rising. The princess shut her eyes against the image and longed for an end to the night.

***

Mr Pyke shifted his attention from the crescent moon in its slow rising progress over chimney pots and returned to his investigation. He moved cautiously across collapsed brickwork and looked for clues between shattered timbers. Beneath his feet the remains of the Gravediggers tavern shifted dangerously, threatening to swallow him up in a crushing avalanche of rubble. Jagged beams pointed randomly skyward, ready to stake him should he tumble over a tripping foot or loosened stone. The smell of recent fires wrinkled his nostrils while wisps of smoke drifted as rising phantoms from deep within the ruin. He imagined himself walking on the roof of Hell itself, but the thought did not cause the pirate to falter on his path. He had to know!

Where are you, Benjamin Blake?

Nothing else could account for the tavern explosion but the spirit boy's intrusion, his sneaking in to press Mr Robinson for information. Pyke had predicted correctly Benjamin Blake's move, and the trap had worked. But was gunpowder enough to deal with a supernatural pest?

Sounds echoed from the streets about and interrupted the pirate's thoughts. He ducked low, becoming one with smoke and wreckage, and watched as two drunken men appeared, each holding the other up in their unsteady progress past the tavern. The companions paused by the ruin and looked over the scene with airs of mourning. They held high the bottles they carried, a salute to the memory of the Gravediggers. A pair of quick gulps followed, next a chorus of belches, and the travellers recommenced their meandering journey with a warbling song to see them home.

Pyke kept to his hiding place a brief time longer and searched for signs of more late-night visitors. As he did, his attention fell on a portion of the tavern and fixed there. His brow furrowed in hard study of what he beheld, and to fading strains of drunken song he eased towards the spot.

The smouldering hole he reached was no larger than his head, a miniature volcano on the chaotic landscape. The buccaneer drew nearer, screwing up his face against the cloying smoke as he peered down into the darkness. This was a void there, formed during the building's fall, and just big enough for…

The rubble beneath him shifted ominously. Stone fell inwards to increase the volcano and Pyke flung out a saving hand to prevent from tipping headlong into the hole. The tremor surged beneath his knees and he prepared himself for the worst until, with a sound like a beast growling in deep caves, the threat began to ebb away. Only when the quake was surely passed did he dare lean closer in examining the coffin-sized space revealed. Suspicion bit hard as he looked on it.

Wiping stained hands, Pyke rose to view the scene from on high. He longed for the gift of tracking a vampire's passing even as his mind speculated on events in this place after the explosion. Turning flinty eyes to follow drifting smoke trails towards rooftops, he wondered what unseen forms might move there even now.

Under his breath, the pirate cursed the night and all its creeping spirits.

The night lowered its weak moon-lantern and caught buccaneers at their villainous work in the shadows. Far from their hideout the five skulked, spectral forms among churchyard trees as they waited for the command to strike.

'We have him, lads,' came a voice from the dark, and the men looked to the hideous form of Billy Buckler rearing up like a nightmare. He in turn surveyed the men before him and was satisfied. Gathered here were the strongest of the Ghostmaker's crew, hand-picked for the grim business to come and wearing sly smiles at the prospect of it. With a thrust of his sinewy head he directed their sight between branches. 'Our target lies yonder. That's where Benjamin Blake sleeps.'

Across a landscape of mist and tilting headstones, a squat mausoleum stood in the lee of the church.

'There,' Billy told his assassins. 'A fitting cell for a demon, eh, lads? At dusk he slips from his coffin there to keep us from our treasure, and there he's now returned like a fugitive. I saw him with my own eye not yet an hour ago. He's at his weakest, dead to the world, and ours for the taking.' He fixed his men with a look of moonstruck madness. 'You have what you need?'

In reply, the eager buccaneers held forth weapons for the fight, stakes and holy crosses, a bottle of blessed water stolen from the church font, all sure protection against any vampire. To a satisfied nod from their leader and a flick of clicking fingers to proceed, the band of cutthroats crept forward.

They fanned out in advancing, making careful movements to avoid dried twigs and dead leaves underfoot. As one they drew on between markers and nearer the tomb, closing on its studded door. There came a sudden shrill activity behind the night, and it halted them and froze their blood. The men held fast as a frightened owl screeched and wheeled away like a whitened spectre. Relieved breaths moved patches of fog, and the attackers renewed their deadly procession.

Hard by the crypt door, Billy gathered his team for final orders.

'Be ready, lads,' he cautioned with the sternest gaze, 'no dawdling. Strike sure and fast and we're all rich men, do you hear me?' He reached for the metal barrier. 'Brace yourselves for action now.'

Billy heaved the iron door and set hinges shrieking.

Determined men raged into the tomb. Baying for action, the pirates swarmed between disarranged coffins, their lids secured and layered in dust. Readied stakes pierced cobwebs made heavy by time and stabbed dank air in the hunt for prey.

'Which one,' a buccaneer demanded in his fury as he swept a crucifix about, 'which one is he in?' He and the others turned back in search of guidance from their leader who stood in the doorway. Billy lingered there with a sixth assassin who shifted and drifted at his side.

Baron Samedi loomed to block all escape and made ready five empty bottles.

'Sorry, shipmates,' Billy said to the disbelieving men, 'but I'm not taking any chances with the spell this time. Best to have more spirits, just to be sure.' He turned his cold attention to Samedi. 'Make it quick.'

Pirates retreated with useless weapons, and the mausoleum resounded to a hellish bedlam of doomed souls.

The night crept on and kept its secrets.

48

Everything floated through the daylight hours.

Feet and inches above the floor of his chamber, books, candlesticks, shoes, paintings, chairs, coins, all manner of items rotated in slow processions about Benjamin where he knelt. He conjured at the heart of all, eyes closed to better sense the soft motions to and fro past his face, seemingly at random, yet each with an ordered precision he commanded.

Concentrating in silence, with hands resting lightly on his legs – just as learned so many years ago from the wisest of holy boys – he focused his mind on the challenge of keeping the pieces in flight while avoiding collisions between the parts. It would not do to have a lighted candle touch the pages of a gliding book, or worse, have a sliver-edged weapon strike his skin. Even as that notion surfaced dangerously, his Roman sword arced by, its fine metal singing on the air close to his cheek. Along its route it passed a portrait of William Shakespeare cart-wheeling lazily in the opposite direction.

After so many years of practice, Benjamin found this conjuration the perfect tonic for a vampire mind made restless through a day of waiting.

And when the night ahead promised so much danger.

Through the magical lifting and lowering of items, he distracted from the agony of dwelling on the countless ways in which his plan for this evening could be undone. Pirates, Pyke, potions, pistols, princess, the many elements offering innumerable chances for disaster.

Permutations endless.

He countered fear with a renewed focus on an object circling closer now. Tilted to a diamond shape on the air, and rotating about opposing corners, a chessboard had become a wooden sun about which its pieces orbited as moons of ivory and ebony. The little collection operated as a perfect system, flowing within the greater turning through the room.

Bottles, bones, Billy, Baron, blades.

Just in time, Benjamin's senses detected a white pawn arcing perilously close to the black king. He quickly reworked their paths, easing them safely apart while keeping control over all besides. Balance was maintained and the soft gliding continued.

This was how it would be tonight, he hoped. The individual movements of children, spirits, pirates and magicians would be guided to a safe conclusion in spite of the best efforts of Billy Buckler. The chaos of pirates would be kept under Benjamin's strict control.

Magic, mother, mayhem, murder, Madigan.

The plan, just like his rolling spell, depended on the numerous parts being in the right spot at precisely the right time. Just as…

Now.

'Return,' he commanded.

The tumbling spell ended. Chairs hovering over their original places descended gently to rest. Books closed their wings and floated to an alphabetic roost on shelves. Benjamin's shirts folded and fluttered to chests where they settled neatly to assigned locations. Ink pots and quills rejoined his writing desk as it touched down, and paintings returned to their hangings. So too his swords and daggers. Crossing in flight, they returned to mountings above the fireplace to the softest note of kissing metal. And lastly the chessboard. The square turned flat and skimmed towards its table, drawing along a train of pieces which alighted in precise formation onto their proper squares.

A cold instant too late, Benjamin recognised a wayward part.

His eyelids snapped open, and he looked quickly to the board to locate his mistake. The smallest of pieces, a single white pawn, had touched down a mere fraction off centre on its square. It was the tiniest miscalculation but enough to doom it. The piece teetered a moment on the board's edge before the fall, and tumbled to the floor to clatter towards him.

He looked on it, this solitary flaw in the otherwise ordered room, and was disturbed by the error in his conjuring.

The disobedient pawn settled before him like a bad omen.

49

Across white-topped waves, Captain Merwin stared to the last rays of sunshine in the west and grumbled nervously.

Holding tightly to the wheel of the Lafitte, more to steady himself than the pitching vessel, he watched the sea blacken under gathering storm clouds, and he shivered. The sooner he dealt with the Ghostmaker the sooner he could be back ashore and free of the infernal threat upon his head. How he longed for the comfort of a warm measure of brandy just now, and his need made him grumble more. What once was the source of his greatest pleasure was tonight made a medicine to be craved for shredded nerves.

A swell from starboard driven by the storm's advance winds struck the boat harshly, and Merwin heard a distinctive sound from his chart table. The bottle that was Baron Samedi's gift to him rolled across the wooden surface, moving in time to the sea's rise and fall. It created a gloomy hollow sound, followed abruptly by a torturous clack! where it struck the table's raised edge and commenced a return journey. Merwin irritably corrected his course to account for the waves and…clack!…tried to ignore the chill of fear fingering along his spine.

Clack!

Gazing skywards to lightning cracks in the cloud cover, he sought to confirm the mast lights were fully illuminated as required for the Ghostmaker. Sure enough, two lanterns glimmered high upon the woodwork, shining yellow like the eyes of some hungry night creature perching against clouds billowing like…just like…a cloak.

Clack!

Merwin shook off the image and swore under his breath with an angry glance at the bottle. Making to reach for it, resolving to fling the accursed object overboard, he was interrupted by a fresh wave-surge which forced both hands back to the dragging wheel. Propelled by heaving waters, the little bottle gained power enough to hop over the table's edge. It hurtled to the deck with a clack! unbroken. As the captain remained caught at his wheel, the Lafitte's shifting tipped the glass to a dancing journey across the boards past him. The churning sea delivered a stronger blast to the hull and sent white water cascading over the main deck. Fishermen swamped by the waves cried out fearfully as lightning again split the sky. Merwin heaved the wheel, forcing the Lafitte into the wind, and he jerked painfully from stinging spray cast into his face. In his momentary blindness, he heard the bottle's rattle towards a rail where it struck with a clack! Coming head-on now, the sea rose up to assail the little craft's bow and it hurled a deluge on the men below who clung on as thunder boomed. Pots and nets were dragged overboard, and the crew scrambled desperately to avoid their own fatal plunge to the depths. Merwin held the wheel as his salvation and fought to remain standing on feet slipping over drenched wood.

And just as quickly as it had come, the tempest subsided. The wind died abruptly in the sails, and foaming water receded to calm black. Waves that had surged and burst on the deck of the Lafitte drained away, hissing back to the deep, and the boat's pitch eased on the calming sea while drenched fishermen stumbled to set the remaining equipment right.

Peering across the deck for signs of damage, Merwin felt the boat's wheel loosen in his hands in reply to the sea's softening flow. He allowed himself a breath of relief and looked quickly to the mast lights again, content to see them flaming brightly in spite of the torrent.

Clack!

Startled, the captain peered down to the deck, and

with a shudder he spied the bottle, neither claimed nor damaged by the flood. Even as he looked, it rolled to him to sit bizarrely on its end between his feet, as though placed there deliberately by unseen fingers.

'Ship to starboard!'

The cry from a deckhand brought Merwin's attention to the gloomy horizon. The sun had finally burned out beneath the waves to make sea and sky one in a blackness torn only by the jagged lightning, and it seemed the Lafitte had reached the very edge of the world. Peering hard into the flickering void, Merwin strained for that which the deckhand had seen, and he caught at last a patch of churning white surf where something set against the background of night cleaved towards his vessel.

Something huge.

To a plume of ocean split by its bow, the Ghostmaker hove from the dark. Its mighty dimensions blocked the lightning and dwarfed Merwin's boat as it coursed along, presenting for the startled fishermen a mammoth nightmare vision. Grim, unlit, and with gun ports shuttered tight, the vessel was a phantom shrouded in ragged sails and twisted ropes, dripping with shadows pulled from a haunted ocean beyond the natural world. When wicked men drowned at sea, the fishermen thought, this was the ship dispatched from Hell's dark harbour to collect them.

Looking to spy signs of life beyond the rails above, Merwin searched in vain for a human form along the length of the Ghostmaker's flank. At a loss how else to proceed, he steeled himself and called out.

'Hello, aboard. Ahoy, the Ghostmaker!'

'You run two lights!'

The voice that boomed across the water seemed to be that of the Ghostmaker itself, and the Lafitte's crew moved uneasily from it to the far rail of their vessel, all hoping to shed the discomfort they felt clawing at their hearts.

'I bring instructions,' Merwin shouted. He dug quickly for Lara's document and held it aloft. 'Preparations,' he explained. 'Captain Buckler summons the Ghostmaker to its rendezvous. He rejoins his ship tonight at the place arranged.'

Something flew through the night from the ship's rail. It fell snaking towards the Lafitte, and Merwin saw a basket at the end of a long rope strike his deck. He stepped to it and dropped the document in. He watched the rope tighten and hoist the container away.

'All will be ready for our captain,' the ominous voice reported.

'I will lead you in,' Merwin offered, 'and signal any danger.'

'Nay!' the voice barked. 'Your part in matters is

played out. You will remain here.'

As fresh lightning cracked overhead, the Ghostmaker rumbled deep within itself, and the crew of the Lafitte looked in dread to its timbered hull. And as they gazed, the ship's gun ports crashed open to gaze back. Too late, Merwin began to haul desperately at the Lafitte's wheel and added his own desperate cry to those of his men. Cannon barrels thrust forth and the night was torn apart by a cataclysm of fire and smoke, loud enough to challenge nature's barrage of thunder. Caught fully by the blasts, the Lafitte was sundered in an instant and flung to smouldering matchwood on the surface of churning water. Collapsing from above, the twin lights on the fishing boat's mast briefly illuminated the scene of utter destruction until they were snuffed out by folding waves and sank, sputtering with the rest.

Cannons withdrew and gun ports slammed. The Ghostmaker eased on, following the storm on its course for land.

50

'Ho there, what's that?'

In the shadow of Buckingham House, Trooper Belmont, a proud officer of the King's Guard, came to a sharp stop on his patrol and peered hard across the lawn. With his musket held at the ready, the soldier squinted into the dark from behind the tip of a sharpened bayonet. Somewhere amid the flower beds and trimmed hedges stretching from him, he was certain he had caught hint of a swift movement, a darting at the very edge of his vision. Beyond the royal garden, made colourless in the gloom, the cloud laden sky flickered and rumbled distantly, offering a dismal vision to the soldier but nothing besides. Garden paths were quiet and deserted in every direction.

Muttering doubtfully, Belmont shifted the weight of his musket and moved along, resigning himself to another boring patrol and, by the looks of that sky, a night of rain to add to his woes.

The soldier forced his thoughts to the guardhouse

fire awaiting him after his watch, and he was in the process of losing himself happily in thoughts of warmth when the clouds sparked again and thunder boomed ever closer. He cast a disgruntled look to the heavens. And in the corner of his upturned sight, by the light of flashing from above, he caught a sure glimpse of movement across the garden. There was no doubting it this time. His eyes had captured a moving form, illuminated by nature's flaring as it sped between the trees. With a racing heart, Belmont pulled his weapon to bear and readied the mechanism for the mystery intruder. Testing the reassuring weight of the musket in his hands, he steadied his breath and advanced on the tree line under the eye of the storm.

Caught by repeated flashes of light, branches jabbed their gnarled fingers towards the soldier and flung dead leaves on the rising wind to peck at his face. He blinked them away and pressed on, probing slowly forward for renewed sign of the trespasser, working all the while to keep his balance against the buffeting gale now rising.

A figure! A human shape to one side of the path appeared against the night. Tall and terrible, it stood rigidly in his way, unmoving in the storm, and though he could not see its face in the dim light, Belmont knew its baleful eyes fixed coldly upon him! The soldier threw up his weapon and prepared his defence.

Forked lightning tore at the gloom and pierced the dark with a resounding crash. Jarring flashes denied the towering form its cloak of shadow and revealed it fully to the quaking Belmont. An angelic statue, posed in marbled glory with empty hands, stared mutely at him from its place among rose bushes.

Belmont lowered his musket and almost laughed aloud at his situation. What would Captain Madigan say to finding him thus, defending the royal family from a carved decoration? Chuckling, he turned to retrace his steps and it was then he spotted a cloaked man lurking just yards away. There was no mistake this time. Belmont swallowed his laughter and silently brought his musket to his shoulder and stepped forward.

The figure stood in a patch of night framed by two overhanging trees and was as unmoving as the stone angel. But this new figure was no statue, Belmont realised. Thankfully, however, with its back turned fully to the soldier, this target was apparently oblivious to his approach. Only by the storm's flickering, which danced on the surface of his cloak, was he visible at all, so motionless did he remain. Just the barest shifting, a slight tensing of the shoulders, became evident as Belmont cocked his weapon loudly.

'Halt!' the soldier commanded in his gruffest tone. 'What are you doing there?'

In reply to the call, the figure rotated its upper portion and presented its ghastly half-withered face and single eye for Belmont's gasp of horror. Billy Buckler widened his skeleton smile to the transfixed man as lightning flared.

'I'm distracting you,' he confessed.

Mr Pyke burst from the gloom. His pistol butt swept down hard and felled Belmont in an instant, sending the soldier crashing to earth, there to dream of nightmare faces.

Billy flung the cape aside and reached for his belt. Fingers clicked in drawing his sword, and for a span of seconds he played its edge in the air to catch the lightning's hypnotic dance. Then, sweeping it high, he called to the darkness.

'Men of the Ghostmaker, forward!' he commanded. 'Our little treasures are waiting!'

The erupting storm gave up the pirate gang. Fractures in the sky illuminated buccaneers emerging from their hiding places, marching as one broad line of faces set in cruel determination on Buckingham House. The moon fell back and drew billowing clouds to shield against the terror coming on. The very trees reared from the terrible rank and its monstrous leader, and the wind shrilled its warning. The thunder replied with a drumbeat of war, and the pirates drew forth their weapons.

51

'Avast there, lads, they've fired their cannons!'

Among the royal children, Edward alone stood in enjoying the flash and clatter of the storm. While the rest of his siblings shifted nervously, listening to blasts thrown against roof and walls of the playroom, the little prince, resplendent in a new buccaneer's hat and with sword in hand, let the tempest feed his imagination.

'On the port side!' he declared as a fresh gust rattled the windows. Leaping onto a couch, he readied his blade against an attack there, only to spin about as the wind howled in the chimney liked a trapped beast. 'No, to starboard!'

'Oh, do be quiet, Edward!' Charlotte snapped irritably and she hugged the frightened Elizabeth tighter to herself. 'George, tell him.'

'Pish posh!' the pirate-Edward retorted. 'I obey the laws of the sea, not the rulers of England!'

'That's enough,' George barked, agitated and nervous as the rest.

Edward sulked.

'You're not king yet. You can't make me.'

George bounded from his chair to chastise his cheeky brother. He had barely taken a step, however, when the storm intruded brutally to end all arguments. With a mighty crash, the wind threw open the balcony windows and shrieked through the playroom, driving toys and frightened children from it. George shielded his face against the tempest and fought past whipping curtains to reach for the clattering frames a moment before his brother arrived to help. They joined in a driving effort to beat the storm and reseal the windows, wrestling the protesting wind until finally they shut it out. And, as calm was restored, the brothers saw through the shimmering glass the armed pirates advancing on their home.

'What on earth...?' Edward mouthed awestruck. He looked to George who was already springing from the window towards the bookcase.

'What's happening?' Elizabeth demanded, made all the more frightened by the concern in her brothers' faces.

'We must raise the alarm,' Edward exclaimed.

'It's too late for that,' George replied. Spilling books aside, he snatched for a box hidden behind and flung open its lid to produce a gleaming pistol. He hefted the weapon up and cocked it sharply.

'Where did you get that?' Charlotte cried as she beheld the gun.

George paused with a perplexed frown.

'Seriously?' he asked. 'The house is full of these things.'

Sounds of harsh disturbance from within the house reached the children's ears. Princess Elizabeth burst into tears at the crashing of glass and metal, and a sudden explosion of gunfire.

George plunged for the door despite Charlotte's protests.

Sprinting ahead of her from the playroom to the head of the grand staircase, he looked down on a scene of unfolding carnage. The palace guard, caught by surprise, blocked the foot of the stairs in a defence against pirates who spilled into the building like rats from a sewer to overwhelm them. Firing, slashing and roaring in their advance, the men of the Ghostmaker bore down on the soldiers, stepping over the bloody fallen to battle deeper into the house amid a choking fog of pistol fire. The last of the soldiers gathered desperately together, bayonets fixed, but all too quickly they too were overcome, and the pirate horde began to climb to the upper floor.

George pushed Charlotte back and retreated fast, dashing to the playroom to lock the doors behind him. Turning from the barrier, he hastily shepherded his family to the farthest end of the room.

'We must hold together,' he instructed. He placed himself boldly between his siblings and the doors, his pistol levelled, again despite Charlotte's pleadings.

Boom! The twin doors shook on their hinges under a great blow and a chorus of foul swearing outside.

'George!' Charlotte tried but her brother pushed her back.

Boom! Again a great rattling of the wood filled the space and drew cries from the smaller children.

'The balcony!' Edward cried. 'We can make our escape that way!'

'No!' Charlotte cried, but her objection went unheard by the children who ran eagerly to the curtained windows, even as the doors began to splinter to admit the first pirate.

Reaching the curtains ahead of the others, Edward tore the material aside, and his shrill cry overcame the storm as he fell back from the awful vision of Billy Buckler he revealed stepping through the window.

Caught on two sides, George swung his pistol between Captain Billy and the pirates who now fanned out across the room from the shattered doorway.

'Hold there!' the prince commanded. 'I warn you!'

Pirates grinned at the boy and his lone weapon, and Billy issued a wet, gurgling chuckle.

'One shot's all you have, boy,' the captain said with a flicking gesture. 'Best pick your target and let us get on with our business.'

'George,' Charlotte pleaded, 'don't be rash.'

The pirates guffawed as George continued to swing the weapon desperately back and forth even as Charlotte tried to control him.

And in the midst of the stand-off, with the pirates laughing yet, Charlotte paused, distracted. The barrel of her brother's gun cut the air to hold all attention but hers. Hers alone shifted from the action to fall on the mouth of the battered doorway where one pirate in a tunic of ragged crimson kept solitary guard with his back to the darkened corridor without. The man smirked with evil relish like his comrades, untroubled by childish threats. But it was not the man Charlotte looked to. No, the princess looked past him and towards a growing point of darkness at his shoulder where, in a blinking, a form young and pale, with razor sharp teeth and silver eyes that locked fiercely on hers for an instant, swept from the blackness. Benjamin's hands clawed up, and the crimson buccaneer was snatched away in deathly silence, unseen by all but her. A single heartbeat later, lightning flashed to illuminate the corridor, wide and empty.

Shaken by the vision and chilled by eyes that had communicated so much, Charlotte quickly collected herself. She reached firmly for George's wrist and forced his pistol down. The act was met by wicked chuckles from the pirates and horrified gasps from her siblings.

'You must trust me,' she said calmly to the children.

'Well?' Billy barked at his men. 'What are you all waiting for? Bring up the carriage and let's get moving!'

Spurred by their leader's voice, the buccaneers closed around the shivering children.

52

The nightmare journey began.

Squealing and biting and twisting and fighting, the children were dragged through the wreckage of Buckingham House by their gruff captors. Out to the courtyard they were hauled to the pirates' carriage where it waited amid a scene of frenetic activity. Horses stolen from the royal stables had been brought up, and as the prisoners were bundled aboard their transport and crammed into its restricted space, pirates raced to claim whinnying mounts.

Exiting last, Captain Billy surveyed events with manic glee. Yet, even as he smiled, he caught sight of activity far off across the garden. Flaming torches darted between the trees and signalled the approach of reinforcements for the already slain defenders.

'Mr Pyke!' Billy roared, drawing his mate to his side. 'Do you see?' And he pointed off.

'Aye, Captain,' Pyke replied, 'we're ready to go.'

'Make all speed,' the captain ordered and he strode to the carriage to take his seat high by the driver.

Seizing the whip from the man's hand, Billy reared up and cracked it hard across the horses' flanks, setting all in motion. 'With me, my loyal lads! Onward to the Ghostmaker!'

The pirate horde surged to a clattering of hooves, leaving but one man trailing. Weighed down by a bag of riches hastily looted from the palace, the solitary, wheezing buccaneer struggled up into his saddle, beaming with delight for his booty of gold coins and jangling silver pots. He hauled on reins and spurred the horse to begin the race after his comrades. In his turning, lightning caught a burst of swift motion to his right but betrayed it to late for him to avoid the collision. What hurtled upon him with a vampire's growl plucked him shrieking from the saddle, and the riderless horse fled in a kicking frenzy of spilled riches.

Avoiding the panicked beast, Madigan and Faulkner raced to the courtyard ahead of a flank of soldiers. Madigan swiftly directed men into the house and followed on, becoming more alarmed as he beheld the devastation inside.

'Search everywhere!' he bellowed to send soldiers running.

'Have we lost the king, sir?' a concerned trooper asked, voicing the fears of all present.

'His Majesty is attending a gala,' Madigan

responded, and his own words raised a terrible alternative. 'The children! Find the children!'

As soldiers spread out at the double through the palace, Madigan took the stairs two upon two, aware of Faulkner chasing after. The captains drew pistols in unison and gained the upper corridor.

'Careful, James, careful,' Faulkner urged him for the long passageway ahead.

Together they advanced as quickly as they dared, pistols raised, and closed steadily on the playroom. On a signal from Madigan, they steeled themselves and burst through the ruined doors.

Corridor candles were not matched here, forcing the men to squint through ember-touched shadows lying over upended furniture and scattered toys. Amid all, only one chair remained upright, and some movement there in the dark drew pistol arms towards it.

'Hold fast there!' Madigan demanded. He now perceived a standing figure, apparently inclining over another seated in the chair. 'Hold fast, I say!'

The standing figure turned and offered his pale face to the men.

It was the boy from the Gravediggers tavern!

The same boy, Madigan realised, and with that same look as before, so fierce it made his eyes glint like daggers.

And in a blinking, Benjamin was gone.

The captains felt a breeze pass sharply between them and they jerked from it to sweep weapons all around. To their astonishment, no target was found in front or behind, and the pair struggled to gather their nerves against disbelief in stepping closer to the only mystery remaining, the shape in the chair.

'A pirate!' Faulkner gasped.

The villain groaned unconsciously in his seat, ignorant of the pistols drifting before him, ignorant too of the note Benjamin had pinned to his tunic, and which Madigan now plucked up to read.

Handwritten words sent ice to his heart.

East. The Ghostmaker.

53

The criminal convoy hurtled through the streets of London.

Whooping and howling as they charged beneath forked lightning, the pirates of the Ghostmaker sent up a tumult of savagery to terrify faces at shaking windows and drive citizens to stampedes of mindless fear on all sides. At the head of the frenzy, Billy Buckler rocked in his seat, seized by his terrible laughter. It was a lunatic cackling drowned only by pistol shots he offered again and again to the night to fuel his amusement.

Jostled and shaken within the chaotic interior of the carriage, the children cried in fear and clung to one another amid the din. Only Charlotte held her tongue, praying silently that promised help was already at hand.

The carriage sped beneath the span of a low bridge, the confined space boosting the explosive sound of Billy's latest shot and the shrieking laughter he flung after it. The pirate cavalry galloped behind, riders whipping sweating horses to greater efforts.

A bearded buccaneer came last, protecting the rear and checking for signs of pursuit as he raced beneath the bridge. Assured the road lay empty for now, he looked to his companions where they cleared the overhang. Lashing his mount cruelly, he gained the spot a second later. He did not see the attack when it came, but felt only hands, a boy's hands, cold as the grave as they reached to envelop his hairy face from above. Razor-sharp nails dug past his beard to find leathery skin, and the man was whipped upwards and away from his speeding saddle.

Mad with fear, the riderless horse bucked and reared, gaining on the column in its frightened charge and overtaking the pirates, one after another. It passed Mr Pyke where he leaned hard over the neck of his own beast. The horse drew his gaze and the sight prompted sharp suspicion within. With a furious roar for interfering spirits, Pyke drove his own horse on.

The convoy clattered through residential streets and turned to follow Billy's guiding of the carriage south towards the river. The abandoned horse here drew level with the vehicle, frothing and galloping as though in a race to the death with it. Inside, Charlotte held Elizabeth and looked to the frightened creature and then beyond it, far off, to a movement black and sweeping against the night. A phantom figure kept pace with the charge, flying with the cape it wore out-stretched in tracking the carriage from a neighbour-ing street.

Faster than all in the chase, Baron Samedi sped through the city. His cloak trailed like smoke from some infernal engine propelling him over the streets and higher, upwards where he coursed across roof-tops, his half-white face shimmering through chim-ney smoke in reply to the lightning. Diving down to draw nearer the speeding vehicle, he stared through a window as though to examine the occupants with a wide-eyed curiosity.

'Courage,' Charlotte whispered to her little sister, 'have courage.'

Together the children cried out again as the car-riage drifted precariously, tilting into a sharp turn, and the vehicle descended with the roadway's pro-gress towards the final destination. Stretching broad and long across the sea-flowing Thames, London Bridge waited.

At his secret post just short of the bridge, a waiting pirate sentry emerged and gave signal all was clear at the stopping point. With pistols prepared, he watched the crazed passing of carriage, horses and howling buccaneers to the water's edge. Then, as ordered, he paused long enough to probe back along the way for whatever fools came in pursuit of Captain Buckler and his crew.

The road snaked into the silent, deserted night. As the buccaneer looked on, lightning sparked to make flickering shapes in doorways and alleys, but no following form was betrayed by the effect, and he grunted his satisfaction. He lowered his weapons and was on the point of drawing back towards the waiting convoy when there came a harsh scraping to his right, like metal drawn across stone. He swung to it, guns up to trace the night for a target. Fresh sound came now, and it was some kind of hissing to his left. He whirled again with pistols aimed. And so it was his back was fully turned when the assault came. The night surged up, and the helpless gunman was snatched away, pulled down by it to a darkness pierced by silver eyes.

Milling about the foreshore, pirates dismounted and swarmed on the carriage, there to haul on doors and wrestle its human cargo. Edward punched a scowling face, Charlotte kicked shins, but nothing allowed for escape, and the children were dragged along, down to wooden wharves hard by the bridge. Billy led the way, his face fixed to a manic anticipation as he stared across misty water.

'Can you feel her, Mr Pyke?' he asked breathlessly of his first mate. 'Out there, cutting towards me. She knows I'm here, Mr Pyke. The Ghostmaker is near!'

Pyke nodded to his captain's words but turned his own frowning attention inland, back along the route taken by crew and carriage. Where was the sentry he had posted? Amid the noisy transfer of the royal brats, Pyke wondered what other dark form might be drawing close.

'Get a move on!' he barked at the men.

A sudden hiss of breath from Billy Buckler stilled Mr Pyke, and he looked to his captain where the half-man stood rigidly with hands extended, clasping as though for some invisible element on the air. Buckler's eye grew huge in his head and his teeth clicked in his torn jaw.

'She's here!'

Carried soundlessly on the rising mist, coming on as though lured by the anguished cries of the children, the forbidding shape of the Ghostmaker cleaved into view.

54

'Haaaaaaalt!'

In response to Captain Madigan's roared command, the galloping column of soldiers drew up behind in a deafening clamour of weapons and armour. Horses stomped and snorted impatiently as Madigan leapt to the road, attracted by what he had spotted in the lee of a church along their path. Closely pursued by Faulkner, he raced forward, hardly believing what he saw.

Strung up to the church gate by his boots, a buccaneer swung in a befuddled state, groaning pitifully.

'Please don't bite me,' the pirate sentry begged woozily of the upside-down captains.

Madigan seized the man's hair and pulled up his scruffy head for clearer identification, though he already knew what kind of man he had found. Another scallywag, yet another to add to those sprawled at Buckingham House and one left dangling from a bridge in the city.

'A trail of pirates to follow,' Faulkner gave voice

to what his friend was thinking, even as loud and hasty activity somewhere past the church caught their attention.

Abandoning the prisoner, the captains ran on to the corner, skirting the church from the main route to spy along the way towards London Bridge. Both gasped at sight of the tall and ominous ship at rest hard by.

'Forward!' Madigan bellowed for his troop, drawing his sword to point the way. 'Make ready to charge!'

As the captains regained their mounts, horsemen spread out to fill the breadth of the road. Polished blades winked to the lightning, and the thunder that followed was the sound of horses spurred to charge on the Ghostmaker, and towards a lone figure waiting between on the water's edge.

As the last of his men scrambled aboard, Billy Buckler stood to stare his enemies down with a leering smile.

'Come on!' he dared the king's men. 'Come and get ol' Billy!'

The speeding cavalry aimed for the river and issued cries of war in reply to the pirate leader's challenge. All paths and every sword pointed the way to Billy Buckler's heart.

The troops spied the snapping open of the Ghostmaker's gun ports too late to react, too late to break the charge and avoid the rolling guns. Cannons exploded about the demonic pirate leader, shrouding him in smoke as they consumed the soldiers in fire.

The earth split asunder. Horses reared, tumbled and fell under the withering barrage. Riders were blasted away on the tearing hurricane to be flung down and trampled. The ordered line of attack shattered and became a chaos of pitiful cries.

Faulkner cried out against searing agony as he was thrown from his horse to a jarring tumble across rough ground. Fighting the pain, he looked to the Ghostmaker easing from shore, and saw on her hull his wicked adversary Billy Buckler clambering up. Spurred by the sight, Faulkner found a reserve of strength to press on bleeding hands and he regained his feet to race for the waterline. Somewhere far behind, Madigan's voice raised in alarm, but he ignored the warning and drew his pistol on the run, sprinting to close the distance to the retreating vessel. At the wharf's limit he halted, steadying himself for the shot and fixing his target squarely.

'Billy Buckler!'

Faulkner watched the pirate captain turn to the calling of his name, and he fired to send the pistol's ball flying across open water. He saw his shot strike in a flash of sparks, not skin or bone, but Billy's sword, and he gasped for the monstrous face leering in triumph for devilish luck. Stunned, Faulkner could only look on as pirates crowded the Ghostmaker's rail to level muskets and pistols on him.

'God save England,' he whispered in the moment before a firestorm of gunpowder sent him to cold water.

55

Overcome by his joy in murder and destruction, Billy pushed from the rail and laughed raucously.

The crew and captives of the Ghostmaker fell quiet to witness his seizure, a crazed merriment that rocked his monstrous frame and arched his crunching spine. His ripped head fell back, the better to deliver that insane laughter to the sky from holes in his cheeks. And so it was, in this upturned attitude, that Billy Buckler regarded after so long the full sails of his ship flowering overhead and heard the rustle of wind in the canvas. The moment was enough to sweep his howls in an instant to an adoring silence. He stood, lost among all, hypnotised by the only love he knew dancing for his safe return. He spread his arms wide as though to pull the whole of the vessel to him in a crushing embrace. Welcome back, he heard her from far away, welcome back.

'Welcome back, Captain.'

Pulled from his reverie by the voice at his shoulder,

Billy found Pyke standing by with a victorious smile of his own.

'Welcome back, Captain,' the first mate repeated. 'Orders for the crew?'

Billy scanned across the faces of his waiting men and those of the terrified children they restrained. None was the face he sought now.

'The girl,' he snapped. 'Bring me the girl.'

'Here, Captain,' Davy said, and he pointed where a gross buccaneer dragged Lara forward.

'Good, good,' Buckler said, clicking white fingers in anticipation. 'Very well. Helmsman, catch the river's flow! Full sail and all speed to open sea! Take our guests below.'

The crew leapt to obey but had barely begun when a stern cry from the ranks stopped all.

'Belay those orders! All hands stand fast!'

Billy whirled in fury to seek the one challenging his authority, and he found and stared on Mr Pyke.

'What's the meaning of this?' he demanded of his mate.

'Do you trust me, Captain?' Pyke asked of his leader.

'Aye, of course,' Billy agreed, 'through storm and strife, and well you know it.'

With a nod, Pyke turned to address the helmsman who frowned from the ship's great wheel.

'Catch the river as the captain commands,' he said, 'and make ready for all the speed the Ghostmaker can muster. But await my order on that!' The ship's wheel turned, and Pyke felt the groaning ship lean hard over to gain the middle of the Thames. He signalled to a cluster of pirates near the rail. 'Run out the plank!'

'What's your thinking, man?' Billy exclaimed. His leathery brow furrowed with a crack in watching crewmen prepare the plank.

Mr Pyke winked knowingly.

'We have a rat problem aboard this ship, Captain, and it needs sorting out.' Without warning, he lunged for the royal children and snatched at the wrist of Princess Elizabeth to drag her from Charlotte's embrace. Ignoring youthful cries, he held her fast as the plank grated to its place over churning water.

'We have no time for games,' Billy warned, 'we still lie dangerously between English shores.'

'No games, Captain,' Pyke declared, and with a jerk he drew the frightened girl towards the rail. Spinning her about on the way, he forced Elizabeth to step backwards onto the narrow plank. And there he held her, precariously balanced on the beam. 'No games,' he repeated, and loudly for all to hear, and for the one in particular he searched for through the ship's dark corners. 'I know you're there! Show your-self, or the girl goes to the deep!'

'Pyke,' Buckler growled his warning, 'the spell.'

'Five bottled spirits and three extra youngsters in hand,' Pyke replied defiantly. 'The spell will work. Show yourself, I said!'

Crew and captain stared on, baffled by this turn of events. For his part, Pyke continued his scan about the ship, high and low, and into the quiet recesses. Displeased at the lack of response to his calling, he moved Elizabeth further off balance so that only her toes remained in contact with the plank, and her eyes held wide and glassy on Charlotte's.

'Enough,' said Benjamin and he dropped from his hiding place among the sails.

The pirates nearest leapt back, startled by the unexpected appearance of a boy in their very midst, and they nervously cleared a path for him to approach Pyke.

'At last,' the pirate snarled, 'the one who has dogged us from the beginning.' His face betrayed the boiling hatred he felt at the sight.

'What's this?' Billy demanded, stepping forward to examine the trespasser. 'Are you the devil named Benjamin Blake?'

'I am.' Benjamin met the monster's staring eye unafraid.

'The interfering night spirit,' Pyke hissed, 'a bloodsucking vampire, if I'm not mistaken.' At this the pirates drew farther back, muttering in heightened fear, while one crossed himself to a muttered prayer.

Billy Buckler held fast and sneered.

'You're the one who took my leg,' he said through clenched teeth.

'The one who sought from the very beginning to undo all we have worked for,' Pyke added.

Driven by a surge of anger, Billy tore a pistol from his belt and aimed at Benjamin's head. Stayed by the boy's unchanging features for the threat, he looked to Pyke and back again, understanding the futility of trying to kill an immortal spirit.

'You spoke in your senses just now, Mr Pyke,' the captain said, his evil smile creaking wide as a plan formed, 'we can spare a little sprat to deal with a rat. Get off my ship, Benjamin Blake.'

'All speed!' was Pyke's roared command and with a final smirk for Benjamin, he released his grip on Elizabeth's tiny hand.

The princess teetered just a moment on the board's edge before the fall, her scream coming in time with her siblings' as she plummeted towards churning waters.

Benjamin followed at once, sprinting to the rail, and with just time enough to catch the brief white eruption where the hungry river took the girl down.

The Ghostmaker accelerated as he dived headlong after her.

56

Benjamin plunged to the river's crushing depths. Searching for sign of Elizabeth, vampire senses were tested to their limits by the impenetrable crush of night waters. All around, the river's vast underworld offered nothing to sight or hearing, while overhead, the Ghostmaker's round underbelly carved a bubbling white trail through the murk until it too receded to nothing, a passing comet lost to the void. Just as in the folds of Baron Samedi's cloak, Benjamin was adrift in a seemingly endless abyss, this one as cold as that held by the spirit, though empty of all, even the dead. But Elizabeth would change that fatal aspect if he did not locate her, and quickly. She was here, somewhere! As he kicked deeper down, underwater currents pushed and pulled at Benjamin and mocked his search for her.

I'm here.

That familiar voice rippled from the endless water, growing to tease him on all sides.

I'm waaaaiting.

Benjamin slammed shut his hearing and mind to all but the lost princess and he hauled furiously on. Now was not the time for the haunting mockery of a wicked book and its spells.

And yet...

Spells. Benjamin pulled up abruptly to hang on the river's blind shifting. Spells, his thoughts echoed, of course, and one spell over others jumped from lost pages to his memory. Hands prepared even as he cursed himself a fool for wasting precious time in clawing aimlessly at the dark when the answer lay at his very fingertips. Bringing the conjuration to his throat, he offered it to bubbling lips.

'Fulmen.'

Power burst from him, growing as an orb of light to defy the river's buffeting currents. An underwater sun was born at his command, so bright the darkness fled the eruption and left its secrets exposed.

Elizabeth floated as a lost angel on the edge of magic's dawning.

She was below, far off and descending, a white and shifting form, and as the light fell back, the edge of her skirts drifted in marking her place.

Benjamin aimed for the spot and dived.

Farther and farther he swam, stretching out for that which rapidly faded from him, hoping for a hand, a hem, anything by which to secure the drowning girl.

But now the vengeful darkness was returning to close steadily round and close off vision once more.

Elizabeth's face! He caught it, the last sure image of her in the gloom, pale and passing as the moon. She fell through the slowest tumbling of hair with all the appearance of one sleeping as the darkness carried her on. Benjamin strained, kicking harder and all at once felt her wrist pass into his grip! Pulling her limp form close he felt the riverbed at his feet and he pushed, seeking the unseen surface without a backwards glance for the swirl of riverbed soil he created, or the symbol-filled pages it disturbed, turning over and back, over and back.

He ascended for what seemed an eternity, pleading to reach the world above before it became too late for the girl. On and on he strove until a sharp flickering light danced across his vision, a signal that, to a mortal brain, spoke of breathlessness and the onset of drowning. But not to a vampire without need of breath. What was this light?

With the next blinding strobe he had it! He beheld lightning from the storm still rolling over the city, glinting on the river's surface. With renewed effort he swam harder and reached higher, and in a burst of waves he met the night air.

Presenting Elizabeth's face to the rumbling sky, he searched for indications of life where she floated limply in his arms, and he drove hard for shore. Quickly gaining shallower waters, he scooped her up and carried her across the last short distance to land.

The moon broke free of storm clouds to behold its imitation in Elizabeth's deathly face, and Benjamin grew alarmed at the sight as he placed the girl on the foreshore, there to search for signs of vitality in her cold form.

'Breathe,' he heard himself urge her, 'breathe. I can't do it for you! Breathe!'

Another spell, he thought desperately, a spell from the countless he possessed must be of use, though as he pored through his store of remembered magic, not one from all formed for a witch's cruelty came to him, and he cursed useless power.

The absence of a spell allowed the faintest sound to catch him then. He stilled abruptly and built all hope on it, soft and fragile though it was, and he was rewarded at last in recognising the faint rhythm of Elizabeth's heart, and next her first catching breath as she roused. Life renewed in the slow opening of her eyes, though the orbs flared at once in frightened reaction to the silvery features staring down on her. It lasted a mere instant, however, as she recognised the boy from the ship's deck, allowing a greater fear to stab at her.

'Charlotte!' she exclaimed tearfully. 'My brothers.'

'Steady,' Benjamin instructed softly.

'But you have to bring them back,' Elizabeth pleaded.

'I will,' he promised her, 'but first things first.' The girl was shivering intensely now and not through fear alone.

Benjamin scanned the vicinity quickly and spotted a ready source of heat for the princess. An abandoned boat lay forgotten on the shoreline, sagging and holed.

'Don't be afraid,' he said and prepared fresh magic. Rubbing palms vigorously together, Benjamin whispered his incantation across them, 'Incendium'. He flung out his fingers towards the wreck. The dry wood sparked aflame in an instant and grew rapidly to a roaring inferno. 'Stay close and warm,' he instructed the little girl. 'Someone will see the fire and help will come.'

'But my brothers and sister must be helped too,' Elizabeth insisted, growing distraught again at thoughts of them even now sailing away, and she peered into the night for trace of the Ghostmaker and struggled against Benjamin's hold. 'They must be helped too!'

In her despair, the princess made to return to the water's edge, even to wade mindlessly into the river. But Benjamin blocked her path, and with a firm grip on her shoulders he seized her gaze with his own.

'Highness, calm yourself!' he commanded sharply, and she became transfixed by silver light dancing in reply the rolling flames. 'There is nothing you can do. You must leave it to me.'

'But what can you do?' she asked breathlessly. 'You have no ship, no horse.'

'No,' he admitted. 'But I am faster than both.'

In a flicker of firelight, Benjamin was gone.

'Quit your jabber!'

Barking against the cries of frightened children as they fought their guards, Billy stalked through the belly of the Ghostmaker, eyeing his crew at their hurried tasks. Under that hideous gaze, sailors raced faster to attend to their duties for the long sea voyage ahead. Pirates who had been ashore hastened back to their posts while those who had remained aboard stole uneasy glances at the thing their leader had become.

Stomping farther on through the creaking, dripping bowels of the ship, Billy led the way to the place prepared for the ritual. Close behind, Mr Pyke shouted orders as men struggled to drive the children forward until all arrived at a stout door guarded by two crewmen.

'Is all made ready for magic?' the captain demanded of the nervous men, and his neck swivel-cracked between them in search of a timely answer. Caught by their captain's diabolical orb, the sentries could only nod in response as they hastily unlocked the door. Billy pushed men and the barrier aside and bounded through the portal.

Arriving in a dismal hold, he paused to examine the space. The slow creak of his smile was heard by those nearest as he discovered everything arranged to his instructions. The crew had worked to remove surplus fixtures to other parts of the ship, leaving behind two items necessary to the proceedings. Made visible by the light of black candles affixed to the ship's beams was a high-backed chair carved over with dreadful symbols, and set before a grand table whose surface was covered by an unsettling display of articles required for Lara's magic.

'Bring them,' Billy ordered, impatient to begin. He stepped aside and glowered as the helpless prisoners were shoved in and lined along a bulkhead by their guards.

Last to come was Lara. Under the close care of a scowling escort, the girl approached the hold. But as she moved to enter the room there came a great disturbance of metal along the corridor behind, that of a cage door and stout lock attacked by the one they held.

'Lara!' came a woman's cry from between the bars, and it held all the power a mother's voice has to spin her child back.

'Mama!' Lara wailed. In a fierce moment she slipped her captor's grasp and darted to her mother's face, clasping for it and the hands that reached, only to be hauled cruelly off and carried towards the hold.

'Snap to it, girl!' Billy shouted irritably. He stomped across the decking to take his place in the grotesque chair, settling between its arms like a monstrous king. 'Get on with it!'

Lara turned and shot Billy a look of burning hate, and for the longest time pirate and girl stared one another down in mutual loathing. Finally, and working hard to collect her thoughts, Lara blinked against her anger and shifted to inspect the table. She walked slowly to examine the items spread across its dark surface, nodding in turn at drawn symbols and the placement of root bags, bottles and candles. With measured care she next circled the chair, halting at a covered earthen jar located at Billy's feet.

'Well?' Mr Pyke demanded.

'All is in place,' Lara confirmed sullenly.

'Then call in our guest of honour and let's get done with this,' Billy ordered with a slap of his hand to the chair.

Pyke raised his voice to the upper decks.

'Baron! Come!'

The royal children looked with growing dread as the first black folds of cloak snaked over the threshold in answer to the summoning. Tattered strands coursed to touch the floor and began to slither forth, bringing on more and more of the one who gave them life. The doorway filled with an expanse of cape and yet more ragged lengths tipped across the ceiling and curled about rafters and beams until at last, emerging from within the swirling mass, the painted face of the Baron beneath his feathered hat became visible and he surveyed all with piercing eyes.

'By stick and stone, and root and bone, I am come,' he declared mournfully.

Lara looked to her spirit, searching desperately for some last sign of hope in his fearsome face, but she found only sadness there. She was still looking to her friend when Mr Pyke leaned forward to whisper at her ear.

'Your Benjamin Blake is gone, missy, along with any plan you had. Think of your mother and get to your task.'

Lara turned back to the chair and its leering occupant. Setting all hope aside, she raised her arms to begin.

'We are in the house of souls now,' she intoned slowly, and the very words seemed enough to dim the candles.

'Don't do this,' Charlotte pleaded in a powerless whisper.

'The candles are lit for the dead,' Lara continued, stung by the girl's words. 'Damballah, you are needed now. I call you. Come!'

From high above, through the thick wood of the decks, came a deep beating of drums, their rhythm seeping down to drive candle-shadows moving. Light and dark played across the ship's interior in a dance of sorcery, swaying and jerking for all to see. In his chair, Billy beat out the rhythm with his skeleton hand and grinned madly on the ceremony.

Lara reached and uncovered the jar, and looked on as a serpent's head began to free itself. Propelled by its unfurling body, the creature came fully into the light and traced the jar's outline slowly down to flop on the decking. Gliding forward, it bypassed the table to coil before the children, there to rear up and hiss at them. Lidless eyes regarded each one coldly as its black tongue flicked on the air for their scent.

At her place by the table, Lara removed a cloth to reveal a circular tray, upon which sat eight corked bottles. Five of the vessels glimmered with the power of green light stolen from dead pirates, but three did not, and five were corked to contain their magic glow, but three were not. The empty bottles stood ready to receive, and with a gesture to the Baron, Lara signalled for him to take up the vessels.

'Damballah,' she continued with her incantation

as the spirit clasped the glasses and turned to face the children, 'Damballah, I call to you in your place on the magic island. There is one who must yet come fully back, a *gros-bon-ange* to be released. Give back in full what was half given, let fly what must surely die!'

The royal children struggled uselessly against restraining arms and tried desperately to push from the Baron as he closed on them and brought the empty bottles along. The drumbeats continued louder overhead as his lips trembled reluctantly for his task.

The earthen jar crashed in pieces where Lara flung it down.

'I serve with both hands,' the girl cried into the dark. 'Damballah, see what I do! The jar of the dead is broken! Remove the barrier! Give me the rest of Billy Buckler!'

The encroaching shadows fell back before surging light. It was illumination with no apparent source, a shining that flowed green among the struggling children and threw a ghastly hue over their dismayed faces. And it grew to catch the weakening in their features, the loss of resistance to the magic taking them. Vision dimmed, and the children heard the Baron's distant whisper as he pressed in on them.

'Forgive me.'

58

Benjamin ran. On and on, he ran.

Rooftops blurred beneath racing feet, chimney pots passed in a flash. Faster than the reckoning of mortal sense he cleared the widest avenues, his speed unchanging up slopes and down. With momentum to outpace the stars, to beat the very sunrise, Benjamin pressed his pursuit of the Ghostmaker.

But could he regain the ship before it reached the sea? Even a vampire cannot run forever and he knew the night tide had already turned, running back from the dying moon to carry the pirate vessel ever faster to open water.

The night became a blur of compressed images on his track of rooftops hugging the north bank of the river.

A derelict building loomed into sight, its roof broken to a wide swallowing hole. Mid-stride, Benjamin sought a safer path but found none. Straight on or stop were the choices. He timed his jump, counted his remaining steps in an instant, and launched over the chasm. Sucking blackness passed below, and the sound of a single loose tile crashing away echoed distantly after as he landed and charged on.

The buildings grew taller as they gave over from dwellings places to the business houses of the city's eastern end. One final low roof, inclining upwards, would make way to those towering stores of the warehouse district. Benjamin powered up a slated ramp and gained new heights. Here the moonstruck river filled his vision where he came to overlook its broad turn at Blackwall Reach, and despite all, he paused with a gasp, there to behold the water glittering directly across his line of travel, and bringing with it the Ghostmaker!

***

'Mr Davy, sir!'

The voice of the watch was filled with alarm and it brought Davy running across the Ghostmaker's sloping deck. The pirate who shouted leaned urgently to the port rail with his eyes locked on Blackwall Reach. Warehouses towered, and seemed to advance on the ship as it was forced to navigate close to shore for the coming starboard bend. Without waiting for his officer to question him, the pirate of the watch stabbed a finger urgently at the threat he had spotted.

'Above, Mr Davy, on the roof!'

Davy looked, straining up for the last of the crescent moon falling steadily behind the warehouses. And his eyes grew wide at the pale arc and the boyish figure it betrayed standing on high. He let slip the name as a curse.

'Benjamin Blake.' Davy spun from the rail and filled his lungs for orders. 'Helmsman, hard over! Make your starboard turn now!'

But the helmsman clung fearfully to his wheel.

'Too soon, Mr Davy! We'll run aground!'

Davy's eyes burned with fury as fists pumped the rail in seeking an alternative strategy against the vampire's return. In an instant of clarity, he had it.

'Roll out the guns port side! Highest elevation! Full salvo!' He listened to the rumble of cannon wheels beneath his feet and the banging of gun ports.

'What target, sir?' someone called.

'The moon! Shoot at the moon!'

***

Benjamin was already into his run when he saw the Ghostmaker's gun ports wink ajar, and was already set on his course as the first smokey boom rolled to him on the air.

A shrieking projectile gouged a roof apart, and

Benjamin felt a cannonball pass dangerously close. He weaved to avoid flying debris, and was instantly forced to change direction again as another blast, and another, tore wood and tiles to pieces all about. The path ahead became a torrent of splinters over collapsing rooftops, but Benjamin pressed on, on towards a new target he sought, one he realised with sudden and excited recall lay directly ahead, reaching from him towards the Ghostmaker's path.

The pirate vessel was at midships to the warehouses as Benjamin burst through smoke and flame, its plumped sails dominating his sight. Across the decreasing space to the ship he spied the route he needed and leaned fiercely into his charge. The final stretch of roof ahead ended to a chasm of night, but Benjamin did not slow. He knew that a few more solid feet and firm inches lay just beyond the tiles, a measure to make all the difference. Without pause he passed from slate to wood, and his racing feet slapped along the warehouse beam holding Billy Buckler's gibbet. In a final surge, Benjamin flung himself into space.

The world passed to a sky of billowing canvas.

Benjamin flew on, his legs kicking hard to fight gravity for as long as possible before the inevitable plunge. The river spread wide and dark beneath, ready to swallow him up should his strength prove insufficient or his aim too poor. A fierce wind tore at his limbs and assailed his ears until, after a moment's floating pause, he at last began his downward plummet. The Ghostmaker's half-skull banner fluttering over the main mast grew huge at the edge of sight. The ship itself seemed to pull him down, and the fall became ever faster as he descended towards the deck with pirates scattering in panic across it.

Benjamin brought his feet together and aimed hard for the wood, praying he was not too late.

59

'Forgive me.'

Green fire cascaded from the children, and Baron Samedi shut his eyes against the dreadful sight of their fear. Life-force ebbed towards his bottles, making each one a glowing lamp whose light dismissed all shadows and illuminated the faces of the royal siblings as one after the other they slipped from waking behind fluttering eyelids.

The same sickly light caught Billy Buckler's features where he clicked fingers and teeth impatiently to the muffled thump of cannon fire. But he allowed himself a smile for the magic's progress, and his glee was shared by Mr Pyke who watched keenly nearby.

'All life is mine,' Billy whispered to himself as he fought the urge to bound from his chair, to snatch those bottles from Samedi and gulp the renewing spirits down.

A sudden and jarring commotion on high drew pirate eyes to the ceiling. Cries of alarm above were followed a moment later by an eruption which sent a shudder of collision through the vessel. An instant more and an explosion of boards and rafters showered down on the assembly as a speeding mass hurtled through the lower deck. And when slowly the storm of dust cleared, Benjamin Blake rose on the wreck and faced Billy Buckler.

The vampire roared.

The animal sound hammered throughout the Ghostmaker, reverberating within its confines to pound the ship's ribs and test the eardrums of all. In the instant of stunned silence after, Benjamin sprang to action.

'Pulvis,' he intoned, and the shimmering bottles in the Baron's grasp exploded to powder. Their glowing contents swept free on the air and flowed back towards unconscious children.

Pirates shook off their confusion to draw swords and pistols for the fight. But, freed from his grim work, the Baron was moving too.

Seizing two men nearest him by their collars, Samedi flung the pair upwards and away screaming through the hole created by Benjamin's landing. A third buccaneer, witnessing the act, turned his pistol on the spirit with a cry and fired, only to see his shot swallowed up harmlessly by the sweeping cloak as Samedi clawed towards him.

With pirate shrieks ringing in his ears, Benjamin spun on the growling Pyke, just in time to see his pistol brought to bear at close range. Whipping an arm forth in response, Benjamin coolly pressed his palm flat to the muzzle as the hammer fell to spark waiting powder.

'Prohibeo!'

Shot and sorcery collided in bursting fire. Held fast to the pistol, gunpowder exploded in all directions and tore Pyke's weapon asunder. The man howled in torment as he was caught by scorching metal shards and he tumbled away clutching his bloodied face.

Movement behind swung Benjamin to meet a pirate already in the act of driving his blade hard, his teeth clamped in furious determination. Benjamin coolly prepared for the strike and as the tip of the blade reached his shirt front, he clapped his hands together, trapping the weapon neatly between. The pirate's face twisted to a mask of frightened confusion and he pushed and pulled against the unbreakable grip. As the man wasted time in struggling, Benjamin swung to kick him, and with such force he was driven up against a heavy beam and knocked cold.

Vampire senses flared, seeking to draw Benjamin in three directions at once. In a single moment of time he saw Billy flee from his chair and witnessed the first signs of renewed life in the children, all while a vengeful pirate advanced on Lara.

With an air of defiance, the girl stood her ground

as the man cocked a pistol and prepared for the shot. And though close by, the Baron was distracted by his own fight with pirates crowding the doorway and was oblivious to the threat. Yet Lara held firm against the murderous form bearing down.

Her words were fiercely offered.

'Damballah's coil hold pirate tight, and I am saved by serpent's bite!'

Unimpressed by her utterance, the pirate drew up his pistol and aimed. It was then he caught first sight of the hissing snake wrapped about his arm and weapon. With a cry of disgust, the man fell back, eyes bulging on those of the serpent as it licked its way along his arm. With lightning speed, the creature struck at the man's face and the poisoned bite took effect instantly. Gurgling his last, the pirate toppled to the floor.

A great crash of wood signalled the end of the Baron's adversaries. Looking to the sound, Benjamin watched as a pirate was flung crashing through the hull of the Ghostmaker to his doom in the river beyond.

'Billy is on the move,' he informed the spirit with a gesture to the empty chair.

'I will take care of Billy Buckler,' Lara interrupted, her stern voice cutting short any argument. 'Get the children to a lifeboat and away. Baron, free my mother.'

Without further word, the girl strode away.

60

'What happened?'

With a weak and drowsy voice, Princess Charlotte rose to regard the scene of destruction. Beside her, George and Edward moved as though emerging from a sleep of bad dreams. They reached to steady one another as best they could. Catching sight of Benjamin, Charlotte's mind quickly sharpened and she lunged to him, her face betraying her fear as she grasped his arms fiercely.

'Elizabeth is safe,' he assured, answering the question in her eyes.

'Can someone explain to me what has been going on?' It was a much confused George who spoke. He looked on wreckage and slumped pirates while Edward cast a nervous eye to the looming Baron.

'Magic, revenge, kidnap, rescue,' Charlotte recited with a smile for Benjamin.

'Billy's revenge failed,' George guessed, and watched uncomfortably as a snake slithered from the room.

'Yes,' Benjamin said without feeling a need to

explain just how close to disaster they had all come.

'It's over, then,' the prince sighed, relieved.

As though seeking to disprove George's words, pounding feet across the deck overhead gave promise of fresh attack.

'Look there,' Benjamin instructed quickly and he pointed to a door at the far end of the hold. 'Go, everyone, and make your way up. I will be right behind.'

With nods of assent, Charlotte and George paused only to scoop up fallen weapons and the children hastened towards the escape route.

'I stand with you,' the Baron said, rising behind Benjamin. The spectre formed his cape to a pair of fearsome black wings above his tall hat. And he scorned his enemies with a snort. 'They come so eagerly against us, we spirits who own the night.' His wings crashed down to create a blast of air across every candle, offering vampire and phantom the greatest weapon of all.

Darkness.

Moments later, pirates advanced slowly through the ship, whispering in the inky black with pistols sweeping in all directions. Their set faces sought ambush everywhere as they neared the hold. Four, five, six pirates entered the room and spread out, probing recesses and places behind beams in search of a target.

'Over here.'

The whisper was a mere breath to test the very limits of hearing, and it jerked the search party to one spot as pistols cocked loudly in the gloom.

'Behind you.'

That same whispering voice, a boy's low tone, came now from a different place and it turned the men on their heels again. And from another location, in deepest shadow behind the buccaneers, a draught sprang up and wafted between their boots to envelop them, chilling each man in its passing. Unconsciously, and as one, the startled men added swords and daggers to their pistols as they retreated from the icy touch. Farther back they stepped, on into the dark where their footsteps grew muffled against some soft black material lying over the wood.

There was a spark to the left! The men gazed in wonder as a lone candle flared of its own accord. A flame to the right! Another light blazed to life. And still another, and another, until the space was once again illuminated. The pirates looked all around in bewilderment until finally they spied a target. There, resting causally in the captain's tall chair of symbols, the spirit boy Benjamin Blake eyed them intently.

'Here be monsters,' he warned and offered his broadest vampire smile as the firing squad hastened to take aim.

Jostled by eager colleagues seeking the best line

of fire, a grizzled pirate lost hold of his dagger and cursed its tumble to the floor. With a dull thud the pointed blade cut through black carpet and stuck fast to a board. Still cursing his mates' clumsiness, the buccaneer stooped quickly to retrieve the blade, only to pause with a frown for what he saw.

Where the dagger pricked the floor covering, torn black strands around its edges seemed to flick with life in answer to the assault. They played softly against the shining metal, and stroking motions gave way to a gentle tapping before the threads began to extend upwards, swallowing first the blade and next the handle. The tendrils stretched on and caressed the startled pirate's fingers, causing the man to snatch back his hand in fear, only for him to discover his feet and legs were already ensnared in the flowering cloak of Baron Samedi.

The phantom surged up as pirates cried against bonds whipping to seize all. Their struggles were useless against the spirit's might, and he pulled each man to him that they might fully see the anger in his face, and the uncorked bottles he drew into the light. The Baron whispered to Benjamin through his hypnotic fury.

'Go and help the children,' he said. 'These wicked men belong to me now.'

Candles burned green and Benjamin sped away, leaving the phantom to his work in the room of screams.

61

The children crept through shadow patches along the main deck.

Across the Ghostmaker, pirates ran with weapons and shouts of warning as they hunted for the source of the attack on their ship and furiously demanded orders to quell all chaos and confusion.

With her own sword at the ready, Charlotte kept a wary eye as she traced the rail with the others and weaved a secret path between barrels. More than once the feet of a buccaneer paused hard by and she heard her siblings catch breaths of fear for discovery. And each time, her grip tightened on the blade as she vowed silently to fight to the death for her family.

On they crawled, inching closer to the ship's lifeboat strung above the deck. With silent signals, Charlotte kept watch as George examined the muddle of ropes holding the little vessel, trying to work out exactly how it was to be successfully – and quietly – swung over the rail and down to the water without disaster. In the midst of his inspection, he felt

Edward offer a soft tug at his sleeve and watched the boy point to a spot on the rail opposite the lifeboat.

'The main rope is there,' Edward whispered helpfully.

'Well done, young prince,' the delighted George replied and he motioned for all to follow.

Progressing to the spot where the guide rope was secured, George attempted to unfasten it while remaining concealed, grunting against the awkward angle of his work. Despite his best efforts, however, the knot held fast. With a cautious search for any pirates lurking nearby, the boy rose to tackle the bond again.

'Hey, who goes there?'

The gruff shout betrayed a pirate approaching with his sword held high. A scarred and bearded face loomed over the prince.

Charlotte reacted in an instant, throwing up her own weapon to clash against that of the buccaneer and forcing the man to leap back. The sound instantly attracted the attention of others of the crew who gathered to assess the situation.

'Back!' Charlotte commanded with as much authority as she could muster. She waved the sword at the sneering pirate.

'Fancy your chances do you, girly?' Her pirate foe swung his blade dramatically through the air as though to transfix the princess. In a flash he struck out, arcing the sword towards Charlotte's head with killer force. Inches from its target, the blade crashed against hers where it swept up expertly to stop the assault.

'Actually, I do,' she informed the buccaneer defiantly and she slapped the attacking sword back. 'My fencing teacher is the best in England.'

Enraged, the pirate attacked again, slashing for Charlotte's body but only to find the move anticipated, blocked and struck aside. A thrust for the guts was deflected with a flourish, a downward slice to the head deftly avoided and countered. The pirate grew all the more angry as his accomplices chuckled for his efforts, and he sought furiously for a new angle of attack.

It came as a frontal lunge, a driving of the sword towards Charlotte's heart. But the princess was watching closely. She nimbly side-stepped the blow to offer her own to the competition and her blade reached to slash the man's tunic. The assembled pirates groaned for their comrade's humiliation.

Driven by the sound, the pirate growled bitterly and launched a flurry of cuts and thrusts in a bid to land at least one blow for wounded pride. Charlotte was equal to the challenge, however, and steel sang again and again until, with a flashing thrust, the princess scored another hit and drew blood from the pirate's sword arm. She withdrew to the rail and took up her ready stance once more.

For his part, the stung pirate staggered back to the line of watching buccaneers and clutched his injured arm. His lips twisted in rage and pain, but slowly he recovered addled senses and brought up his weapon again. He peered along its length at the waiting princess.

'You're finished,' he hissed.

'Indeed I am,' Charlotte agreed, and she brought forth the dagger concealed in her skirts. With a swipe she cut the lifeboat's fixing rope and sent the vessel crashing down on the heads of the gathered pirates.

'That,' Edward declared as he emerged from hiding, 'was exceptionally good.'

'Thank you,' Charlotte said with a smile and a swish of blade. She gestured to the fallen lifeboat. 'Quickly, both of you, we have our chance.'

Moving fastest to gain the severed rope, George ushered his brother and sister into the vessel and rounded his shoulders for the work ahead. He leaned back to haul on the line with a grunt for the effort and began drawing the loaded boat towards the ship's edge. With aching arms the prince struggled to make progress and he became frustrated as the keel of the boat knocked repeatedly against the rail. He watched with growing desperation as the rope slipped slowly through his tiring hands under the weight of the load.

'You should join the others,' Benjamin instructed suddenly at the boy's shoulder. 'You'll need your strength for rowing ashore.'

Startled, the breathless George nodded and scrambled to join his siblings.

Without strain, Benjamin drew the boat higher and stepped close to guide it over open water. But as he prepared to lower away, there came to him a soft rumbling, felt as much as heard from the deck under his feet. Looking there, he was horrified to discover a small barrel of gunpowder rolling slowly towards him. Black dust poured from its uncorked top to trail across the wood as the container trundled lazily past his boots and came to rest with the slightest thump. Benjamin could only watch as Billy Buckler followed, stepping into the light with grating laughter and a readied pistol aimed squarely at the barrel.

62

'Caught like a fish on a line, young vampire.'

Billy Buckler drew on, chuckling over the thump of his wooden leg on the deck. He gestured dangerously with the pistol to his enemy's hold on the rope.

'Quite the conundrum you've set for yourself there,' he mocked through snapping teeth.

The cursed pirate was correct, and Benjamin knew it. The children, so far above the water, would surely drown if he released his grip suddenly on the rope, but if not, they would be consumed by fire should Billy let loose his shot. And Benjamin's hands, so tight to the rope, could not work a spell against the threat. He held firm, unable to do more than glower at Billy's obvious delight.

An amusing thought seized the watching pirate.

'Do you know the best thing about the shaky memory I now possess?' he asked, choking on his merriment. 'I can't remember the last time I had this much fun!' The joke sent the pirate captain into fresh spasms of laughter.

'So what will you do?' Benjamin demanded, cutting through the monster's amusement. 'Whichever method you choose, the children die and you are left with nothing.'

Collecting his senses, Billy grunted sourly for the vampire's reasoning.

'You're not half as clever as you think, are you, boy...spirit....spirit-boy, whatever you are? Whether these scamps drown or burn, I'll have stabbed England in her rotten heart, and it won't be hard to gather up another few kiddies for the sacrifice. Of course, we can stand here all night and leave the little dears swinging, but in case you haven't noticed, my night-walking friend, the Ghostmaker's heading is due east and our destination is sunrise.' Billy tittered to himself. 'Everyone dies but me.'

'You can't kill me.' Lara appeared, stepping over unconscious pirates to stare hard at Billy.

'Pah!' the pirate scoffed. 'Everyone thinks they're the smartest in school tonight. You're a slave, remember, my slave! You're worse than dead.'

'Not any more,' the little sorceress snapped. Reaching through her clothes, she drew out a small bottle filled with brown powder. Without hesitation she flung the container at the deck where it shattered at Billy's feet.

Billy Buckler frowned at the small, dusty explosion, and grinned for the stillness that came after.

'Looks like you're out of tricks too,' he said and gave over to more booming laughter.

All watched the pirate captain fling back his head in manic amusement for spells and spirits, and they looked on as he bellowed his triumph to the stars. And all saw then how he hiccuped through his laughing, as though caught by the intensity of his fun. And looking on, they saw the first cough become a fit of choking, of guttural eruptions from the creature's mouth, and the laughter abruptly ceased in the buccaneer's sinewy throat. Billy's mad eye rolled for curious sensations rushing through his frame, and he turned his hands over and back as though to see in them the source of unease afflicting his body. With rising dread he looked to his feet and beheld what everyone else now saw.

The dust on the deck touched the pirate's boots, and where it settled, that place too became dust, and the effect climbed steadily, a magical transformation spreading higher to turn ankles, then shins and knees to powder. Like a crawling infection, the rot advanced hungrily over the whole of the pirate's body and began to consume his bones. Tearing at his shirt with a cry, Billy exposed his pulsating heart just as it too was overcome and became a dried-up husk that flowed like sand between ribs already flaking. At the sight, and understanding at last his dusty decay, a look so strange came to overwhelm the pirate's face, one that startled all who saw it for the very first time.

Billy Buckler was afraid.

The buccaneer rounded on Lara, and the motion crumbled the powdered legs that had supported him. He tumbled towards the deck, thrusting forth his hands for protection but only to find them eagerly devoured by the bottle-dust they touched. More and more of the pirate's body sundered under its own weight until just the head remained unaffected. Billy's face turned in a last silent pleading to Lara.

She spat her words at him.

'Gathered at midnight, and gathered right well, dust from a crossroads to send you to Hell!'

The pirate's look of terror froze to the magic that claimed him, and the last of Billy Buckler crumbled to a cloudy pile on the deck.

A howl of anguished despair filled the night. Unseen till now in shadow, Mr Pyke staggered forward and cried out against the death of his captain and for the loss of his only path to treasure. The man's features contorted in torment, and were made worse by the ugly cuts and scorching inflicted by his ruptured pistol. He looked glassy-eyed on the remains of Billy Buckler and reared up, consumed by rage and confusion. He glared on Lara with his battered mask of hate, unable to form curses foul enough to hurl at the girl. In place of words, he brought up a weapon and aimed.

The rope that had been Benjamin's impediment became his weapon. Holding the lifeboat steady, he whipped the trailing length forward and snared Lara's ankles. As Pyke's pistol flashed and crashed, he pulled her feet from under and sent her sprawling onto the deck. The ball meant for the girl's heart whistled safely by and was lost to the night.

Thwarted again, Pyke shrieked as a man possessed and grabbed at his belt for a weapon, any weapon, to continue the fight.

'Lara, move!' Benjamin shouted and he freed the rope to let it run swiftly through his hands.

To startled cries, the lifeboat bounced against the rail and began a dizzying plunge to the water, its pace controlled by Benjamin's grip as he kept eyes on Lara where she sped forward. He watched the girl leap after the vessel and fall safely among the other children. A moment after, the boat struck waves and began its drift from the Ghostmaker.

Pyke screamed at Benjamin on staggering legs and pawed yet at his belt as the boy clambered onto the rail.

'We're not finished, Benjamin Blake!' he roared

hysterically. 'I'll see you sent to the bottom of the ocean! I'll grind your bones and drink from your skull, you interfering dog!' His hand found what it sought at last and without pause he drew and fired a fresh pistol at the powder barrel.

The night became fire.

63

The gunpowder's eruption flung Benjamin headlong.

Smoke filled his eyes, flame enveloped skin, and on all sides blasted wood pounded his frame as the explosion worked in vain to tear him apart. He flew in the midst of the pummelling detonation as though falling through the heart of the sun, barely aware of his descent towards the river.

Heat and light gave over to icy depths in a plume of water. Benjamin kicked hard and quickly regained the surface to find he had landed at a spot between the lifeboat and the ship. At his back, the children huddled from cascading debris. Before all, the Ghostmaker pitched tremendously as smoke billowed from a jagged hole torn high in its side.

By the gaping wound, Mr Pyke appeared at the rail, holding his shattered body upright in scouring below for prey. He fixed on Benjamin's face, white against the night waves, and he bellowed his hate across the water. Whirling about, he roared his order to the heart of the ship.

'Run out the guns!'

The Ghostmaker's heart groaned and rumbled. Along the length of its flank, the gun ports drew open to free cannons, each wide muzzle coming to bear on the tiny lifeboat. Pyke straightened himself and brought up his sword with baleful relish as his lips parted for the final command.

Baron Samedi rose up.

The night became black behind Pyke where the phantom filled the sky and devoured the stars, huge and terrible in his appearance. His cloak flared wider than the broadest sail on the main mast. Its ragged ends drew rigid to form massive claws that turned inwards on their target, and Mr Pyke, sensing all with a fearful dread, turned his sword to the phantom in a futile defence. The spirit plunged on him, and the pirate's terrified wailing echoed away to the unending darkness of the spectre's cloak.

Pyke's fallen hat rolled across the boards as the Baron sped on.

Smashing through the upper deck, the collector of the dead sped below in a maelstrom of destruction, tearing his way through floors and supports and snatching up pirates on his way. The Ghostmaker became a vessel of dreadful sounds, of crashing, snapping, bursting, and pitiful screams. Along the gun deck, the Baron's cape tore cannons away and used them to batter the hull still further. The Ghostmaker screeched and hissed against the first invading water that came gushing through its ripped keel. And the Baron roved on, leaving nothing complete in his devastating wake. Up among the masts and rigging he travelled to sunder beams and hack sails. The debris cascaded through the body of the ship, creating more splintered holes for consuming waves. Samedi followed, ripping the ship's wheel to sticks before descending again to the interior. He careered through barrels and chests in a blizzard of wood and gunpowder and passed on, the trailing edge of his cloak finding a burning lamp and tipping it to the midst of the wreckage.

The Ghostmaker was consumed, dying before the eyes of the children in a billowing fire that touched the very sky and transformed night into day. Lifted upwards by a gunpowder blast, the ship broke under its own weight at the centre, casting its parts far and wide before settling back on the foaming water to surrender itself to the deep in a slow glowing descent.

The churning Thames rolled in, and the Ghostmaker was lost.

64

The lifeboat reached a shoreline covered over by smouldering wreckage.

Driving the little boat onto the sand, the young survivors of the Ghostmaker clambered gratefully ashore and looked back where Billy Buckler, his pirates and their ship existed now only as foul memories.

'Safe,' Charlotte breathed, weary but happy.

'Safe,' Benjamin agreed. He looked to the city about. 'The explosion will have been seen for miles. Soldiers will arrive soon.'

'They will never believe the story we have to tell,' George chortled as he looked for proof of it in his blade.

'Then tell them only what they can believe,' Benjamin advised with a wink.

The Prince of Wales nodded his understanding and moved to join his siblings where they rested nearby.

Benjamin left them and walked quietly to the shoreline, and to Lara, where the little girl stared across the water, her eyes probing desperately for a sign, any hopeful sign amid the floating debris as her fingers knitted anxiously together.

'I can't find them,' she whispered forlornly, not taking her eyes from the water.

'That's because you're not looking in the right place,' Benjamin explained softly, and he pointed the way.

Along the water's edge, at one with the darkness but for his painted features, the Baron stood alone. Under that tall feathered hat, the spirit peered back sombrely at Lara as his cloak fluttered lazily on the breeze. He made no move to approach but merely looked on his mistress as the stray edges of cape continued their idle dance, to and fro, hither and thither, winding and unwinding to at last reveal the first of a woman's face, with eyes like Lara's searching from the dark and lighting up at sight of her daughter.

With a joyous cry, Lara dashed headlong, kicking up mud in slipping and sprinting towards her mother.

'Levitas,' Benjamin was inspired to intone, and the girl's final steps were on air as she sailed into her mother's arms.

For his part, the Baron smiled at the kindly use of magic and tipped his hat in salute.

The gesture was the simplest act of courtesy in a world set to rights. Benjamin stood between calm water and peaceful land, between reunited mother and daughter and happy children.

And he smiled too.

65

The crescent moon came and brought with it the ghost.

The Boy of the Tower remained faithful to whispered tales and drifted in shade towards the battlements, there to peer east in welcoming the night.

Be about your business, Benjamin Blake.

He smiled, though not for fireside stories. Nor was it the moon that drew him tonight, but that which rose against it, slender and crossed and bedecked with rope and canvas. Among the many ships crowding together on the dark river, the mast of the cargo vessel Leveau rose highest in seeking the Pole Star to guide its imminent journey. Even now the ship's crew worked speedily to cast off lines and pull in the gangways in preparation for departure.

It was easy to pick out Lara and her mother, already on board. Motionless amid the hustle and bustle and holding close together at the ship's bow, mother and daughter looked forwards, not back, and traced the shimmering line of the river to the possibilities for them beyond. By kind arrangement of the king, they had passage on the fastest ship to their chosen destination. They were bound for New Orleans in the New World, and with a chest of coins stowed for new beginnings.

With her senses for the supernatural attuned as ever, Lara turned her gaze up towards Benjamin's dark perch and she waved happily.

Oh, but where are you, Baron?

Across the length of the ship Benjamin searched but found no hint until the phantom decided to give himself away. Rising from his hiding place atop the sails, where his cloak was perfectly disguised among flag and flowing canvas, Baron Samedi raised his hat in high salute, the motion timed perfectly with a westerly gust that caught the sails and set the Leveau on its way. The spirit's jubilant laughter crossed the wind, and his white painted face defied the pressing darkness as he called back a final time.

'From this night on, till time's last end, Benjamin Blake, I am your friend!'

With a smile, Benjamin offered a wave to the departing Baron and tracked the ship's smooth progress downriver, watching until it became one with the night and could be seen no longer, even by vampire eyes.

Breaking his lingering gaze at last, and feeling a

measure of sadness in seeing his friends depart, he turned to walk the precincts of the Tower, once more and as ever alone. On his way he looked for London to distract him, and he surveyed its mighty form in following the graceful line of the river under a star-filled sky. Over the battlements the city twinkled to the power of a thousand candles, radiant and alive with possibilities. His place in the Tower was an island of shadow on a sea of magical gleaming, and he became enthralled by the city's luminous beauty, his vampire senses enraptured.

And yet, bedazzled as he was by the scene, Benjamin was not entirely captivated. The adventure of Billy Buckler had placed a thought in his mind early on, and now, if he dared, tonight was the occasion to draw it into the moonlight.

If he dared.

Why shouldn't you dare? She won't bite.

Benjamin smiled, and scolded himself for a cowardly vampire.

He plunged into the night.

***

'My lords and ladies! The children of the Royal Household.'

At the instant of announcing, expectation reached

fever pitch across the ballroom. Assembled dignitaries surged to the marbled staircase and erupted in cheering and applause. Necks craned excitedly for the first glimpse of England's heroes, and a mighty cheer rose in greeting their first glittering appearance.

Arrayed in royal finery, the children swept into view and lined out at the head of the stairs, there to graciously accept the warmth of the deafening salute. Allowing for a suitable interval, the princesses advanced, smiling radiantly and waving to well-wishers along the way. How they had stood defiantly together against the worst excesses of the vile pirates was the talk of the land. It was said Princess Charlotte fought like a tiger against every ruffian, while Princess Elizabeth had braved the dangers of the deep, leaping boldly into perilous waters to summon help at the height of the kidnapping. The tales of daring brought hurrahs from all for their safe return.

The princes' steps after their sisters encouraged new levels of cheering, their courageous reputations going before them among military men and wide-eyed debutantes. There was clever young Edward, whose knowledge of naval ships had secured the lifeboat for escape while Prince George had seized an enemy weapon to lead the rescue from enemy hands. The Prince of Wales now raised the same sword of liberty to joyous exclamations. At sight of the warrior prince, Lady Sara Caitlyn fainted in her bloomers again while the over-excited Lady Matilda of Warwick was seized once more by hiccups.

Pausing to allow her brothers to catch up, and while Elizabeth pushed eagerly on towards the cake table, Charlotte looked over the faces of her adoring subjects, nodding thanks and bestowing grace on one and all, left and right, near and far. The action allowed for her subtle search across the faces for the one she sought, though at first he was nowhere to be found. And then the wigs of the Dukes of Marlborough and Greenwich parted and he was there. Captain Madigan, splendid in his best uniform, moved through the crowd and beamed for the hails and salutes offered by fellow soldiers for his part in the children's adventure.

And Charlotte saw he escorted a young lady.

They walked arm in arm, her smile shining as brightly as his as she attended to him, brushing a gloved hand delicately to the medal awarded by Papa just this morning. The lady's actions did little to dissuade a group of pursuing debutantes who hemmed the happy couple round and thrust dance cards and hopeful requests to the heroic officer.

Only vision beyond mortal capacity could have hoped to detect the brief flicker that threatened Charlotte's smile. But her royal bearing held, and she descended and crossed a sea of curtsies to pass through balcony doors where the night air cooled her cheeks before they could burn. Securing the doors, she kept her back to reflecting windows and made no move to walk on into the garden where night pools shimmered like black mirrors. Instead she held, gathering herself quickly because in that moment, somehow, she knew she was watched.

'I have read that vampires cast no reflection,' she said, and her words drew him from his hiding place.

'You have been reading about vampires?' Benjamin teased her.

'It was a sensible thing to do,' she replied airily.

'Well, it's true,' he admitted, 'I cast no reflection, but it hardly matters. I never need to shave.'

'Or look on yourself when you've been a fool,' she sighed.

'I read somewhere that princesses use mirrors for hours in perfecting their royal demeanour, and never look foolish.'

She grinned despite her mood and struggled a moment in regaining her composure.

'You have been reading about princesses?' she said, with an added sniff of indifference for effect.

'It was a sensible thing to do,' he said. 'But I was disappointed not to find one answer I was looking for.'

'Oh? Perhaps I can help.'

He drew closer in a blinking, and dared to speak.

'Is a vampire permitted to dance with a princess?'

She considered the question for the appropriate length of time.

'If she wishes it, yes,' was her conclusion, and she offered a soft hand.

Benjamin smiled and paused just long enough to conjure, and as he reached to entwine Charlotte's fingers, balcony doors clicked open to release the first strains of a Viennese Waltz.

Perfect.

The night was theirs, and they danced till dawn.

Benjamin Blake will return in
The Witches of Whitechapel

ACKNOWLEDGEMENTS

As ever, there are those labouring behind the paragraphs who share in the completion of any Benjamin Blake book. They deserve a mention (and more) and my gratitude for that:

Ciara O'Hara of Purple Crayon (www.picturebooksnob.com), whose editing skills have been key to keeping Benjamin in line without spoiling his fun.

Alba Esteban (Instagram – @alesturadesign) and Alexis Sierra (Instagram – @alexissierraart) for their cover design, layout design and illustrations.

Paula Nolan (PEN Graphic Design and www.paulatnolanphotography.com) for her layout skills.

Mags Gargan, for her eagle eye and truth-telling on the written word.

Erin Fox, avid test reader and social media whizz.

And Ita, who knew Benjamin Blake before anyone else.

Thank you, always.